FRIENDS SHE KNEW

(Katie Parker Book 3)

CR HIATT

AMB

Copyright

This is a work of fiction. Names, characters, places, and incidents are the product of the author's imagination or used fictitiously, and any resemblance to actual persons living or dead, events, or locales is entirely coincidental.

AMB Publishing

No part of this book may be reproduced or transmitted in any form or by any means, electronic or mechanical, including photocopying, recording, or by any information storage and retrieval system, without permission in writing from the publisher or author.

AMB

Copyright © 2022 by CR Hiatt

First edition, June, 2022
Printed in the United States of America

Friends She Knew/CR HIATT

Printed in the United States of America

Author's Note

Human trafficking is estimated to bring in global profits of about **$150 billion a year**—$99 billion from sexual exploitation, according to the International Labor Organization.

Liberties were taken with law enforcement rules for purposes to entertain in this book.

PLEASE NOTE: this novel depicts sexual and human trafficking abuse. Some descriptions could cause an emotional reaction that I wanted readers to be aware of. Even though the story, as written, is fiction, some of the circumstances and victims depicted, were based on real situations as told to me by those victims.

TABLE OF CONTENTS

FRIENDS SHE KNEW

Copyright
Author's Note
TABLE OF CONTENTS
PROLOGUE
CHAPTER 1
CHAPTER 2
CHAPTER 3
CHAPTER 4
CHAPTER 5 - THE TEACHER
CHAPTER 6
CHAPTER 7
CHAPTER 8
CHAPTER 9
CHAPTER 10
CHAPTER 11
CHAPTER 12
CHAPTER 13- THE TEACHER
CHAPTER 14
CHAPTER 15
CHAPTER 16
CHAPTER 17
CHAPTER 18
CHAPTER 19
CHAPTER 20
CHAPTER 21 - THE TEACHER
CHAPTER 22
CHAPTER 23
CHAPTER 24
CHAPTER 25
CHAPTER 26

CHAPTER 27
CHAPTER 28
CHAPTER 29
CHAPTER 30
CHAPTER 31
CHAPTER 32
CHAPTER 33 – THE TEACHER
CHAPTER 34
CHAPTER 35
CHAPTER 36
CHAPTER 37
CHAPTER 38
CHAPTER 39
CHAPTER 40
CHAPTER 41
CHAPTER 42
CHAPTER 43
CHAPTER 44
CHAPTER 45
CHAPTER 46
EPILOGUE

PROLOGUE

THE MAN, WITH his face hidden behind a Roman Greek Emperor mask, stood on the balcony overlooking the decorated room down below. He was immensely proud of this evening's expected accomplishments. It was a glorious night; a celebration to show off what they achieved over the last few years. He was already envisioning how much money they were going to rake in from this evening's event, with a huge pay-out to come soon, that only a select few knew about.

His dark eyes took it all in. The wall-to-wall mahogany bar was filled with the finest liquor and wine from all over the world. They set a lavish casino up with tables for poker, blackjack, roulette, and slot machines. The large flat-screen TVs were for those interested in fantasy football or online gaming opportunities, horses, or fight clubs that were illegal everywhere else. And the recent addition of young women and men dancing in cages, but not like those of a 70s strip joint or nightclub. The costumed participants inside added an air of mystique and class. They meticulously planned everything in their design to appeal to the rich and sometimes famous who just wanted to allow their inner inhibitions and desires to be revealed without the paparazzi putting them on the front pages of every tabloid magazine.

That amused him. He knew there were reporters and photographers in the crowd right now, but only because they, too, were living out their secret fetishes. With everyone masked, they didn't have to reveal their identities unless they wanted to. That was the beauty of his events. Everyone was incognito. There were politicians, members of school boards and churches, well-known celebrities, law enforcement, and even a judge or two, but everyone's secrets were safe as long as they signed the contract.

It was a thing of beauty. Magnificent, he mused to himself. All our beauties were dressed and molded to perfection and all in one room. Look at them, doing what we trained them to do. There was only one thing that could make the evening more exciting…

And there she was. He smirked. Even wearing the mask and wig, he knew it was her. He knew everything about her, every inch of her. It made him go weak in the knees when he watched her walk into the room. The sexual heat went straight to his groin. Her toned body looked exquisite in her turquoise sequins gown. It fit her like a glove as if painted on. The slit up the side showed her long, muscled, and naturally tanned legs as she worked the crowd. He nearly choked when he realized the dress barely covered the sweet spot he craved, but could no longer touch. She was the one thing he could never completely control.

What was she up to tonight? He glanced toward his private security. With a nod from him, they put their eyes on her.

~~~

She saw him the minute she walked in, lording over his loyal subjects from the balcony. He was truly evil. She was thankful the patrons to this evening's shindig were incognito, so she could blend in. She only prayed the ruse worked so she could complete what she came there to do. All eyes were on her as she waltzed through the room. Eye candy, that's all she was to them. She observed all the phony people. Men in tuxedoes and women in gowns dropped hundred-dollar bills down onto the bar for a top-of-the-line of whiskey, wine, or liqueur. They dropped even more onto a silver platter with the offer of companionship—their pick. With the right amount, several sexually clad women and men would parade themselves in front of the paying customers. His or her eyes would devour the perfect specimens and add more money to the platter once they made a selection. Then the paying customer and their auctioned selection would exit for a private room.

As despicable as she knew that was, she acknowledged it was the only way she could pull off her plan. She walked toward the bar and placed two hundred-dollar bills on the granite top. She chose two tumblers of Jameson Whiskey for this evening's charade. When a silver platter arrived in front of her, she dropped the entry fee. Turning her back to the bar, she caught the smirk on the face of the man on the balcony. She knew he was watching and knew his minions were watching her, too. She had to force back sarcastic laughter when she noticed the selection that was paraded in front of her. The lord and master, the man in charge of everything that occurred on the premises, was showing his humor.

They offered her six to choose from. All gorgeous men dressed in nothing but black satin briefs, six-pack abs, tanned and glistening. All Gladiator-types, which seemed to be a requirement. Everyone chosen and trained by the lord and master to take part in this evening's event had to be in perfect shape. No excuses. There was a full-sized gymnasium on the bottom floor for that purpose. She knew all the rules. They were despicable. Her goal was to bring it all down.

She dropped the amount and chose one man offered. He was merely a pawn in her plan. That he was roguishly handsome didn't matter. She wasn't here for pleasure. She picked up the tumblers of whiskey, and the male specimen followed her like the paid servant he was. Before entering the elevator that would take them down to another floor, she glanced once more toward the balcony.

The man in the Roman Greek Emperor mask was gone.

Inside a private room, she ordered her escort to sit on the bed while she freshened up. He would do as she ordered. Paid escorts did what they were told. The private rooms were not all the same. Some were rooms she would never enter. In this one, the walls were dark wood, the floors the same, and the sconce lighting merely decorative. The housekeeping staff placed freshly lit, scented candles on tables on both sides of the bed. They also scattered rose petals across the white satin comforter. Hand cloths, bottled water, scented soaps, various types of makeup, and adult paraphernalia sat atop an antique dresser. If it was anywhere else, the room would be romantic. Here, she loathed it.

She walked to the opposite side of the room, removed a small vial from inside her bra, and poured the contents into a tumbler of whiskey.

She walked back toward the escort and handed him the drink. She had to be careful. Some escorts were willing participants and in good with the lord and master. She couldn't take a chance on giving herself away. She gulped down her drink in one shot. He did the same.

"Stand up in front of me. Let me look at you," she said, knowing she had to make the charade seem real.

She noticed the perfect white teeth when he smiled, and his chiseled jawline. He was easy on the eyes. She stroked his muscled chest and inwardly cringed when she saw his penis immediately rise. Too easy.

She leaned in close and whispered in his ear. "Touch me as if I were a China doll."

She couldn't tell the color of his eyes in the dark room, but she noticed the gleam through the dark mask. He moved slowly, allowing the fingers of his right hand to stroke her along the cheek, just underneath the mask. They continued down the side of her neck. His eyes held hers as he lowered his lips to hers; his tongue danced around the edges, as his fingers continued their journey.

She had to fight off her arousal when he unexpectedly rubbed his palm over the nipple of her left breast. It sent a shiver up and down her spine. When he devoured her luscious lips with his, she could almost feel her legs parting to allow him entry to the sweet spot the lord and master wanted to own. When he rubbed his palm up and down her thigh, she nearly had an orgasm the moment his fingers brushed against the edge of her vagina.

She was about to step away from his touch—she had a job to do—when she felt him swaying. Once he lost control of his body and slumped forward, she maneuvered him toward the bed. She kept up the pretense until she knew he was out. His hands stopped moving, showing the tranquilizer she poured in the vial kicked in. She checked his eyes, to be sure. Yep, he was out.

"Damn," she said to herself, looking at his gorgeous body. "He was good. Well trained. I might have enjoyed what he offered if this was another place, another time, and not some sham."

She studied him once more to make sure he was asleep, adjusted her dress, and then stepped out of the room. In the dark hallway, she strutted past several doors until she came to the one painted black. She punched the combination into the lock. The lord and master would have a stroke if he knew she discovered that some time ago. When she heard the click, she opened the door and hurried inside.

She had little time. Her escort could wake up, or the security could come looking. They could only enter the private rooms if it was an emergency. They would consider this an emergency if they knew what she was doing. She studied the cameras, tripod, and filmmaking equipment that were used for nefarious purposes, and anger surged through her. She couldn't stop now. She studied the wall-to-wall bookshelves of DVDs, the massive computer, and the drawers full of documents. She couldn't take it all. She knew that. And she couldn't call the police. There were cops upstairs enjoying the party. She wasn't sure which ones she could trust. She just needed a few items of evidence. It would be easier if she could just steal a flash drive, but she knew they kept those hidden in places she couldn't get to.

She strode toward the DVDs and perused the names on the labels. She grabbed two, opened the cases, and tucked the silver DVDs inside the front of her dress, tight against her skin. Then she opened a drawer and grabbed a stack of photographs and secured them, too.

She heard a noise. Damn. Time was running short.

She took a deep breath, crossed the floor to the door, opened it, and peered outside. The hall was empty, but she could hear the elevator coming. She hurried out into the hall and closed the door behind her. Instead of going back toward the way she came, she ran in the opposite direction. At the end of the hall, she arrived at a thick door that looked like it was from an old, historic mansion. It also had a combination lock. A bout of anxiety kicked in as she struggled to remember the numbers. The two locks weren't the same. Once she calmed down, she punched in the numbers from her memory, heard the click, and pulled it open. There was a light above where she stood, but all she could see inside was blackness. She knew there was a corridor that led to a set of stairs. It was an old tunnel that was there from bootlegging days, years before. The problem was; that she didn't know what was waiting for her if she got to the other side. She debated turning back, but the footsteps got louder, which meant they were closing in on her.

The man she referred to as the lord and master was coming for her.

A bullet suddenly shattered the wall light just above her head. Broken glass rained down on her.

She didn't hesitate. Ignoring her fear of the unknown, she raced into the blackness and shut the thick door behind her. Even if they knew the combination, at least she had a couple of minutes to gain ground.

As she ran, she heard the squeaking noises of the rats and the horrific crunching sound when her stilettos stepped on one of them. She shivered at the thought that something was crawling on her and pushed through. There was light shining underneath the doors on both sides of the path. She hated to think of leaving them behind, but she had no choice. Her escaping was the only way to help set them free.

Finally, she saw a spotlight just ahead. It was always on for those that gained entry from this direction. Few knew of this area. Those that did, she hoped, wouldn't be waiting for her.

When she reached the door, she punched the button on the top right of the wall and braced herself for trouble. Once it opened, she felt a moment of relief. It was a pantry fully lined with shelves of food. And there was nobody there.

But she wasn't out of the woods yet.

Stepping inside, she felt along the wall behind the food and pushed another button. The door slid shut behind her. Now was the hard part.

She walked through the panty to the other door, put her ear up to it, and listened. She couldn't hear anything. She looked down at the space under the door and didn't see any shadows from a person standing nearby. She cautiously opened it and looked around at the recently renovated kitchen. It felt like she stopped breathing until she verified she was alone.

Instead of walking out the back door to the alley—where she assumed security would expect her to exit—she stepped into the hall that would take her to the front entrance. Anyone lingering there wouldn't know what was going on inside the private function.

Once you walked through those doors, everything was supposed to be top secret.

As she suspected, men and women were waiting in line, hoping to get permission to enter. Other than admiring her figure and the gorgeous mask, they paid little attention to her. They focused on the gold door to gain entry.

Once she made it to the front door, she thought she was home free. She slipped past the red carpet entrance and finally made it to her car. It wasn't until she was turning onto the highway that she finally removed the mask and wig, and allowed herself to breathe easy. When a luxurious black SUV pulled up on her left and the window rolled down, she knew she was still in danger.

Shit!

The lord and master, himself—still wearing his Roman Greek Emperor mask—and she could tell he was smirking at her.

Without hesitating, she punched the gas pedal and hauled ass.

CHAPTER 1

I HEARD THE sons of anarchy ringtone from my cell phone but thought it was just a dream because the clock on the nightstand showed it was three-thirty in the morning. Who would call at such an ungodly hour? I raised my head off the pillow and looked around. Maybe the events over the last few months had been nothing but a nightmare and the phone interrupting my sleep was too.

Nope, I was still living in the RV Derek Jameson parked in my driveway. A glance outside showed my cottage was being rebuilt after being torched. My Golden Retriever, Bailey, was sprawled out at the foot of the bed, trapping my feet under the sheets. The ringtone finally stopped. I returned my head to the pillow, only to hear it start up again seconds later. Somebody was desperate to get in touch with me. A phone call in the early morning hours wasn't good.

A feeling of dread settled over me, followed by visions of Finn in jeopardy. Finn, the devastatingly handsome police officer I convinced myself was worth putting my fragile heart on the line for. Of course, that was after my twenty-year marriage fell apart because of my husband's betrayal. We only had a few dates before the department sent him on an undercover assignment and he went off the grid. Those dates, and the passionate phone chats in between, revealed the attraction was stronger than what I experienced with my former husband. Just thinking about Finn made my body react.

Please, don't let it be Finn.

I untangled myself from the sheets and tried to reach for the phone, but knocked it off the nightstand by mistake.

"Crap," I muttered to myself, only to receive an annoyed look from Bailey for waking her up, too. "Sorry, Bailey, somebody wants to talk to me."

I swear she rolled her eyes at me before returning to her position.

I scrambled toward the floor and fumbled for the phone. Not a simple task. The space is tiny in the bedroom of an RV. I finally grabbed it and swiped the screen.

"Hello," I said, trying to keep the fear out of my voice.

At first, all I could hear was heavy breathing. It sounded like the person had just stopped running and was trying to catch their breath. There was also vehicle traffic in the background. That was odd, considering the hour. Then, I heard the voice of a female. By the tone, she sounded scared.

"Katie, are you there? It's Jillian Moore."

I gasped. It wasn't someone giving me bad news about Finn. It was a voice from the past. I wouldn't have believed it if I wasn't sitting on the floor shivering from not having the warmth of my comforter.

Jillian Moore was my college roommate. We were inseparable during those years. Once we graduated, she returned to live with her father. For the first few months, we got together a few times at a local coffee shop, but then she just stopped calling or responding to my calls. We drifted apart. Now, here she was, on the phone in the middle of the night.

"Jillian?" I confirmed, stunned to hear from her. It had been so long. She didn't even come to my wedding all those years ago. "It's good to hear your voice. How are you?"

"Katie, please listen," she said, speaking fast, as if she had little time. "Did you get my package?"

"Package? What package?"

"Katie, I'm in trouble and I'm running out of time. I need your help."

"Okay. What is it?" Something was going on with my old friend. I did not know what, but there was no mistaking her fear.

"I know it's been a long time and I'm sorry about that. Can you meet me somewhere?"

"Of course, but why not just come to my home?" And then I remembered I no longer had a home and was sleeping in an RV.

"That wouldn't be wise," she said.

That statement gave me pause. Why wouldn't it be wise to come to my home?

"Can you meet me in the alley behind the coffee shop where we used to meet after college? Katie, this is important. I'll be in the alley behind the coffee shop on Tuesday, at midnight. Can you be there?"

"At midnight? The coffee shop is closed at midnight." Many ideas were racing through my head right now, and that only brought on more questions.

"Please Katie, I know I'm asking a lot from a friend I abandoned, but you're the only one I could trust. I'm in serious trouble. Please. Will you be there?"

"Of course, Jillian, I'll be there." How could I not? We might have lost touch, but she was my best friend throughout college. I would never turn her down.

I heard screeching tires, which told me she was outside somewhere.

"Oh no, I have to go," she blurted out unexpectedly.

And before I could respond, the line went dead.

Now that I was wide awake and in a state of panic, I wanted to talk to her some more, but she was no longer there. I looked at my phone. The call came in from an unknown number, so I couldn't call her back.

She was gone, again.

Frustrated, I stood up and sat down on the edge of the bed. Bailey was also awake now. She knew I was upset about something. She crawled toward me and placed her head on my leg.

"I'm okay, Bailey," I said, petting her behind the ears. I tried to think about what I could do to track Jillian down. After looking at the clock, I had to face the fact there were no options. I would have to wait until a normal hour. What was she involved in that was making her so desperate she needed to meet me in an alley at midnight? And why did she have to rush off the phone? I noticed she didn't say the name of the coffee shop. Was she trying to be secretive about meeting me? Was someone listening?

The coffee shop she was referring to was a spot we used to meet to catch up after she went back to her dad's house. It was a central location between our respective homes. I moved Bailey over and climbed back under the covers. Alone with my thoughts, all I could do was speculate on what was going on with her. Unfortunately, I had the feeling whatever it was;

it wasn't good. I couldn't help but fear for the safety of the friend I once knew. I hugged Bailey and tried to put all the morbid thoughts out of my head, but I knew sleep would not come.

CHAPTER 2

A FEW HOURS later, I was wide awake. Honestly, I don't think I ever went back to sleep. Stretching before climbing off the bed, I tried to recall everything Jillian said before she unexpectedly disconnected the call. She said something about sending me a package. I haven't received a package yet. Nothing else she said made sense. After a few moments, I gave up trying to analyze. I would just have to get through today and tomorrow and meet her as she asked. Maybe the package would arrive in the meantime and give me some answers.

After cleaning up, I took Bailey for a run. An hour later, we had some breakfast, and then I spent a good thirty minutes with the contractors confirming the plans for my new cottage. Once I was sure we were on the same page, I loaded Bailey into the SUV, checked the mailbox—there was no package—and then headed for the office in Onset Village. I parked in the lot across the street and grabbed my backpack and Bailey from the back seat.

"Time to work, Bailey," I said, once I unlocked the door and entered. First, I turned up the thermostat to get the moisture out of the room, and then I positioned myself in the leather chair behind the desk and switched on the laptop.

Bailey did her usual nose-detecting of each room to verify we were alone. After a few minutes, she returned and positioned herself by the front window to watch outside.

I read through emails and responded to those that needed attention. I was finishing the report for a recent case when the sound of laughter interrupted my thoughts. It was the middle of December and the weather outside was gorgeous. The temperature was mild, mid-fifties, high for this time of year, and the sky was as blue as I've ever seen it. That could explain the reason for the unusually heavy foot traffic in the area, considering the weekend tourists went home, and it was now Monday.

When I glanced outside, I saw the smiling faces of several locals strolling along the sidewalks without a care in the world. Some were admiring the recently added Christmas decorations on the storefronts. Others were getting coffee at their favorite café before checking out the boutiques. It didn't help that Bailey kept staring at me with her sad puppy-dog eyes, trying to convince me to do the same.

"I already took you for a run, Bailey," I said to her, which earned me a heavy sigh of boredom when she plopped her head down on the floor in frustration.

"I hear ya," I commiserated

I forced myself back to the computer and was about to do a Google search on my friend, only to find myself elated when a woman unexpectedly walked through the door. Bailey got excited too. She bounded over to greet her, only to be disappointed when the woman's hand went up to block her from getting close. It took me two seconds to realize she was not a dog lover. Should have been a sign, but I let it go.

"Bailey, come," I said, motioning her toward me. Thankfully, she complied and sat down by my chair.

"Sorry," I said to the woman. "Bailey thinks it's her job to inspect everyone who enters."

I discreetly studied the woman as she overtly studied me. She was attractive and her confidence showed by the way she carried herself. I could tell she was successful, or wealthy, by the matching Gucci handbag and briefcase. Her hair was brown with highlights cut to just below her shoulders in an expensive salon style. Wispy bangs feathered her forehead, and she airbrushed her makeup to hide any imperfections. I recently discovered that technique when tabloid media interviewed me during the trial of my stalker. Long story.

She wore a fitted black skirt over a white-tailored blouse, a suede coat, and matching ankle boots. I realized her rebuffing Bailey was probably so she wouldn't get dog hair all over her designer attire.

She gave me a dubious look as she approached my desk. It was the same look I received from other clients who walked through the door since I opened up shop as a private investigator just a few weeks ago. After a few moments of her sizing me up, I felt like I was under a microscope and she was giving me some sort of rating.

"Are you Katie Parker," she finally asked, "the woman who was all over the media recently because her husband was leading a secret life with two different women?"

On the one hand, I hated that potential clients were coming to see me because they learned of my story via tabloid media. On the other, it was free publicity.

"Unfortunately," I said. Thankfully, they never had to ask for the sordid details, because the gossip reporters spelled it all out.

"And now you help those under similar circumstances?"

I pointed to my credentials hanging on the wall. "Licensed and everything. Am I not what you expected?"

"I didn't know what to expect," she said, still staring.

"How can I help you?"

From the outside, the front of the office looks like a New England colonial house. It was only the interior that was converted into an office. The entry, which used to be a living room, has four leather chairs situated around a square coffee table with magazines and a floral arrangement on top. The walls are white with framed photos of the ocean beaches along Cape Cod. Fitting for the area.

I sat behind the desk, my laptop in front of me, and a PC monitor and printer on a console table to my left. In the middle room, there were three more desks with computers and printers on top, cabinets for the files, and a closet to keep the office supplies and miscellaneous equipment from cluttering up the space. A kitchen, lounge, and full-sized bathroom made up the entire back area with a back door that exited into an alley.

"My name is Sarah Miles," the woman finally said, holding out her business card. "I need help with a personal matter. My attorney recommended you after seeing you on the news."

I briefly glanced at the card. She was the owner of

the Miles Modeling Agency. It showed the main office to be in the beach town of Nauset Bay, about twenty minutes away.

I wondered if her attorney was someone Derek Jameson knew. He was the man who set up the office and offered me the position. He put the word out the minute I accepted it and asked friends to refer clients my way.

"Have a seat," I said, motioning to the chairs opposite my desk. "Can I offer you something to drink?"

"I'm fine." She sat down and put the briefcase on her lap, placing both hands on top of it. The purse remained over her shoulder.

"So, how can I help?"

"My husband has been cheating on me."

"I'm sorry," I said. There wasn't much I could say since I just went through it myself. She was also the third client who had walked in claiming adultery since I hung the shingle outside. Derek joked it was becoming so common for divorce attorneys to hand out business cards when they attended weddings. I assumed he was joking, at least I hoped.

"What makes you think he's cheating?"

"A couple of reasons; he's a partner at a prestigious law firm, yet he still claims he has to work on nights and weekends. He had that schedule when he was a junior associate."

I nodded while making a mental note. I remember when I worked at a law firm during college; the partners were gone by six most nights.

She reached into the briefcase, pulled out an envelope, and handed it to me. "I started receiving calls at home, at all hours, even after I'd gone to bed. Sometimes the caller would hang up when I answered. Other times, they would just breathe into the phone until I would get angry and hang up. The envelope has a copy of our most recent phone bill. I circled the numbers that I'm not familiar with."

I looked at the phone bill. All the circled numbers were local. "Mrs. Miles, it sounds like you already know how to verify your suspicions."

"Please, call me Sarah."

"Sarah, if you have this information, why waste your money hiring me?"

She rolled her eyes. "Knowing isn't good enough. I need proof since finances are involved and I don't have the time."

"Is your husband aware of your suspicions?"

She smirked. "Oh yes, he knows," she said, showing her disdain for the man. "The first time I brought it up, he laughed and said I was crazy. Then I told him I wouldn't put up with it and that I wanted a divorce."

"How did he respond?"

"He stormed out of the house like a spoiled child and didn't come home for several days. When he finally showed up, he laid down the law. He reminded me I was his wife. He said I belong to him and he was going to continue to do what he wanted. He said if I tried to interfere, he'd go after everything I owned, including the modeling business I made a tremendous success of."

"So you want me to prove your husband is cheating and get you the evidence to help with any settlement your attorney may present?"

She nodded, but added, "Or evidence of any questionable behavior he might be involved in; anything you think might be relevant."

I stared at her. "Anything?"

"Anything. If it looks suspicious, check it out."

She was giving me a lot of lead-way. I wondered if she realized how expensive that could get. "Have you filed divorce papers yet?"

She shook her head no. "My attorney advised me to get proof of the affairs and anything else he was involved in before we served him. He said we should be prepared first."

"I would require a retainer."

Without hesitating, Sarah reached into her briefcase and pulled out a pre-written check. "Will that suffice?"

I glanced at the check and tried to hide my surprised expression. It was from her account for five-thousand dollars. Money wasn't a problem for Sarah Miles, but I wondered why so much up front to a P.I. she didn't know.

"I'll keep an itemized account and keep you updated."

She handed me a few other items. "Here's a photograph of my husband and his business card."

The man in the photo was lounging on a sailboat, holding a beer in one hand and offering a friendly wave to the camera with the other. All I could garner about him from the photo was that he dressed like the usual Cape Cod yuppie one might find wandering the local marinas. He wore a pale yellow polo shirt with the collar standing up around the neck, a sweater draped across his shoulders, and tan deck shoes.

"I have clients waiting at the office, so if this is enough to get you started," she said, gathering her briefcase and standing up.

"It would help to know the make and model of his car and any places he frequents."

"He drives a red Porsche Boxster convertible with the letters HOTATY on the license plate."

By the snarky way she repeated the license plate, I gathered she didn't agree with his choice. Nothing like a woman scorned.

"And his hangouts?"

"I've been told he's a frequent visitor to Pier 25. I really have to get back to my office." She offered her hand again, thanking me, and left the office.

Bailey followed her to the door then glanced back at me to say: "Let's go."

After Sarah left, I wrote a note to myself to ask Derek if he referred her to me.

For now, I had to give in to the puppy-dog eyes and take Bailey for a walk. "Okay, you win," I said. I slipped on my coat and then grabbed her leash and dog bags on the way outside.

CHAPTER 3

MY NAME IS Katie Parker. It's been almost two months since I accepted an offer from Derek Jameson, a billionaire businessman, to open up shop as a private investigator in the beach village of Onset, Massachusetts. Before that audacious invitation, I was an author who became homeless after a mentally impaired woman torched my home, burning all the manuscripts I had written over the last several years. Thankfully, I currently have a few books published, one of which is being adapted into a TV series, so I still have some income. It wouldn't be enough to sustain me, though. Since I'm currently sleeping in an RV, rewriting the manuscripts had to be put off for the time being.

To prepare for my new gig, I had to pass a background check, and even though I already had a gun permit, I took another firearm safety course, and practice shooting from time to time. In Massachusetts, you need three years of investigative or law experience to get a P.I. license. To qualify, the State Police went through my work as a writer. Except for my last two books, my characters were investigators, and one, a spy. It was determined that the heavy research I completed over the years, along with the knowledge I garnered riding with detectives and patrol officers during their shifts, was enough to pass muster. It also helped that Derek Jameson was a licensed investigator who had connections. A five-thousand-dollar check to cover the mandatory bond validated the deal.

Now, I'm a fully licensed, bonded, and armed P.I.

Derek also allowed me to use his RV while my cottage was being rebuilt. That way, I could monitor the contractors in between the P.I. work, but still maintain some independence. If you're wondering why he is helping me; it was his stepdaughter who stalked me, attempted to kill me, and made the order for my home to be burned to the ground. He carries an overwhelming burden of guilt, no matter how many times I remind him he wasn't responsible. My stalker met her demise when a police officer shot her after she threatened to stab her attorney during the trial.

Olivia and Madison, my editor and publicist in my former career as a writer, are now what I call my co-conspirators in this investigation gig. Somewhat. They only spend weekends at the Cape during the spring through fall, but normally, they come if I call. They helped me add décor, plants, and pictures to make the office more welcoming.

"Now, if I could get you into a K9 course, we'd be a kick-ass team," I teased

Bailey. Her brown eyes looked at me as if to say: "How about you take the training and I'll watch?"

Most private investigators are usually retired police officers or officers who were tired of the bureaucracy. After a little research, I discovered I'm the only female investigator in the vicinity. Three weeks in, clients have been steady. With the divorce rate rising and morals on a decline, referrals keep coming. If I learned anything during my time on Cape Cod; residents hide their scandal and sin inside the ornate homes of the coastal communities.

Technically, I share the business with Derek. He opened an investigation firm in Boston over a decade ago to do background and security checks on potential employees for his development firm or tenants for his luxurious apartments. He doesn't do the work himself, he's just the LLC behind the company, or as he jokingly says: the money man.

Truth is; the man is filthy rich. He owns various properties throughout New England: cars, a yacht, a plane, and the motorhome he's allowing me to use. The home he lives in is twelve-thousand square feet and sits on the ocean in Woods Hole. He has a floating dock for his yacht, which is currently being painted, and there is a spot in his front yard for landing his private plane. His home and stature in Woods Hole equal that of the Kennedy compound in Hyannis.

In the three weeks since I started, he's only stopped in a few times to see how the business was doing. Mostly, he just sends me an email or text with the referrals. If I need to track him down, I can usually find him at one of the local golf courses, or working from home and hanging out with his two Golden Retriever dogs.

CHAPTER 4

WHEN WE RETURNED from our walk, I added some fresh water to Bailey's dish. She lapped it up and then curled up on the dog bed I purchased for the office. "Good girl," I said, petting her behind the ears.

Back at the desk, I reviewed the information Sarah Miles gave me. I have no reason to doubt any of it. However, recently, a local cop taught me a very important lesson. He said I should stop being so trusting and show a little more cynicism. Using his advice, I try to verify information before I start an investigation so I don't get blindsided later on.

To do that, I placed a call to Roger Grainger, one of Derek's IT specialists for his Boston security firm, only he works remotely. We met here at the office the day Derek presented the offer to me. He used to be a police officer with Finn Nichols, the man I'm currently dating, somewhat, considering he's undercover and off the grid. They went through the academy together and were partners for a while. After a few years on the streets and many nights away from home, Roger called it quits and went back to civilian life when his wife said she was pregnant with their first child. She was terrified she would raise the child alone.

"Hey Roger," I said when he answered. I

knew I didn't have to identify myself since we had each other listed as contacts and my name would show up on his cell phone screen.

"Wow," he said without preamble. "That's scary; I was just going to call you."

"Really? I guess I beat you to it."

"You're probably just more organized than I am," he said with a laugh. "I take hours just to get focused each day."

After spending years on the streets as a cop, I would imagine it was a big change to sit in an office dealing with computers and paperwork every day. "What were you going to call about?"

I heard movement and then the sound of a door closing. Then he whispered into the phone, "I just wanted to know if you've heard from Finn."

At the same time I took this gig as an investigator, Finn transferred to a different department to do undercover work. "He called me a couple of weeks ago, just before he left for this latest case."

"You haven't heard from him since?"

"No, I haven't," I said, trying to keep the feeling of angst from invading my mind. "Why do you ask?"

Roger sighed. "It's probably nothing. I was just checking."

"Roger, if it was nothing, you wouldn't have brought it up. What is it?"

He was quiet for a moment. "It's better if I wait until I know more."

Now, I was worried. "Sounds like you're back peddling."

"I'm sorry, Katie, I shouldn't have said anything. Tell me why you were calling before I interrupted you."

"You're not keeping anything from me, are you?"

"No, I promise," he said.

There was something in his voice that made me think he was holding back, but I didn't have a right to push. He no longer worked at the department, but he still got inside information. I tried to reason with myself that everything was okay, but I couldn't. Still, I just started seeing Finn. If there was a problem, the department wouldn't contact me. Roger and Derek were my only go-to, but if they had anything serious to report, I was sure they would. I brushed it aside for the moment and focused on the purpose of my call. "Can you run a background on a company, get me the ownership information?"

"Sure, but it will take some time," he said. "I've got something running right now for Derek. Just give me the name of the company. I'll run it when this task is complete and then email it to you."

"Company name is The Miles Modeling Agency. The owner is supposed to be Sarah Miles. The business card says the office is in Nauset Bay."

"Got it," he said. "I'll email the info. And Katie, don't worry about Finn. I'm sure everything is fine. I was just curious if you'd heard from him."

"You know Finn better than I do," I reminded him. "But one thing he warned me about was that he might not contact me when he was undercover for fear of compromising his position."

"Yeah, I know," Roger said. "Why do you think my wife wanted me out? She couldn't handle each day of not knowing where we were or what we were doing, especially in the current climate. Finn can handle that kind of life. Hell, he thrives on it. Maybe you do too."

I laughed, knowing he was being sarcastic. "I chase down adulterers and runaways, not gangs and dealers with automatic weapons."

He chuckled. "I don't know. Sounds like you do more than that. Derek told me about your first case and that stalker that uprooted your life. You may be new to the P.I. world, but you've already dealt with some scary shit."

Unfortunately, he was right. One of my ex-husband's mistresses was diabolical and obsessed with getting rid of me. It took everything I had to go up against her. And then my very first case scared the life out of me. I thought it was a simple runaway case of a thirteen-year-old girl, and ended up being caught up with members of a group in Boston, the most dangerous gang in the City. They'd shoot you just for driving down the wrong street or wearing the wrong color.

The clients hired me to find their teenage daughter. I quickly learned that she wanted attention from her rich and pre-occupied parents, so she snuck out of the house and ended up on the streets of Dorchester. By the time I found her, two gang members were in a war with each other over the girl, and things turned ugly. The Boston Gang Unit was called in to save my sorry butt. At least I brought the girl home safe and sound and ended up with a bonus to keep it quiet. The rich don't want their dirty secrets in the media.

"That case *was* pretty scary."

"And yet you keep plugging away," he said, amused. "I'll email those documents as soon as I can."

"Thanks, Roger. Keep me informed if you hear anything about Finn."

"You got it."

Roger asking me about Finn bothered me more than I wanted to admit. He knew more than anyone that Finn wouldn't call home for fear of jeopardizing his whereabouts—or possibly his life by taking the chance that someone was listening. I tried to remember my last conversation with him. He led me to believe there wasn't anything unusual about the case; just a routine undercover job. His team had been trying to bring down a group distributing a recent batch of fentanyl that was causing a lot of deaths. I called Derek to see if he heard anything through his connections. There was a reason Roger was inquiring, even though he had a complete turnaround in the end.

I dialed Derek's home number in Woods Hole. I don't like to bother him on his cell phone in case he's busy with clients or out on the golf course.

"Hi Loretta," I said when his live-in housekeeper picked up. "It's Katie. Is Derek around?"

Along with being Derek's housekeeper, Loretta is also his home secretary, chef, dog walker, or any other task she believes he requires. Years ago, an employee murdered his wife. He never re-married and rarely dates. That's a long time to be alone. He tells me the dogs keep him company. I suspect Loretta might too.

"Oh, hi hon," Loretta said. "Hang on. I'll see if I can catch him. He was heading out to the club." I heard her feet shuffle on the floor and the pitter-patter of the two dogs following.

When she came back on the line, she said, "Sorry, hon, I missed him. Why don't you try him at the Club? He should be there in a few minutes."

"That's okay," I said. "Can you just tell him to call me when he gets home?"

"Sure, is everything okay?"

"Everything's good. I just wanted to ask him a question about Finn."

It seemed to be a monumental affair once I consented to go out with Finn. Everybody knew, even Derek's housekeeper. I knew they just wanted to see me happy after what I went through with my ex-husband and his stalker mistress. I understood their feelings, but I wanted to take it slow. Bailey and I needed time to regroup. That didn't stop the butterflies in my stomach every time someone mentioned his name. It blew me away how much we bonded in such a short time. And the chemistry between us was off the charts.

I loved Jake before I learned of his betrayal. But I don't remember feeling the way I do now, maybe because it was so long ago. It could also be because we got together in a working capacity when we first met and became friends before becoming a couple. We didn't date, per se. As a writer doing research, Jake drove me around to different training classes for a few months. After, we went out to restaurants and pubs, as a group, with other first responders. The relationship just took off from there. Thinking back on it, there was never any romantic chase involved in us getting together. We just kind of gelled.

It's different with Finn. We don't know each other from work. He calls, texts, and attempts to romance me with breakfast, lunch, and dinner, walks on the beach, and by communicating. Jake didn't have to do any of that because of our proximity. I think it's probably true to say that we just took it for granted that we were going to be together. With Finn, it feels like I'm being pursued. And I enjoy the pursuit.

"Okay hon, I'll tell him you called," she said, bringing me back to the present.

"Thanks, Loretta."

If Derek was heading off to the club, that meant he'd be there most of the day playing 18 holes of golf with his buddies. Then they'd have a few beers in the clubhouse after. Any fears for Finn's safety would have to be on hold for a while.

CHAPTER 5 - THE TEACHER

Sometime ago

THE TEACHER WAS out hunting for a new victim. Another human being he could add to his already massive collection. Possessions he could mold into the perfect specimens, and train them to earn a huge profit for his future endeavor. This was the best part about his new goal. He loved the hunt. Secretly, he knew all men did.

He scoured the streets of New York City in search of the students out partying past curfew, or the runaways that nobody would miss. He noticed her the minute she stepped out of a local convenience store. She was a runaway; he could tell. He didn't know if she ran away from a troubled home, or if she was just another wannabe actress hoping to be seen? They all came to hang out near the *New York Film Academy*, hoping to get their big break, believing they could get noticed just by being nearby.

He smirked. He didn't care. She was the one he wanted.

He continued to watch her.

Follow her.

Stalk her.

She was a tall and thin brunette beauty with sparkling green eyes, almost like emeralds, and a look of innocence that summoned his attention. She was new to the streets and still feisty, but that would change. After a few days, he was familiar with her routine, where she hid her stash of money, in which alleys and doorways she slept.

After a few nights, he paid a vagrant to steal her money. On another, he paid someone to steal her belongings. Then he paid someone to rough her up, but avoid leaving any visible marks.

Soon, she wouldn't have food or money to buy more. Soon, she wouldn't be able to sleep, for fear of what might happen when she did. He could take her now, but she still had a fire in her. He'd wait until desperation set in. Desperation made them hunger for anything other than the streets.

After another week, he knew it was time. She had been hungry for days, rifling through dumpsters for scraps, sleeping in parks during daylight hours. At dusk, he made his move. She wandered about, looking in the doorways of the shops for a place to feel safe, to close her eyes for just a moment. The sound of an NYPD chopper hovered overhead, drowning out the sounds on the street.

The man retrieved a handkerchief with an acrid-smelling substance on it. When there wasn't anyone around to care, he approached her from behind, wrapped an arm around her slender frame, and placed the rag over her mouth.

Shocked, but not beaten, she struggled to fight him off. She kicked and punched, but he was too strong, the smell overpowering. When she was limp as a rag doll, he picked her up and carried her to the black SUV with a driver waiting nearby.

To the vagrants on the street who might have noticed the expensive car, or the occupants who looked like models off the cover of a popular magazine, it was just another person picking up a runaway sibling.

There wouldn't be anyone out looking for her.

There wasn't anyone who cared.

Soon, she would no longer matter.

Now she belonged to him.

CHAPTER 6

THERE'S A LOT of grunge work involved with being a P.I. I've only been doing this for a short time, but have already spent hours searching public records in a cold drab courthouse and doing research in the old public library. Thankfully, the internet could handle most of the grunt work for this case.

Sarah gave me a list of phone numbers she claimed were from someone calling and hanging up. I assumed she passed them along because she thought one of them was the woman her husband was sneaking around with. I pulled up Google on the computer and accessed a reverse phone directory. It could provide the name of the person or business that belonged to the number and the address.

Two of the numbers were unlisted, but the prefix showed they were local. I put those off for the time being. You had to have connections to get information on unlisted numbers. Derek was my connection, but there was no reason to use that route yet. Two others were for home phones in personal residences. One belonged to a Tracy Donovan with an address in Sandwich. The other belonged to a Jessica Carter, with no address listed. The last number came up as a company called The Tapestry; a business with an address on

Casper Island. It used to be fifty acres of land surrounded by water, but now, there's a mile-long road, Casper Road, that takes you to the waterfront community.

I picked up the phone and punched in the number. After two rings, a female answered, "The Tapestry, how can I help you?"

"Who am I speaking with?" I said in a friendly voice so she wouldn't get defensive.

"Tracy," she replied.

"Hi Tracy, I found the number for your business on my phone bill, but don't remember calling it. It might help if I knew the nature of the business."

"We're an exclusive dating service."

Whoa! I admit the response took me by surprise. But then it crossed my mind that Thomas Miles could use the service for his own needs.

"Hmmm, I don't know why I would have called your service."

"Maybe you were looking for a date," she said with a snippy reply, though I considered it was just a poor attempt to be humorous. I might need to call her again in the future, so I kept my thoughts to myself.

"Thank you for your help Tracy," I said, forcing the words out of my mouth. As I was disconnecting, I wondered if she was the Tracy Donavan whose number was on Sarah's bill. I was betting she was.

Since social media was the catalyst to discovering my ex-husband's secret life with two women, I searched the popular sites for Thomas Miles. The first Facebook profile that popped up was the image of him on the sailboat, so I knew it was the right page. When I clicked on it, all I could see was his name and about status. He had his privacy settings so visitors couldn't scroll through his page. I checked Instagram, Twitter, and TikTok and discovered the same with those sites. That meant nothing, on its own, but I remembered my ex did the same before he made an entirely fake page to carry on his affairs.

I also searched the names that showed up on the phone bill: Tracy Donovan and Jessica Carter. The profiles that matched the location on the phone bill for both women also had privacy settings. There were no listings for The Tapestry or a website. That was odd.

Next, I checked the information for Thomas Miles' office and called to check his schedule. It's easier to set up surveillance when you can narrow down a subject's timeline. I punched in the number and asked the receptionist to patch me through to his secretary. A woman with an Irish accent came on the line.

"Thomas Miles' office, this is Molly; how can I help you?"

"Hi Molly," I said. "How are you?" Something I learned when I worked for a law firm was always to be nice to the secretary. They could be your best friend and an enormous source of information. Or they could hinder you from getting any information at all.

"I'm fine," Molly answered. "Thank you for asking. What can I help you with?"

"I'm calling from Caulfield's Florist and have a delivery for Mr. Miles. Is he expected to be in most of the day?"

"I believe so. Let me check."

She placed me on hold and I hummed along to the classical tune.

After a moment, she returned. "Ma'am?"

"Yes, Molly."

"Mr. Miles leaves the office at noon, and he's expected to return around two. The rest of his day is clear. He usually leaves by six."

"Great, I'll schedule the delivery for after lunch. Thank you, Molly, you've been very helpful." Thomas has been lying to his wife about working late, as if that wasn't expected. I had nothing pending, so I thought a stake-out was in order.

"You want to go for a ride, Bailey?"

She bolted off the dog bed and was in position by the door before I was even out of the chair.

"Sheesh, I guess that's a yes?"

Before leaving, I double-checked my backpack to make sure the cameras, binoculars, and recording devices I purchased were all inside and then locked the door on the way out. I walked across the street to the parking lot next to the marina, gave the ticket to the attendant, and retrieved my keys.

Bailey took her place in the back seat and stared at me until I put the window down. When we pulled out of the parking lot, she extended her head out the window and her ears flopped from the wind as we rolled along.

Nauset Bay is one of the popular resort towns on Cape Cod and is only twenty minutes away. During the summer, the drive extends to double the time battling the traffic going over the bridge by tourists flocking to the various beaches along the shore. There are miles of beaches and marinas, streets lined with shops and restaurants, and some popular locations to ride the e-bikes. I joined Olivia and Madison on one ride that took us along a winding path with trees and scenery all around, and ended in Woods Hole where we had lunch and a drink by the water, and then the ten-mile ride back home.

When I turned onto Main Street, I checked the buildings for the right address. It was the HOTATY license plate that caught my attention. I saw it on the back of a red Porsche parked in the circular drive of a four-story modern structure.

I parked on the street, a few cars away, to study the area. I was also in the position to monitor the door. If Thomas Miles walked outside for lunch, I would be ready to follow.

When noontime had come and gone with no sign of him, I assumed he left through another exit and walked to one of the local restaurants. It would be a waste of time to wander the street, hoping to find him. My best bet was to wait till the end of the business day.

My cell phone buzzed, signaling I had an email. It was from Roger. I clicked on it and reviewed the documents. As she told me, Sarah Miles was the sole owner of The Miles Modeling Agency. Roger provided the financials as well. The business did very well each year, more so in the last two years. I understood her fear and need to be prepared before having her husband served. Massachusetts not being a community property state meant her husband would have to provide a valid reason for the court to give him a portion of her business. Did he contribute financially to her business? She was right to protect herself. Proving he committed adultery, or was involved in something shady, as she seemed to suggest, could help her case.

That was a good reason to check out The Tapestry while I was in the area. It was only a few miles away from Thomas Miles' office. And Sarah told me to check out anything suspicious. There was a reason their number showed up several times on Sarah's bill. I found it odd that they chose

Casper Island as the location to open the alleged dating service. Most of the residents were older and purchased their homes years ago before prices skyrocketed.

Several years ago, my ex-husband, Jake, took me to the Island Grill, which was the only restaurant and bar in the area back then. There were three levels, and the kitchen offered most of the popular seafood plates known on the Cape, plus various pasta dishes, pizzas, and all-American hamburgers. There was also outdoor seating on each level, with perfect views of the ocean. The major attractions were the volleyball, bocce ball, and paddleball courts on the private beach outside. Jubilant customers packed the place. Unfortunately, the community didn't like the noise. They put in so many complaints that the owner eventually shut it down.

I suspected that the owner of the exclusive dating service that Tracy described now occupied that building. That street was the only spot on the island that offered business opportunities. If I was right, whoever purchased the building knew about the noise problem. They probably had to guarantee it would never be an issue, or a lot of money exchanged hands. Of course, it was all speculation at this point.

"You like taking rides, don't you, Bailey?" I said, glancing back at her. She was in heaven. Her chin rested on the open window and her tongue was hanging out, revealing her smile. She didn't even glance my way.

"I'll take that as a yes."

I took the turn off the MA 28 rotary and followed it until I reached Casper Road. Turning onto it, I followed it for the mile. Cape Cod homes with the traditional Cape Cod shingles lined both sides of the street. No traffic and no children were playing outside. As I neared the area where the Island Grill used to be located, I confirmed I was right. Someone had completely renovated the building. The former restaurant and grill was now a contemporary location with a stone walkway out front that ended at a cobblestone circular drive. Another addition to the area was the grocery mart and a café with outdoor seating. They built an enormous stone wall around the businesses to separate them from the community, which probably helped to block any noise.

I drove further up the road. They landscaped spacious corners of each block with massive-sized rocks, perennials, azalea bushes, and hydrangeas growing all around them. The rocks were perfect for what I had in mind. I parked behind them, but I could still observe the front door through the binoculars and remain out of sight. When I noticed a few dogs being walked at the opposite end of the street, I took the time to do the same. That allowed me to get a close-up view.

From the exterior, The Tapestry resembled a residential property. It was more modern than the typical shingled houses of Cape Cod. Probably stucco, with lots of windows on all three floors. It looked as though the builder took pains to make it blend in, instead of being recognized as a business. It was not what I expected.

I got the impression the owner of the building hired the same landscaper who perfected the street scenery. The same lush greenery lined the stone walkway to the door, and they layered the front of the building with colorful perennials that could have captured the eye of home magazines.

When foot traffic to the grocery mart and café picked up, I returned Bailey to the back seat and resumed my surveillance. I didn't know if The Tapestry played into Sarah Miles' situation yet. But since the number was on her phone bill, it seemed necessary to find out. If it turned out to be irrelevant, I could keep it off my last bill.

It was early afternoon when several people started showing up and entered the stucco building. Expensive cars pulled into the circular drive and parked along the side. Then a parade of individuals started entering and exiting at hourly intervals. I immediately understood why they wanted the wall. They wanted to isolate the business from the community, so homeowners wouldn't complain about all the traffic.

What I found interesting; the women that stepped out of the vehicles were all young, no older than their mid-twenties, and extremely attractive. They arrived at the same time and remained inside while I observed. Yet, the men who entered were a mixture of ages and only remained inside at hourly intervals.

That piqued my curiosity; dating service, my ass.

CHAPTER 7

MY CELL PHONE buzzed while I was fighting the traffic back to Main Street to continue surveillance on Thomas Miles. The caller ID showed it was Derek Jameson.

"What's wrong, Katie?" he said the minute I answered.

I sighed. "I thought you were golfing."

"Loretta left me a voicemail. I just got it and checked in. She said you sounded anxious."

"Derek, you know Loretta worries." The last thing I needed was Derek to go on a tangent. "I just called to see if you heard anything about Finn or his mission?"

"Only the usual," he said. "He's investigating a drug gang bringing in fentanyl."

"Have you heard from him?"

"Katie, what's going on?"

"I'm sure it's nothing," I said, cursing myself for bothering him. "It's just that I was talking to Roger earlier... he made me feel uneasy, that's all."

"Roger gets inside information."

"Hence the uneasiness," I said.

"You think he's heard something?"

"Honestly, I don't know."

"I'll make some calls."

"I'm sure everything is fine," I said, not convinced, though. Roger wouldn't say anything unless something got his attention.

"Maybe it is," Derek said. "If it is, there's no harm in checking."

"You should just go finish your golf game," I said. "We can talk about it later."

"Yeah, yeah—okay."

"Derek!" I said in a voice that was a little harsher than intended. I knew what he was doing. He was placating me. The minute he got off the phone, he'd be making calls and making waves until he knew Finn's whereabouts. Finn would not be happy.

"Katie, I'm just going to call Nauset Bay headquarters and speak to my buddy. He can at least verify that Finn's okay without giving me any information. I'll tell him to keep it quiet."

"Then why don't you let me do it," I said. "You go finish your game. If there's anything new to report, I'll call the club and let you know."

"Katie," Derek said in his authoritative voice. "I'm going to make the call. You don't have the connections. They won't tell you anything."

I knew to back off when he issued an order. He earned the right. "Okay," I said. "Call me if you hear anything."

"Will do."

"Thanks, Derek."

"Be safe, kiddo."

Be safe, kiddo. That's how he ended

every call with me and anyone else he cared about. They were words that had a specific meaning, and only his elite circle knew what they meant. I knew when he used those words. He was telling me he cared about me, to be careful, and not do anything stupid and get myself in a dangerous situation. Derek and I had gone through a lot when my ex-husband had a sleazy affair with Derek's stepdaughter, Lexy. She did just as much damage to him as she did to me during her escapades over the last few months. Derek felt partly responsible for her actions. It was an employee of Derek's company who kidnapped and ultimately murdered his wife, Lexy's mother, when the ransom payoff failed to go as planned. Lexy had mental problems as a child, but her issues worsened when she lost her mother. Not only was she a narcissist, but they also diagnosed her with a histrionic personality disorder. If she was still alive, she would still be trying to ruin our lives.

Twenty minutes after arriving at Thomas's office, I spotted him walking toward the Porsche.

"Whoa," I said, noticing that he looked a lot different now than he did in the photo his wife gave me. I pegged him around forty. In the photo, he looked healthy and happy. This man looked harsh and rough around the edges. He still dressed like a conservative attorney; a blue suit over a light blue shirt. His red tie hung loosely around his neck. I definitely wouldn't grant him the title, HOTATY. But then again, I spend my time fantasizing about Finn. With his disheveled appearance and rock-hard abs, he had a *Gerard Butler* thing going on. Who could compete with that?

I heard two beeps. He turned off the car alarm, which was my signal to restart the car. He walked around to the passenger side, opened the door, and placed his briefcase on the seat. Then he removed his suit jacket and tie, and then placed them on the seat as well. Two minutes later, he was driving down Main Street.

Bailey extended her head out the window again as I tailed him from a few cars back. I could tell by the direction he traveled that Pier 25 was his destination, one of his hangouts, according to his wife. Once he parked and walked inside, I circled the block a few times until I found an open spot on the street.

"Watch the car," I said to Bailey. "Mommy has to go check out her mark. I'll be right back."

Bailey looked at me as if she understood. The minute I stepped out, she jumped in the front and took my place in the driver's seat. Good thing I bought those leather seat covers.

The target was at the bar ordering a drink when I entered. With his back to me, I walked toward the hostess's desk and pretended to study the menu. Within a few minutes, it was clear Thomas Miles didn't respect his marriage and pictured himself as quite the ladies' man. He had no boundaries and was overly flirtatious with women at the bar. I got the impression he knew them. Yet, even though they didn't appear to be interested in his unwanted attention, they still put up with it. I wondered why.

After a few minutes, he got bored with them, because they weren't as receptive as he hoped. He swiveled around on his stool and checked out the other women in the establishment. He smiled when he spotted a blonde woman sitting alone at the opposite end of the bar. He grabbed his Martini and strutted in her direction.

I couldn't hear the conversation from my location, but her body language was clear. She had no interest. When he didn't take the hint, she grabbed her drink and walked away, calling him an expletive as she did. That didn't sit well with him. He didn't like being rejected. He threw back the last of his drink, dropped a wad of cash on the bar, and sulked out of the bar.

I watched from the door. He stumbled over something on the pavement which gave me the chance to exit and reach my vehicle car unnoticed.

"Get in the back, Bailey," I said when I opened the door to see her lying down in my seat. She looked at me for a few seconds, confused, as if I interrupted a dream, and then she slowly complied.

"Good girl."

When the Porsche sped out of the lot, I waited to allow another car to get ahead of me before following. Ten minutes later, I was stunned when he turned onto Casper Road. His wife told him she suspected his behavior, so it surprised me he didn't bother to hide the fact that he was going to an alleged dating service. He warned her he was going to continue to do what he wanted. I guess he meant it.

I drove on by but kept the sight of him in my rearview. He parked at the far end of the circular drive, stepped out, and strutted inside. From my observation earlier, the men who visited were only inside for an hour. I wondered if that would be the same for Thomas Miles. While he was inside, I couldn't catch him in the act, but I was still getting plenty of info. I parked in the same spot as before and looked around the area. Other than a few stragglers walking out of the grocery mart, I didn't see anyone else around from the neighborhood. Most of the residents were probably inside having dinner.

"Are you hungry, Bailey?" She responded by licking her jowls and staring at me.

Bailey coming with me on jobs was still a trial basis. I knew she could be a good bodyguard if I got into a tight situation, but I was also worried that she would get bored and whine. So far, that hasn't happened. I considered putting her in a doggy daycare for a few hours, but haven't found one nearby that would work time-wise, yet. And she seems to like stakeouts. Maybe because I talk the whole time, and make it sound interesting.

I packed her food and water in my Go bag and keep a collapsible rubber bowl behind the driver's seat. I stepped out and opened the back door. When I grabbed the bowl, she put her belly down on the seat in anticipation.

"I don't know if it's good that you're already used to eating in the car," I said to her while pouring two cups of food into the bowl. Her brown eyes just stared at me.

I placed the bowl on a rubber mat in front of her and watched her devour the food. It took less than two minutes. After she finished, I wiped the bowl and added a bottle of cold water. She lapped that up, too.

"Good girl."

She seemed to grasp we were back in working mode. She got back into her position by the back window and placed her head outside, watching.

I put everything away and returned to my seat. I was getting hungry myself, but didn't think to pack any snacks. I glanced over at the grocery mart and then looked around. No movement at The Tapestry and I still didn't see any residents outside in the community.

"Watch the car, Bailey. Mommy is going to the store."

I stepped out and quietly shut the door. One more look around, before I walked across the street and entered the grocery. The store was like a convenience store, except for a wall of fresh fruit and vegetables, and a deli that offered meats, homemade pasta, and fruit salad. I headed to the refrigerated drinks in the back of the store and perused the labels in search of something healthy. I settled for a V-8 juice. The elderly gentleman behind the counter was talkative. I suspected he was a former Navy man, a fisherman, or he loved the film Jaws. He had the tattoo of a large shark that covered an entire arm and an anchor on the other.

"Good evening," he said when I reached the counter.

I put the V-8 juice down and glanced at his name tag to confirm it was the same as on the door. I smiled. "This will do it, Charlie."

"Can I get you anything else?"

"I just needed something to tide me over until I get home."

"That will be three ninety-nine."

I silently gasped. The last time I bought a can of V-8 juice of that size, it was less than half that amount. Inflation was killing the average American.

He smiled through the whole transaction like he knew the prices were high, but if he was pleasant enough, maybe you wouldn't notice.

I handed him a twenty and watched him go over to a small safe behind the counter. When he came back, he made small talk while handing me the change. "Beautiful day, wasn't it?"

"Yes, it was." He seemed friendly. I thought it might be a good idea to find out what he knew about The Tapestry, without being too obvious. "How long have you been here?"

He leaned against the counter behind him and smiled, reminiscing. "I've lived on Casper Island for forty-something years. The powers that be didn't permit me to open the store and café until the last few."

"You own the café, too?"

He nodded. "My daughter runs it."

"You're lucky. The island is awesome. What's the building next door? That used to be the Island Grill, didn't it?"

He knowingly followed my gaze. "Beautiful, isn't it? Some residents complained about all the construction trucks for a while, but I didn't mind."

"It looks like they completely renovated the building."

"Major renovations," he said jovially.

"Did they just add on to the existing building?" I knew it used to be the Island Grill, but it looked nothing like it used to.

"It was a total revamp. I hated to see the trucks leave."

I smiled. "I bet business was good when they were here."

"They had visitors in from New York viewing the renovations."

"Really," I said. "What kind of business is it?"

He eyed me speculatively. "You a cop?"

I shook my head, but I don't think he believed me. I got the impression Charlie was very observant, but also discreet.

He looked around the store to see if anyone else was inside and listening. "They don't think I know, but I see things."

"Oh?"

Charlie enjoyed talking. He seemed to know things about what went on inside, but when a couple of locals entered, he clammed up.

I took the hint and made an excuse to exit. I didn't want to take the chance of many locals getting wind that I was investigating. Small talk is one thing; overtly asking questions is a clue.

Back in the car, I gave Bailey a few of her blueberry treats and finished the V-8. It gets dark earlier in December, so I took her for another walk. We were pretty much incognito since the streetlights weren't on yet. It was almost pitch black, except for the light over the door of Charlie's store. When we returned to the car, it was nine p.m. The grocery mart and café closed, and Charlie, along with the woman I assumed was his daughter, hopped into an old Ford truck.

They drove toward the water, where I assumed they both had homes.

It was at that same time that the traffic at The Tapestry picked up. I witnessed the same pattern of behavior that I observed earlier in the day. Men continued to arrive and leave at hourly intervals, yet Thomas Miles remained inside. I didn't have to be a genius to conclude something was going on behind doors, and it wasn't just a dating service. When Sarah Miles instructed me to investigate anything suspicious, I wondered if she knew that all along.

CHAPTER 8

THE RV WE were staying in was a forty-two-foot luxurious home on wheels. It had an open floor plan with two slide-outs that opened on both sides and ran down the length of the rig. The only negative was the windows on both sides that made me feel like I was living in a fishbowl when the automatic blinds were open.

The door was at the front of the rig opposite the steering wheel. The leather captain seats swiveled around and turned into recliners in the living area, where two off-white leather sofas lined both sides. The floor was Cape Cod laminate gray oak. I walked into the kitchen area. The cabinets were white, with granite countertops and stainless-steel appliances. An entire wall opposite the stove had a built-in bookcase with a flat-screen TV and fireplace below. They built the refrigerator into the wall behind it at the beginning of the hall. The bathroom offered a walk-in shower, washer and dryer, and porcelain incinerator toilet. And the master bedroom had a king-sized bed with an entire wall of closets, drawers, and another built-in TV and fireplace. When they finished rebuilding my cottage, I might be sorry to see it go.

I opened the refrigerator, grabbed a bottle of water, and poured it into Bailey's bowl. She looked up at me and stared.

"What, water isn't enough? What do you want?" As if I didn't know.

She was facing me, but her eyes kept moving to the side toward the cookie jar on the counter. "What, you want a cookie?"

She gave me a half-assed bark. When I didn't immediately reach for the jar, she barked louder. "Just give me the effing cookie!"

"Okay, okay. Sheesh."

She followed me to the counter and put her paw up, already prepared to shake. I reached for her paw and gave her a cookie. "You were a good girl today."

I felt a little guilty that she had to hang with me all day and didn't get to play. But she seemed to like it. Normally, we would get in a couple of rounds of tossing and chasing the tennis ball. We both had to get used to a different routine with this new gig. I could deal with it, but I wasn't sure it was good for her. She didn't act out, though. She just followed my cue.

I was a little restless, so I put on some comfortable clothing and sat down on the sofa to watch some TV. Instead of joining me, Bailey curled herself behind the driver's seat recliner. That was her go-to space when she was tired before bedtime.

I scrolled through the channels. Seeing nothing of interest, I switched over to Paramount and looked for something to stream. I settled on The Good Wife. I never saw the show when it first came out. It was a long day, and I was tired, but the first episode had me intrigued. I dozed off during the second but was wide awake when I heard the Sons of Anarchy ringtone on my cell phone. Derek's name showed up on the screen. I hoped he was calling to tell me not to worry about Finn.

"Hey," I said. "How was the golf?"

"Hey kiddo," he said, somewhat somberly.

I immediately knew something was wrong. "What's up?"

"Did I wake you?"

"No, I was just watching some television."

"I don't have good news."

Oh, God. I was now sitting on the edge of the sofa, bracing myself. "What is it?"

"I spoke with my buddy at Nauset Bay P.D. There's no way to sugarcoat this, Katie, so I'm just going to say it. The crew Finn was working with lost radio contact with him." There was a tension in his voice that usually wasn't there.

"So what does that mean, exactly?"

"They said we shouldn't worry just yet, that Finn is probably in too deep, and just can't make contact."

"When was the last time they heard from him?" Even though I just started dating Finn, we already talked about how we'd handle this situation if it came to pass. But preparing for the possibility and dealing with it, in reality, were altogether different.

"It's only been two days, so they're not overly concerned yet."

"Two days of no contact?" I confirmed.

"Katie, we have to think positive," he said. "I've known Finn for a long time. He's been in some pretty difficult situations. He's always come out of them."

I sighed. "Thank you for saying that, Derek."

"We have to believe he's fine. He's with some good cops and they watch each other's backs. He'll be just fine."

Derek was right, thinking negatively wouldn't help. But I couldn't get rid of the uneasy feeling in the pit of my stomach. I had to hold strong. Finn wouldn't want it any other way. It was too soon for me to meet his son, but I immediately thought of him. I wondered if they informed the ex-wife. Probably not. There could be several reasons to explain why he was out of radio contact. "I'm okay, Derek."

"Yes, I've seen how strong you can be. Hold on to that," he said. "As soon as they get in touch with me, I'll let you know."

"Thanks for looking into it." It had to be okay. What else could we do, go undercover looking for him?

"Okay then," he said, and then he was quiet for a moment. "You be safe, kiddo."

"Ditto," I said.

When I got off the phone, I wondered if Derek remembered to say those words to Finn before he left on this latest mission.

I'm sure he did. The two of them were close. Finn was a young officer when one of Derek's employees kidnapped and murdered his wife. They formed a bond during the ordeal, and after. I had to believe Finn was fine. He was just in too deep, like they said. It had to be.

"*You better be alright or I'll kick your ass,*" I said to myself.

CHAPTER 9

Years ago

IT WAS THE day of registration for my freshman year at college. Dozens of students waited in line to sign in, and collect schedules and information about classes. Most of them were with a parent, or parents, except for me, and another eighteen-year-old, Jillian Moore. She stood directly in front of me, acting independent, just as I was, over the fact that we were handling this monumental life change all alone.

"Hi, I'm Katie," I said with my hand out in the introduction. "Looks like you and I were the only ones brave enough to tackle this new challenge without a parent hovering over our shoulders."

She turned toward me and returned the handshake with a smile. That was the first time I could see how gorgeous she was and with very little makeup. She wore a pair of skinny jeans, a white blouse tied at the waist, and sandals, designer brands, but still unassuming. "Jillian... I see what you did there."

I shrugged and smiled back. "Better than admitting my father couldn't get the day off work to be here. Makes it sound like it was my idea, at least that's my story. Yours?"

She smirked. "My father is a multi-millionaire who prefers spending his time making more. He shouldn't be here. He would have his phone stuck to his ear, which would only irritate me. What about your mother?"

"Left when I was a toddler."

Jillian looked at me as if she was just seeing me for the first time. "Mine too," she said, stunned. "We have something in common. The nanny and butler raised me while my lawyer dad schmoozed with wealthy politicians and CEOs, smoking cigars and drinking Cognac."

There was an edge to her voice when she talked about her father. The line inched forward and we with it. We were walking side by side now.

"My early years were with a father who was a beat cop, and the neighborhood boys, hence the tomboyish attire."

She glanced at my cheap boyfriend jeans with holes in them, the ribbed tank top, and white converse tennis shoes on my feet.

"You know holy jeans are the trend, right?"

I laughed. "I know nothing about clothing and makeup. I just dress for comfort."

"Well, it works," she said, genuinely. "You look great. Comfortable, yet stylish."

That was how my friendship started with Jillian Moore. From the moment we met, there seemed to be a connection between the two of us. Both of us revealed things about ourselves that we ordinarily wouldn't.

Both of our mothers left home, so our fathers raised us. Not too many could relate.

Her father, an extremely wealthy and prominent attorney, enlisted the help of a nanny and butler. She grew up in a luxurious waterfront home on the New England coast and attended private school. My father, a police officer, enlisted the help of a neighborhood full of boys until he met the woman who became my stepmother years later. I attended the only public school in town.

Howard Moore, Jillian's father, wanted her to follow in his footsteps, so he used all his influences to help her with her education, and she ended up with a full scholarship at the school he graduated from. She declined the scholarship, much to her father's disappointment, and made her own choice, which was how we ended up as roommates. I wasn't sure about a future career, so I opted for the criminal justice program. It was the perfect situation. Jillian and I came from different worlds and financial statuses, but we ended up being best friends.

During our time in school, Jillian focused on her goals and had a firm grip on what she wanted to do with her life. Studying was her priority, while I only did so when I had to. She was conservative and conscientious. I was carefree and always looking for an adventure, which convinced me to switch to creative writing in my third year. She graduated with top honors, and some of the top law schools were sending her applications. I was just happy to finish.

After graduation, I moved in with my grandmother, whose health was going downhill. That's when I started writing books so I could be at home when she needed me. Jillian went back to her dad's house. And everything changed. We kept in touch and met up a few times for the first several months, but I could tell things were different. I just didn't know why. Not long after, I heard a rumor she was having difficulties with her father and decided against working at his law firm. When my grandmother passed away, she showed up at the funeral and we went to lunch. I could tell she wasn't the same young woman I went to college with. And then one day, she moved out of her father's home but didn't give me a forwarding address. When I met Jake, the man I was to marry, I called her dad's house several times and continued to get the same message; that he didn't know where she was. I also talked with the nanny and butler who helped raise her, but they didn't know where she was. She just dropped off the face of the earth, or someone was lying. For her to leave home didn't surprise me. But to leave without keeping in touch with me, something was wrong, only it was too difficult to tell me.

That was the last I heard from her, until now, asking me to meet with her. Not for lunch or dinner, but in the back of an alley at midnight. She said it was urgent. And I could tell from her voice that she was terrified. But of what? What happened to Jillian that I didn't know?

CHAPTER 10

WHEN I WOKE up after only a couple of hours of sleep, my body felt like I had been in a kickboxing match, only I didn't get any kicks in. Between worrying about Finn and dreaming about Jillian, all I did was toss and turn until I heard the alarm clock. I dragged my body out of bed and went to the bathroom. Bailey was still curled up on the end of the bed, oblivious that it was morning.

To get motivated for the day, I decided a long run was in order. I threw on a pair of tights, a t-shirt, and my Adidas jacket and running shoes. After pulling my hair into a ponytail, I grabbed my phone, Bailey's leash, and keys off the counter. That was all it took. Bailey jumped off the bed and we headed out the door. I waved to the builders working on the cottage, bummed that it was going so slow. That was to be expected in December. The weather was mild, but it was still winter.

We started at a slow jog and took a left out of the driveway. We headed toward the recreation center. Bailey could do her business and I could place it in the dumpster. We ran around the track. After about two and a half miles, we did a U-turn and headed back.

I put food and fresh water in Bailey's bowls and then hopped into the shower.

While I waited for my hair to dry, I went into the kitchen and poured myself a glass of unsweetened green tea, and made two pouched eggs and whole-wheat toast. While eating, I observed the work on the cottage, wondering if I would like the new layout. I viewed the blueprint. It was an open floor plan, like the original design, with the kitchen and family room together. Derek suggested adding a ten-by-ten loft over the area that I could use as an office, with French doors leading to an outdoor deck. The addition would give me a view of the ocean, but I could still see Bailey if she remained down below. She used to enjoy sitting by the sliding glass door off the kitchen/family room, watching the ocean, and seeing if any new dogs walked by.

Once I finished breakfast, I cleaned up the mess and went about getting ready for the day. I slipped into a pair of boot-cut jeans, a white-collared shirt, and my red cowboy boots. When I got my license to be a private investigator, I kept my gun in my backpack. When the case of the runaway girl took me into gang territory, it was unsettling when I couldn't get to my gun in a pinch. Keeping it in the backpack had to go. Derek bought me a leather gun belt and suggested I try that. Now, the gun sits in the holster at my right hip. To keep it out of sight, I wear a lightweight blazer or windbreaker.

"Okay, Bailey," I said, reading the notes

I wrote the day before. "The first thing we need to do today is to check out the address for Tracy Donovan."

Bailey tilted her head to the side as if she was listening to my every word.

"She was one number on Sarah's phone bill," I told her. "If the Tracy on the bill is the same woman who answered at The Tapestry, she could be someone Thomas Miles was having an affair with. It's a place to start, anyway, don't ya think?"

Bailey walked toward the door and looked back at me, as if to say, let's go.

"So you agree," I said. She just stared.

The address I was looking for was on this side of the bridge, so we didn't face the morning traffic. When I pulled onto the street, there was a white convertible Mini Cooper parked in the driveway. I wrote the license plate number in my notebook and surveyed the house from down the street. It was a small house with Cape Cod shingles, two blocks away from the water, which meant it wasn't cheap. All the houses on the street were the same, two or three-bedroom homes. The large picture window in the front made this house unique.

At the house next door, two young women were on the front lawn with strollers. They were talking and stretching, getting ready to walk or jog. To keep from looking suspicious, I pulled a map out of my glove compartment. In some neighborhoods, you could sit all day with no one noticing. Seeing the neighborhood watch sign, I assumed someone was observing.

As luck would have it, I didn't have to wait long before a female walked outside and stepped into the Mini. She looked to be in her early twenties, with long, brown hair that fell to the middle of her back. She wore a tight-fitted royal blue dress with a pair of three-inch stilettos, and enough makeup for an evening out. Interesting attire for a receptionist, I thought. That only encouraged me to follow her.

When the Mini reached The Tapestry, she pulled into an alley behind the building. I didn't notice it during yesterday's surveillance. She parked next to a red Corvette Stingray. When she stepped out of the vehicle, she checked her image in the mirror, and then entered through a back door.

I chose a different corner to park, grabbed Bailey's leash, and took a stroll, cutting across the street towards the alley. I added the plate number of the Stingray to my list. While in the alley, I mentally noted that the back door to The Tapestry was a standard steel door. On the way back to the car, Bailey took part in our charade by leaving a deposit, which I had to pick up with one of her dog bags. Since there was no dumpster, it meant we'd have to suffer from the smell until we could find one.

"Thanks, Bailey."

I swear she smiled.

CHAPTER 11

THOMAS MILES WAS the target of my investigation, but all the numbers on Sarah's bill pointed to The Tapestry. I wanted to know the connection. Sarah said, check out anything suspicious. And the place *was* hiding secrets.

While it was quiet, I called Connie Fulbright at Derek's Boston firm to ask a favor.

"Hey Connie," I said when she answered.

"To what do I owe the honor? Let me guess, you're working a fresh case?"

"How about dinner at your favorite restaurant?"

"You already owe me dinner."

"Okay, so add on a cheesecake."

"Only if you add strawberries and whip cream. So what's new since the last time we talked?"

"Finn's currently unaccounted for. His team lost radio contact."

"He's missing? Oh, Katie, I'm so sorry. You must be frantic."

"What can I do? It's the part of the job that's tough to handle, but you have to deal with it when it does. I feel bad for his son."

"Do you think there's anything to worry about?"

"Too early to tell."

"Shit, you've been through so much

already. If you need anything, just call or text."

"Thanks, friend, I appreciate it, but I'm keeping positive thoughts that he's okay," I said. "However, since you offered to help, I could use a favor."

She laughed. "I walked right into that, didn't I?"

"That you did. Could you check your computer and see if you can find any records for a company by the name of The Tapestry, Inc.?"

"Spelled as it sounds?"

"Yes." I heard her fingers on the keyboard.

"Sorry Katie, I don't see any corporate docs under that name."

"That's what I expected."

"Well, good, but I still expect dessert."

"I'll check my schedule to see when I'm available," I said. "Maybe you can fit me in if you're in between dates."

She laughed. "You make it sound like I go out every night."

"You do."

We both laughed.

"I'll pray for Finn," she said. "Keep your chin up."

"Thanks, Connie."

Connie said there weren't any records for the company I requested, and she can access any business that files for corporate status. So, it probably wasn't a legitimate dating service, as I suspected.

From my spot, I noticed Charlie walking in and out of the store, placing items out front. Around ten, a couple of employees showed up to prepare for any lunch crowd at the café. Not long after, I noticed a change at The Tapestry as well. All was quiet on the street, so you couldn't help but notice the five attractive women who arrived at the same time. Even at rush hour in the city, it would have been hard to miss them. They looked like they were dressed for a New York or Hollywood nightclub. And just like yesterday, the male customers arrived at noon.

Noontime dating. Interesting.

Even though the males were all different in age, they all drove an expensive vehicle. Reasonable to assume money was required to date the women at this alleged dating service. That was fascinating all by itself. Derek taught me that investigations sometimes veered off in different directions. That appeared to be the case here.

After an hour of watching, a black Range Rover drove past me with three men inside. Watching through the rear-view mirror, I saw them continue for a few blocks. Then they did a U-turn and slowed as they drove back toward the circular drive. On Cape Cod, a Range Rover is a semi-popular SUV. It wasn't the vehicle that got my attention. There was just something about the three men that made me take notice. It was the obvious way they studied the surroundings as they passed and then pulled into the circular drive. If this was Hollywood, I would have thought they were actors filming a scene. Since this was Casper Island, a quiet, waterfront community, I thought there might be a shakedown.

"These guys have me all kinds of cynical," I said to Bailey.

Her head was out the window, breathing in the fresh air. But I swear she had her eyes peeled to the men, just as mine were. Maybe she was a good K-9 dog without the training.

The driver was the first to exit the vehicle. When he did, he stood with his back to the SUV, as if on the lookout for something sinister to appear. He was over six feet tall, with a wide-barreled chest and a very thick neck. Once he cleared the area, he signaled the front seat passenger, who exited in the same fashion. The overt manner of searching the area was rather obvious. When he reached inside his jacket, I followed the movement: he clasped his fingers around the gun on his hip. He was packing heat.

Both men wore black jeans, black leather jackets, and black boots. Once he, too, concluded the area was clear, he opened the door for the backseat passenger. I couldn't help but laugh. The man who stepped out wore an Armani suit with a white-collared shirt opened at the neck.

Instinctively, I looked around for another

vehicle to come in as backup. All three men were similar in size. This one had thick-dark hair, slicked back, not a strand out of place, and a perfect tan. As cliché as it was, it felt like I was watching the Sopranos.

It was difficult to place their nationality; could have been Italian, Hispanic, Portuguese, or even Greek. I reached into my backpack for the binoculars, hoping to get a close-up.

Walking toward the entrance, the two in leather jackets blanketed the backseat passenger between them. All three kept their eyes focused on any unwanted threats. One didn't need a college education to conclude they were bodyguards. The question was: who was the guy they were protecting, and why did he need protecting? I waited a few minutes to make sure they weren't coming back out. Then I zeroed in on the back of their Range Rover and added their New York license plate to my list. Interesting. Charlie mentioned out-of-state visitors.

I figured that would be all the excitement I'd see for the day. I was wrong. A few minutes later, a dark sedan turned into the circular drive and pulled up to the stone walkway. The driver stepped out and opened the backseat door. My mouth dropped open. The man who stepped out was a public official for the State of Massachusetts, only I couldn't remember his name. He stood at the door for a few seconds, looked around, and then walked toward the door and disappeared inside. The driver jumped back into the vehicle, pulled toward the end of the parking lot, and backed the vehicle into a spot. It was out of the probing eyes of the public, but he could still see the front door.

With the recent visitors arriving, I hung around to see what else was going on. Thomas Miles was still at the office for a few more hours, so plenty of time to catch up with him. Besides, The Tapestry was getting interesting.

During the downtime, I checked in with Olivia and Madison. They wouldn't be coming down to the Cape until the weekend, but they liked to keep up with the cases. I put them in a joint text:

"Hey girls, just checking in.

Olivia texted back: *"Hey Katie, Madison is here with me. We're on the back deck enjoying the mild weather and planning our upcoming cruise for New Year's Eve. Sure, you can't come?"*

I laughed to myself. I could picture both of them viewing locations and brochures on the internet and planning a shopping spree for new outfits. *"I wish. I need to stay behind and monitor the cottage rebuild. Next time, though. What country did you settle on traveling to?"*

"We're currently debating that. Madison says we should try Greece, so she could check out the Greek men. The cost is off the

charts, though, so we'll probably settle on Mexico."

"What is Madison going to do with Ted while she's swooning over the foreign men?"

"LOL," she texted back. *"Since the weather didn't cooperate on our last cruise, they canceled the zipline adventure. We're booking them for the one in Mazatlan, which will also take them on a four-hour moped tour. We'll have an entire day to ourselves. So how is that new hunk you're dating? Is he still on his UC assignment?"*

"Yep, Finn is still on assignment, so our dating is on hold." I didn't have the heart to tell them he was unaccounted for. They went through so much with me dealing with the stalker, the craziness that followed, and then the trial. I thought it best to wait until I had facts. Let them enjoy some peace while planning their cruise.

"That sucks," Olivia texted. *"So what else is going on, working on anything interesting?"*

"It has potential."

"Potential?"

"It started as a typical case of adultery, but now it's looking more intriguing."

"Tell us everything!"

"Too early, really, just suspicions. You'll never believe it, though; I got a call from Jillian Moore last night."

"Jillian Moore? Your college roommate? After all this time? What's going on with

her?"

"I don't know. She called me at 3:30 in the morning. She said she was in trouble. She sounded scared. She wants to meet tonight."

"What do you think is going on?"

"The way she disappeared, I just don't know. I think something happened between her and her father. I'll let you know after I meet with her and I'll fill you in on the case when I see you."

"Keep us updated."

We disconnected, but mentioning Jillian got me thinking. During college, her father never dropped by to visit. I thought it was odd. He sent checks, but when they arrived in the mail, she ripped them up. That's why I got confused when she wound up moving back home after graduation. I knew there were problems between them, but she would never tell me what they were. I was worried that those problems, whatever they were, were coming home to roost now.

CHAPTER 12

WHEN EARLY EVENING rolled around, I dropped Bailey off at the RV. We already put in over eight hours in the vehicle. I fed her, gave her fresh water, and took her down by the water to toss the ball. We walked toward the mailbox to check the mail; still no package, and then I made sure she was in her bed when I left to resume my surveillance on Thomas Miles.

Like clockwork, he came out of his building following the same routine as the day before. When he pulled out of the lot, I knew he was going to Pier 25. I wanted to send an alert to the women at the bar that a snake was on the loose.

I found a spot in the bar's corner and ordered a Michelob Ultra. He ordered a Martini for himself, but this time, was generous enough to offer a drink to the women who had to put up with his roving hands the day before. Observing him, I fully understood how Sarah felt when she smirked about his license plate.

After several minutes, he received an unwelcome call on his cell phone. He got into a heated exchange, screamed obscenities into the phone, and continued the conversation in the hall. I could hear his loud voice from where I was, just not the substance.

While I waited for him to return, I looked around the bar. I noticed a woman with long, wavy red hair. She was sitting at a corner table with a view of the marina, locking lips with a very muscular man. The red hair looked familiar. When she stopped kissing the gorgeous man, I got a good look at her face and was stunned. It was Connie, Derek's IT gal, who, along with Roger, gathered the information for me.

Outside of the office, Connie was a vivacious woman. Even though she dated several men, she was particular about those she got intimate with. It looked as if this guy was someone of importance. If I wasn't on surveillance, I would have loved to bust her chops, but it would have blown my cover. I would have to check in later to get the goods.

When Thomas Miles returned, his expression was strained. He downed the rest of his Martini, threw money on the bar, and left without even acknowledging the women. Somebody ruffled his feathers.

When I rushed to follow, I was pretty sure where he was going. I noticed two things when he parked in the circular drive: the Range Rover and dark sedan were still there, and every available parking spot was full. I couldn't help but wonder if those things had something to do with Thomas Miles' heated conversation. Once he was inside, I dreaded another night of sitting in the car, not being able to catch him in action. It was also rather strange that the number of visitors seemed to have doubled. Did it have something to do with the visitors from New York?

I got a bigger surprise when a dark blue Ford Mustang Mach-E pulled into the parking lot, and less than a minute later, an unmarked car pulled up next to him. I was sure the Mustang was an undercover police vehicle. Something significant was going on at the club, and it wasn't just a social gathering.

The driver of the unmarked car stepped out and joined the man from the Mach-E outside his vehicle. They had their backs to me, so I couldn't see their faces. But there was enough light from the street lamp to make a mental description of other attributes.

The driver from the Mach-E was on the thin side with brown hair and highlights that he wore spiked and gelled. It was clear he was undercover. His attire reminded me of a member of a rock and roll band.

The guy from the other car was Irish. As a cop in Massachusetts, he was required to keep his tattoo hidden while on duty. But I got a brief glimpse of his Shamrock when his short-sleeved shirt stretched up over his muscled arm.

They huddled in close for what I assumed was a private conversation. They kept looking around to verify they were alone. Once they finished, they bumped fists. The rock and roller walked into the back door of the club, and the Irishman jumped back into his ride. That's when I got a look at his face, and the ice-gray color of his eyes sent a shiver up my spine. What were the police officers doing at the club? I added the plate number of the Mach-E to my list. Maybe I could narrow down the driver through the department. When it was clear whatever was happening inside was going to go on for some time, I left to talk to a detective I knew.

A couple of weeks after the trial of my stalker, Derek had a Thanksgiving feast at his home in Woods Hole. He invited Finn and me, along with Olivia, Madison, and their husbands. Several members of the Nauset Bay P.D. and their families were there, as well. Detective Maldonado and his wife, Margie, were there that day. I spent some time with Margie while her husband engaged in a fun game of competitive poker in Derek's family room.

During my first case of the missing teenager, I met up with Maldonado again. The parents originally went to the police department, but since they considered her a runaway, there wasn't a lot of traction on the case. They hired me soon after. It was after interviewing several of her friends that I learned she was in the middle of a teenage love triangle between two gang members in Dorchester. When I wound up facing off with the two gang members, Detective

Maldonado called in the Boston Gang Unit to bail me out. Since then, he said I could call on him anytime. So I do.

CHAPTER 13- THE TEACHER

Sometime ago

A HUGE STORM threatened to hit the northeast, forcing a seventeen-year-old girl to brave the elements in search of food to feed her family. She begged for scraps from nearby restaurants and stood helpless with her hand out, hoping locals would have pity.

For days, a man had been lurking in the background with the teenager in his sight.

He continued to watch her.

Stalk her.

He knew her daily routine, where she lived, and all about her family. She had a mother at home who suffered from addiction, and a baby brother that needed diapers, food, and clothing. The father was gone, leaving the teenager responsible for providing for the family.

They lived in a one-bedroom apartment owned by the New York Housing Authority on the lower east side. Heat, water, and electricity were luxuries they couldn't afford. The Teacher devised a plan. He could grab her, just like the others. But it was better if the mother didn't put in a missing-persons report. Instead, he offered her food and promised to help her family. He knew she would accept. She was desperate.

Unaware of the evil intentions, the teenage girl accepted the aid. Together, they went to a local market to purchase necessities and then carried them to her dismal home. After the family ate and were grateful to the angel who stepped into their lives, The Teacher took the mother aside and presented the plan: give up the girl and accept the money he offered, or suffer the consequences when social services showed up to remove both kids. He knew she wouldn't refuse. The instant he showed her the money, her eyes got huge, and she thought about the crack she could buy.

The following morning, the teenage girl was told she was going with The Teacher to start a new life. As a private Cessna airplane lifted off the tarmac at Long Island MacArthur Airport, the teenager was told she would never see her family again. With a signed document from the mother, airport security had no reason to question them.

There would be no missing report filed.

There wouldn't be anyone out looking for a seventeen-year-old girl.

There wasn't anyone who cared.

Soon, she would no longer matter.

Now she belonged to him.

CHAPTER 14

OFFICER GREG HARDESTY was on front desk duty when I walked into the Nauset Bay Police Department. He was a professional football player before he became a cop. A few years back, he suffered a major knee injury that took him out of the game and forced him to retire. Lucky for him, the injury wasn't bad enough to keep him from getting into the department. The powers that be said he was a top-notch police officer. Not to mention, he had no fear—possibly from getting one too many hits to the head.

"Evening Officer Hardesty," I said. I already knew several officers at the department from my connections to Derek and Detective Maldonado. Some knew I was dating Finn, but only a few, since he was fairly new to the department. He worked for Malden P.D. for ten years, but recently changed positions when he learned of the opportunities for advancement in Nauset Bay.

"Hey Katie," Hardesty responded with a smile. I always had to do a double-take when he spoke. His voice was so soft-spoken that you would hardly know it belonged to a gigantic bear of a man. "How's the best-looking woman on Cape Cod doing this evening?"

I groaned. Hardesty was always teasing me when I stopped by. His wife said it was his sense of humor that made her say yes to getting married. "You only say that because you're stuck inside the station, and I'm the only woman you've seen."

He laughed. Coming out of the mouth of a man his size, it surprised me the entire building wasn't shaking. "Not true Katie," he teased. "I went to the jail. I saw plenty of women there."

"Comparing me to the jailbirds, how can I respond to that?"

He smiled. "So, what brings you here this evening?"

"I stopped by to see Maldonado. Is he in?"

"When isn't he?"

"That's what his wife says."

He laughed again. "The day Margie married him, she said she knew he was married to the job, and she was just the happy mistress."

"That woman is a rock," I said, recalling the time we first met. She knew her husband was a dedicated member of the brothers in blue. And she was proud of that fact. Instead of pressuring him to cut down on his hours, she found a vocation to keep her occupied during his absences. One of those endeavors was volunteering to help victims of violence and children without a home. It wasn't long after that the couple signed on to foster two young children suffering from abuse.

"Go on back. He's in his office."

I've been to the station a few times, but they honored me when they let me walk around without an escort. Most departments were close-knit groups; to make it inside their family was something extraordinary. Of course, as in all families, there were rivals and competitions. There have been a few outspoken critics who didn't think I was qualified to be an investigator and made their opinions known. I understood their concerns, but it wouldn't stop me either way.

It was my close connection to Derek that helped me get accepted. He has connections in many police departments and clarified that he has no problem with me being in the field. Most of them came around, but there were still a few who couldn't control their anger or indifference.

When I walked into Maldonado's office, he was sitting in his chair with his feet up on the desk. He held his phone in one hand and was shooting paper balls into a trash can with the other. For a guy who spent so much time at work, he looked like he lived on the beach. With his head of white-blond hair and bronzed tan, one would think surfing was his full-time job, instead of just an early morning hobby. He wore his usual Jos. A. Bank suit, but the jacket was hanging on the door, and his tie loose around his neck. When he saw me in the doorway, he motioned me in and made an excuse to get off the phone.

"You up for a Margarita?" I said when he hung up.

He eyed me for a moment, and then his lips curved into a grin. "What do you need?"

"I resent that," I joked. "Why do I have to need something?" I handed him the list of license plate numbers I collected.

His eyebrows widened in surprise. "You expecting me to run these?"

"Can you?" I gave him an innocent smile.

He threw a paper ball at me. "What is this, anyway? Somebody ding your precious car, and you're trying to narrow down the suspects?"

I laughed. "Nah, just a bunch of good-looking guys. Thought I'd look them up. You know, maybe drop in and introduce myself."

"Does Finn know you're already stepping out on him?" he teased.

I smiled but refrained from speaking about Finn. He knew we were dating, but it would be unprofessional of me to mention that I knew there was an issue with his undercover gig. I had to act oblivious, which took effort on my part.

"Seriously, what are they?"

I gave him a look that said: "don't ask", which he understood all too well.

"I'll see what I can do, but can't guarantee anything."

"That's all I can ask. Oh, and by the way, do you know of any undercover operations going on in town?"

"No," he said rather evasively. "Why?"

"If there was such an operation from another department, you would know about it, though, right?"

"We'd receive a heads up, yeah. What's going on?"

"I was just wondering," I said, trying to make light of it.

He studied me for a moment and then glanced at the clock. "Shit, I gotta go," he said. "I promised my daughter I'd come home tonight and help her with her science project."

Even though the girl and boy living with them were foster kids, he and Margie still referred to them as their own. Last I heard, they put in papers to make it permanent. Though I heard the natural parents were fighting it.

"I think you'd better get going, then? It's late."

"She's already in bed. I just have to finish forming her clay volcano."

"How'd she talk you into that?"

"Bribed is more like it," he said. "I didn't make it to her soccer game. It crushed her. She's working the guilt aspect."

"Little girls are good like that."

He gave me a knowing smile. "You would know."

I returned the smile.

He cleared his desk and put some documents in a folder. "How's Derek doing?"

Most of the Nauset Bay, and surrounding police departments, as well as the local FBI, knew Derek from the kidnapping and murder of his wife by a former employee. I didn't know him back then, but a lot of police officers worked tirelessly on the case, even off-duty. After she died, there was a memorial service. Local police officers and FBI Agents lined the streets showing their support. To show his appreciation, Derek has donated millions over the years to local police department causes and helps to provide the equipment needed to fight crime. He funded most of the body-cams local departments were required to use. They all formed personal friendships along the way.

"He's doing okay," I said. "Since he has such dedicated employees these days, he spends most of his time golfing and enjoying a semi-retirement."

"Good for him. That's how I want it to be when I'm through here."

"You've got a long way to go."

"Got that right," he said, glancing at the clock again. "But if I don't get home, it's going to be sooner than we think."

"Then I suggest you get moving." I stood up and headed for the door. If I didn't push to leave, he would keep talking. "Give Margie and the kids a hug for me."

"Come for dinner on Sunday and do that yourself."

"I'll check the schedule, but don't think I'm your excuse to get out of dish duty."

"Oh c'mon Katie, why do you think I keep inviting you?"

"Good to know."

After leaving the station, I headed home to fix myself something to eat and hoped to relax before it was time to meet Jillian. I didn't know what to expect when we got together, but I was feeling anxious.

When I walked in the door, my cell phone notified me I had voicemail messages. They must have called while I was at the station. I punched in my password. The first message was from Connie. She sounded exuberant, yelling into the phone that she met the love of her life. She wants to tell me all about it next time we meet for dinner. The second message was from Roger, telling me what Derek had already found out; that Finn was out of contact. He followed it up by reminding me that Finn's fellow officers had his back. So stop worrying. Right, Finn was undercover with known bad guys. How could I not worry?

CHAPTER 15

Midnight meeting

JILLIAN SAID MIDNIGHT, but I arrived early to scope out the area. Things had changed since the last time I was here. It had been two decades since I met Jillian at the coffee shop. Back then, it was like a 50s diner, and they called it Rosie's. Now, it was a modern coffee house, similar to a Starbucks, only privately owned. The name stayed the same, only with a modern calligraphy style. There were new stores on the street. An Italian restaurant two blocks over. New businesses too. I spotted a sign for a hotel two blocks the other way. And a nightclub was further down the street, which explained the traffic since everything else was closed. Other than the echoes of those coming out of the nightclub down the street, there wasn't anyone else around.

Ten minutes to go.

I parked in a spot on the street, two buildings down from Rosie's. And watched. Where would Jillian choose to come in from? Would she just park in the alley? I had no way of knowing. There was a day when I could read what was going on in Jillian's mind. Now, I didn't even know if she looked the same.

Five minutes.

I looked up and down the street once more. No sign of her. I stepped out of my

SUV and stood for a moment to get accustomed to the sounds. I could hear the trail of voices at the nightclub. They were enjoying themselves, oblivious to anything else going on. The traffic was still busy near there, but not much in this area. I started towards Rosie's, watching the shadows as I did. It was dark, and anyone could walk around and surprise the crap out of me. Not that I was paranoid, just being cautious. After everything that happened to me in the last few months, there was no excuse not to be.

Rosie's was closed, which I expected. Back when it was a diner, it closed at ten o'clock. Now, I did not know about closing time. I admit I was curious why Jillian wanted to meet in the alley. Was it just a coincidence, or was there some significance? Or was it just because it was our private place? A location she and I used to meet at, with nobody else involved, where we could share our secrets. I assumed that was the reason she wanted to meet now. She had a secret to share.

When I got to the corner lot of Rosie's, I started toward the alley and paused. I realized how dark it was, both in front and behind the shop. There were overhead streetlights, but the bulbs weren't working. I looked north at the other section of the alley, and then south. Those areas were well lit. This was the only section in the dark.

Something wasn't right.

I retrieved the gun at my hip and held it out in front of me. I cursed myself for not bringing the flashlight. My heart raced, kicking my adrenaline into high gear. With the gun out, I slowly crept into the alley.

Where was Jillian?

I thought of calling out her name, but my instincts were telling me not to speak. What the hell? It took my eyes a couple of seconds to adjust to the darkness. In the meantime, I relied on my senses and I felt someone's presence. If it was Jillian, she wasn't letting me know. I walked deeper into the alley. Suddenly, I heard two loud popping noises that made me stop in my tracks and get down on the ground in a defensive mode. I've heard the sound before. Just recently, in fact, when I was taking target practice at the shooting range. Then two more... someone was shooting at me. Was it Jillian? Why would Jillian shoot at me? If it wasn't Jillian, then who was it?

I tried to analyze where the shots came from and pointed my gun in that direction. The time seemed to stop. Just as soon as the shots began, everything went quiet. I'd heard four shots, then nothing. A moment later, my senses still alert and listening to every sound, I heard another noise. It sounded like footsteps pounding the pavement. Somebody was running away from the scene. It was so dark I couldn't see them. I could only detect the sound, which gave me a sense of their direction. Then the sound of squealing tires and everything went completely still.

My body froze. From shock, I assumed. I was beside myself, not knowing or even understanding what had just happened. I couldn't see anything. I reached for my cell phone, dialed Nauset Bay P.D., and asked to speak with Detective Maldonado. He wasn't in, which I already knew, but after identifying myself and telling them it was an emergency, they patched me through to his cell phone.

"Maldonado," he yelled into the phone. I obviously woke him since it was after midnight.

"It's Katie," I said. "I'm in the alley directly behind Rosie's Coffee Shop… somebody is shooting at me."

"What the hell!" Maldonado yelled. I could hear him getting out of bed, knocking things down along the way. "Are you hurt?"

"No," I said. "I heard somebody leaving the scene, but I don't know if there's more."

"Do you have your weapon?"

"Yes."

"Stay down. Officers are on their way. I'll be there as soon as I can."

"Okay."

At the same time I was disconnecting from the call, an unmarked car barreled around the corner and parked at the end of the alley. My first thought was he must have heard the shots. Maldonado didn't put the call out yet. The plainclothes officer got out of his car with his weapon drawn and headed into the alley. Because of the dark, I could only see his silhouette through the glare of the headlights. He couldn't see me either, since I was crouched down and out of sight. I felt a moment of fear that the officer didn't know who I was, and was coming for me, ready to shoot, thinking I was the perp.

I was just about to announce myself when I heard sirens in the background. It was odd that the officer didn't hold his position and wait for them.

"Officer, it's Katie Parker," I yelled out to identify myself, "Detective Maldonado's friend."

I noticed a slight hesitation in his movements, but his silhouette frame continued. At the moment, I was thankful he couldn't see any more than I could for fear he would shoot first and ask questions later.

In the next moment, he unexpectedly stopped. I didn't know if it was because I yelled out my name, or because two patrol cars and a van rolled into the area. Their headlights lit up the alley like a spotlight. It was at that moment that I recognized the officer who was first on the scene, and I was thankful the others showed up when they did.

It was the officer I dubbed the rock and roller who showed up at The Tapestry earlier. He wasn't a fan. Officer Jimmy

Smith. He was one cop at Nauset Bay P.D. who didn't think I was qualified to be a P.I. We made eye contact, and I made a mental note of how hesitant he was putting his gun back in the holster.

"I heard gunshots," he yelled when other officers stepped out of their vehicles. He needed to explain why he was first on the scene.

I nodded but continued to speculate about his being in the area so soon after I heard the shots. I didn't like the look he was giving me.

"You okay?" he asked, trying to show concern now that others arrived.

"I'm fine," I said. But I wasn't fine. It scared me to death, and I wanted to know what the hell happened.

He started looking around the alley, rather anxiously, as if he were searching for something or someone. When his eyes reached the back steps of the coffee shop, his expression changed.

I followed his gaze. It was then; with the lights from the other patrol cars lighting up the alley, that I could see what he was looking at. It was the body of a female sprawled across the back steps of the coffee shop. The body position looked distorted as if she'd fallen, and her legs were in the opposite directions. That's when I screamed.

When I pulled myself together, I noticed blood was flowing like a river down the steps and onto the asphalt. My hands were shaking so badly that I had to use both to put my gun back in the belt. I started toward the body, fearing the outcome, but needing to know. My mind reasoned that I'd be contaminating the crime scene, but I couldn't stop myself. I had to see. As the tears flowed, memories of Jillian flashed before my eyes. I tried to pick up the pace to get to the body, but my legs were like lead, keeping me from getting there. I didn't realize it, but Officer Smith was holding me back.

Other officers on the scene were busy searching the perimeter to see if the perp or perps were still in the vicinity. A woman that arrived in the van walked toward the body. She wore a navy blue jacket identifying her as the Medical Examiner. I was in a daze, watching her, as she slipped on a pair of latex gloves. After confirming the body was deceased, the ME pulled her hair away from her face so I could see my friend one last time. When I was close enough, my knees nearly buckled. It was Jillian. She was dead... murdered. Her beautiful face was now marred by a bullet hole, right in the center of her forehead. Was the killer so close that he could make a direct hit? Did Jillian see who killed her?

Officer Smith pulled me away from the body and held on tight. I kept calling out her name as if it would bring her back to life. After a while, I gave up and my body went slack in his arms as the dam burst, releasing my pent-up emotions.

I was like that for a while before Maldonado arrived and called me over.

When I pulled free from the officer's arms, I noticed scratches from where my nails dug into him. I tried to voice an apology, but there was something in his eyes that kept me from speaking.

"You're okay, Katie," Maldonado said when I was by his side. He walked me toward his police-issued Dodge Charger and placed me in the backseat to regroup.

"Thanks," I said, with what energy I could muster.

"Here, take this." He handed me a thermos filled with coffee. "Will you be okay for a minute while I converse with the officers?"

"I'm okay. Thanks." I don't normally drink coffee, but I needed something to warm the chill inside me. I was shaking like a leaf. Seconds later, I tried to jump out of the car and threw up everything I had eaten earlier in the day. Some of it soiled the side of the car.

In the backseat again, I placed my face in my hands and my mind was in a fog. It felt like I was living through a nightmare and couldn't wake up. When I looked out the car window, I had to face the fact that this was real, and the ending wasn't good.

They had already placed the yellow tape around the perimeter to let everyone know there was a crime scene. They maneuvered patrol cars at both ends of the alley, keeping bystanders from entering the area and contaminating possible evidence. Officers were out canvassing the neighborhood for witnesses, while crime scene techs combed the area, and another tech took photographs. The medical examiner had already covered the body but was conferring with the detectives before removing it from the scene. It all just seemed so surreal.

While I waited for Maldonado to come back, I ran things through my mind. There was just no way to make sense of it. Jillian called me out of the blue, asked me to meet her, and then she was gunned down where she wanted to meet. When she called, she sounded scared, but of what? I had so many questions. But the only answer I cared about was who killed her? I felt an intense rage inside me like I'd never felt before. I just lived through the worst time of my life after my ex-husband's betrayal, the stalker's antics, and then the trial. Finn was out of communication with his team, and now Jillian... it was all just too much to handle.

CHAPTER 16

MALDONADO CAME BACK to his ride after making sure all the details were being covered on the crime scene and the detectives were in charge.

"You okay?" he asked me.

I nodded. "Your coffee wasn't too good. Some of it found its way onto the side of your car."

He glanced at the area where I had regurgitated a few moments ago. "Looks like you had some pasta for dinner."

Being a veteran police officer who has been through his share of crime scenes, he was trying to show his cop humor. He reached into the glove compartment for a package of handy wipes and handed them to me so I could clean up.

"It was V-8 juice." I accepted the baby wipes. "Thanks."

"So, what brings you out on a night like tonight?"

I couldn't help but stare at him. How were cops able to muster humor and keep detached from all the evils out on the street? I knew he was only doing it for my benefit.

"The victim was a friend of mine." I replayed the vision in my mind of her lifeless body lying there in a river of blood.

"I'm sorry, Katie." He reached for my hand and patted it, just as a concerned parent would do. "Who was she?"

"Her name is—was Jillian Moore." It hurt to remember her in the past tense.

He gave me the once over, trying to decide whether I was up for a brief question and answering. "Can you tell me what happened?"

"I think so."

He took out a pad of paper, ready to take notes. "Go on."

"Jillian called me at three-thirty in the morning Monday. She said she was in trouble and she sounded terrified. She said she needed my help and asked if I'd meet her here at midnight."

"Any ideas of what she was afraid of, or why she'd want to meet you at midnight?"

"No," I said. "None. I haven't heard from her in years. Her calling me took me by surprise. I agreed to meet her because she sounded so scared."

He looked around at the dark alley. "Why here?"

"After college, she and I would meet at Rosie's to catch up. It used to be a diner. I do not know why she chose the alley when the place was closed."

Right at that moment, the Medical Examiner was removing the body from the scene and it all became real.

Detective Maldonado watched, along with me, as officers carried her body into the ME's Van, and then the Van as it pulled away from the scene.

Jillian was gone... gone forever.

He gave me a few moments to collect myself and waited for me to acknowledge that it was okay to continue. "So, what happened when you got here?"

I wiped the tears and cleared my head. "I parked my car. There wasn't anyone around, except for the customers at the nightclub down the street. The lights were out as I walked toward the alley. I got suspicious, so I drew my gun. I walked into the alley and immediately sensed someone's presence. Because of the darkness, I couldn't see who it was, and then someone started shooting."

"Where were you, exactly?"

I pointed to the location. "I was crouched down directly under the lights, but as you can see, the bulbs aren't working."

Maldonado looked up at the lights and frowned. "How many shots fired?"

"I heard four."

"Could you tell where they were coming from?"

"Only general direction." I pointed to an area near the building on the opposite side of the alley.

"There's a window in the building, but I couldn't be sure the shots came from there. There's also a small space in between the buildings. Whoever was shooting could have been standing in there as well."

He was writing the information down and drawing diagrams. "Continue."

"After the shooting stopped, I heard

footsteps pounding the pavement like they were running away from the scene. Then I heard squealing tires."

"Like someone was leaving the scene?" It was more of a statement than a question.

"Timing was right."

Maldonado radioed a message to one of his detectives, advising that he'd be there in a few minutes with more information. When he was done, he looked at me again. "So, you don't know what your friend has been doing; or anything about her life?"

"Unfortunately, no."

He was making a final notation in his notebook. We both got quiet and looked out at the chaotic scene. Maldonado made some comments, then barked out orders on the radio to two officers who were supposed to be blocking off the pedestrians from entering the area.

"Have you planned for anyone to make a notification yet?"

He thought about it for a moment. "Not officially. It'll probably be me."

"I'd like to go," I said. "Even though I haven't seen her in a while, she was my best friend in college."

"Think you can handle it?"

"I need to."

"Sure, let me check in before we go."

Twenty minutes later, Maldonado came back to his ride, and I joined him in the front seat.

"You know where her family lives?"

"Beachwood Road, Nauset Bay," I said, relieved we were at least moving away from the horrific scene.

"Great!" Maldonado said. "I hate dealing with money."

I said nothing, but I knew what he meant. The wealthy normally questioned every move of the detectives, which made their investigation harder. Being a detective in Nauset Bay County, you'd think he'd be used to it by now.

"What does her father do?" He probably wanted to get a sense of what he was up against.

"Howard Moore is a senior partner for his law firm," I said. I rambled off a few names of his clients to let Maldonado know just how high profile he was.

"That means the media will be swarming."

I hadn't even thought about the media. During the trial of my stalker, I was in the media spotlight. I wasn't looking forward to dealing with them again. "Mr. Moore hasn't seen his daughter in a while," I said, trying to give him some understanding of their relationship. "I don't know that he'll care enough to give you a hard time." I got that feeling after dealing with his attitude during our conversations after she disappeared all those years ago. Every time I called to see if he heard from her, he always said that he hadn't, and gave me the impression he didn't care.

Maldonado looked at me, somewhat surprised. "What about her mother?"

"She left the home when Jillian was a child." That Jillian and I were toddlers when our mothers left home was something we had in common. It helped us to form a closer bond with each other. I always believed Howard Moore forced Jillian's mother to leave the home; I just couldn't confirm it.

"Tough deal."

"Yeah."

"But what kind of father wouldn't care if his daughter takes a hit?"

"Guess we'll find out." I didn't want to talk about it anymore, so I laid my head back on the seat and closed my eyes. I just lost a friend. Even though we hadn't seen each other in years, I still felt that special bond with her. I needed some time to reflect. I was afraid I could hit overload soon.

Detective Maldonado was cognizant enough to respect my wishes. He gave me some time. We were almost at the location before he spoke again.

"I'm sorry about your friend."

CHAPTER 17

WHEN YOU PULL up to the Moore residence, a black wrought-iron gate automatically opens to a paved driveway. They lined the outer landscape with beautiful trees and beautiful arrays of perennials throughout the grounds. A stone walkway leads you to the front porch with four cathedral columns that only add to the magnificence of the home. They customized the exterior with Ivory-colored wood siding and shingles. An Italian stone giving the home an air of opulence framed the front entrance, which was protected by the roofing over the columns.

"This place is incredible," Maldonado said, as he looked around at the posh surroundings. There were some pretty spectacular homes on Cape Cod, but this area had historical appeal.

As we headed up the stone walkway toward the mahogany wood door, I thought I noticed a movement in an upstairs window but chalked it up to my imagination. It was the middle of the night. Nobody knew we were coming. Did they?

Detective Maldonado rang the doorbell, and we waited patiently for someone to respond. A few moments passed before the butler, Jose Hernandez, opened the door and peeked out. He recognized me immediately, but was hesitant to open the door all the way. He kept looking behind him as if he was waiting for someone to appear.

Maldonado reached inside his pocket and pulled out his badge and identification. "Detective Maldonado, Nauset Bay Police Department," he said.

Jose realized he had no choice. He opened the door and allowed us to enter.

The entryway we were now standing in was exquisite. They had renovated the house since the last time I was in the home during college. White, Italian marbled tiles covered the floors and expanded onto a circular staircase that was in the center of the entry, leading to the upstairs. An exquisite chandelier hung down from the cathedral ceiling, directly over the staircase. It was beautiful.

"It's good to see you, Jose," I said, trying to break the ice.

Jose looked around nervously, as if he was afraid someone was watching. He cautiously approached and gave me an awkward embrace. The warmth that he showed me years earlier when I visited Jillian at the house was missing. "How is Isabella?"

His face softened.

No sooner had I asked than an older Hispanic woman with gray hair pulled into a tight bun came bursting into the entryway with her hands flailing in the air from the excitement of seeing me. She embraced me in the same welcome she gave me so long ago. She didn't care if anyone was watching her. "My precious Katie," she cried with excitement as tears rolled down her cheeks.

It was good to see them. Yet, I knew the news about Jillian would probably hurt them more than it would Howard Moore.

I looked at the two of them. "Jose, Isabella, this is Detective Maldonado of Nauset Bay P.D."

Maldonado offered his hand first to Isabella, who was hesitant to accept; then to Jose. "Nice to meet you," Maldonado said, noticing their hesitancy to speak to the police.

"He's here to speak to Mr. Moore," I said. "Is he home?"

Jose and Isabella exchanged glances. I couldn't help but notice a look of fear on their faces. They knew something terrible had happened. Isabella was making signs of the cross, as Jose excused himself to let Mr. Moore know he had guests. A moment later, Isabella guided us toward the den. I knew from earlier visits that it was the room where guests were greeted.

It was a room nearly the size of a gymnasium. Floor-to-ceiling bookcases covered three walls, with books on every shelf, and extended at least twenty feet high. An antique ladder with wheels rolled around to reach the higher shelves. They refinished the hardwood floors with ash wood. Tapestry rugs, the colors of burgundy and gold, protected them, and two white sofas were centered and opposite each other, with end tables at each end. To add more conversation areas, burgundy-colored wingback chairs sat in corners throughout the room.

I recognized the gold cart that Jillian used to describe that delivered Cuban cigars. The room screamed out wealth. She used to describe the parties that were held in the room. The cigar-smoking aficionados would sit in the wingback chairs and debate the political speeches or commentary viewed in the days before.

Maldonado and I waited in the room while Isabella went to make coffee. I wandered, thinking about the one time she invited me to a dinner party and how unusual it was. It wasn't a political event; just an intimate dinner for some of Howard Moore's esteemed friends. There were six couples invited, along with Jillian and I. Isabella served appetizers and drinks here in the den, but it looked different back then. When dinner was served, we moved into the dining room. Even the seating arrangement was odd. Howard Moore said the only way to have a successful dinner was to separate the couples. That evening, he proved his point. He placed us between two of the married men who fawned all over us all evening, while their wives sat at opposite ends of the table and glared. I felt strange about it and never attended another dinner. That night was the first time I got a glimpse of some of the odd things Jillian used to say about her father.

We waited a good twenty minutes before Howard Moore graced us with his presence, bellowing about having visitors at this time of night. He continued his tirade until he walked into the den. When he saw me, he got quiet. And for a moment, I thought I noticed a pained expression on his face, but it disappeared rather quickly.

He walked toward me and pulled me into a hug, but it felt cold and forced. "Katie, it's been a very long time," he said. "What brings you here this evening?"

There was something in his voice that just wasn't right, like maybe he already knew why a police officer was in his home. I was hoping it was only my imagination. I never liked the man, but I didn't want to think he was involved with his daughter's death.

Being the observant detective, Maldonado watched the interchange between the two of us and sensed my discomfort. Flashing his badge, he said, "Mr. Moore; Detective Maldonado. I'm with the Nauset Bay Police Department. We're very sorry to disturb you at this late hour."

Maldonado was trying to be as diplomatic as possible. He knew Howard Moore could use his wealth and position to be difficult if he didn't like the treatment, and then we wouldn't get anywhere.

"It's no problem Detective, I'm sure you're here because you have something to tell me."

"It's about your daughter, Jillian," Maldonado said. "I'm sorry to have to tell you this, but your daughter is dead."

We both observed him, looking for some display of emotion, but his face was devoid of expression. A moment later, he seemed to realize how it looked. He paced the room to give the appearance of being shaken. It was a little too late for me. It wasn't sincere. He also didn't appear to be shocked by the news. Now, why would that be?

I was so busy observing Howard Moore I didn't immediately notice the muffled cries that were coming from the other end of the room. When I looked in that direction, I saw Jose and Isabella huddled together. When they heard the news, Isabella got hysterical and was crying. Jose had a tough time ushering her out of the room. I waited until they were out of earshot.

"Mr. Moore," I said, trying to act like a concerned friend. "Have you heard from Jillian recently?"

He wouldn't look me in the eye, but I could see there was at least a touch of sadness. There was something else there as well. He sat down on the sofa, and for a moment, he almost looked defeated. "Katie, you know I haven't talked to Jillian since she moved out. I told you that on your repeated calls all those years ago."

I nodded, but my instincts told me he was lying.

"Mr. Moore," Maldonado said, trying to direct the attention back to the investigation. "Could you tell me where you were earlier this evening?"

Detectives considered everyone a suspect when investigating a murder, even the family.

Mr. Moore appeared to be taken aback by the question and was immediately on guard. "Why?"

The two men stared at each other. You could feel the tension in the room, each of them daring the other to look away first. It was at that moment that Jose walked back into the den and nervously advised Mr. Moore that he had a phone call. Mr. Moore excused himself, cutting the connection between himself and Maldonado. He walked out of the room, leaving us to wonder who would call in the middle of the night and what was so important to make him leave a conversation about the death of his daughter? It felt contrived.

When he returned, he tried to make an excuse by saying it was a neighbor calling with a concern about police officers being at his house. We knew he was lying. We were in an unmarked vehicle. How would a neighbor know cops were visiting? I couldn't help but wonder if the killer just called to say the deed had been done.

"Mr. Moore," Maldonado said, talking in

a sterner tone and trying to regain control of the conversation. He was probably thinking the same thing I was. "We're going to need you to come down to the station tomorrow."

Howard Moore sat back down on the sofa. He briefly looked at Maldonado. "I don't know what help I could be. I told you I haven't talked to her."

I could tell from the clenching in his jaw that Maldonado was losing his patience. He didn't like the fact that this guy didn't seem to give a shit about his daughter, but he knew he had to continue to handle him delicately. The last thing he needed was a swarm of attorneys landing at the police department. "I understand what you're telling me, Mr. Moore," he said diplomatically. "But it's just routine procedure. We need a family member to identify the body, and make a statement to that effect."

"I see," Mr. Moore said. But he didn't buy it. Once in a while, we would get a glimpse of emotion; then a moment later it would be gone as if it never existed. Out of the blue, he glanced at me with curiosity in his eyes. "Katie, how did you get involved?"

Since I didn't think Mr. Moore was being very truthful, the last thing I wanted to do was share any information about Jillian. "She called me," I offered. I didn't lie. I just didn't feel the need to elaborate.

He looked at me warily; worried that I

might have some grave dark secret. "Jillian called you?"

I nodded. I didn't want to get into the specifics of Jillian's call. But after seeing her father's reaction, I couldn't help but wonder what went on between father and daughter? And why did I suddenly have the feeling that he already knew she called me?

Mr. Moore wanted to hear more. He looked like he was going to say something else, but glanced in Maldonado's direction and changed his mind. It was possible that whatever he wanted to say; he didn't want to say it in front of a detective.

I could tell by Maldonado's expression that he'd heard enough and wanted to leave. He knew he would not get any information out of him. He looked at me and motioned toward the door.

"I'm sorry for your loss, Mr. Moore," Maldonado said, trying to maintain his professionalism. "I'll see you at the station."

Mr. Moore nodded but refrained from speaking.

Maldonado placed his hand under my elbow and guided me towards the front door. I was just as eager to leave. Mr. Moore remained on the sofa and didn't bother to get up. There was a definite chill as we walked into the night air, though it wasn't from the temperature.

CHAPTER 18

WE WERE BOTH shaking our heads as we walked back to his car. I knew it was probably because we were thinking the same thing: that Mr. Moore's behavior was indeed bizarre.

There were a few things that struck me as odd, but the one that stood out was him not asking how she died. And I suspected Jillian had been at the house recently, only he didn't want us to have that information. It also bothered me that he said nothing about funeral arrangements. She was my best friend. I could understand it if I thought he was so tormented by her death that he wasn't thinking clearly. But I didn't get that impression. I got the sense he was almost relieved she was gone. Right now there wasn't anything to prove that, only my gut feeling. Sometimes that's all you have to start with.

Maldonado was good enough to give me some space while we drove back to my car. He could tell I was analyzing everything in my head. Like, for instance, when Jillian called, she asked me if I got the package—what package? There was also something about the shooting that bothered me. I wanted to discuss it with him, but it was a can of worms I wasn't ready to explore yet. I needed more information.

When we arrived near the crime scene,

officers had expanded the area with yellow tape to keep the media out. They'd shown up in droves. There were news vans and cameramen from every local station. Helicopters were flying overhead. We had to go around several blocks and bypass several reporters before we could get close to where I parked my SUV. Maldonado finally found a spot to park his vehicle, and we headed on foot towards mine.

As we got closer, I noticed something odd around the SUV. Maldonado noticed it too. We both looked at each other and took off running. When we reached it, we realized somebody had shattered the front passenger window. There was glass scattered all over the sidewalk.

"What the hell?" I yelled. At first, I thought it was just vandalism.

Maldonado raked his hands through his hair, frustrated. "How the hell could somebody vandalize a car with all these uniforms around?"

When I went to open the driver's side door, I knew it wasn't just vandalism. "Whoever did this was looking for something. They tore the car apart. They pulled everything out of the glove compartment, and center console and ripped the side panels off the doors."

Maldonado stared at me. "What were they looking for?"

"I don't know," I said, though I couldn't help but feel this was a little too coincidental. It had to have something to do with Jillian. What do they think I have?

He lost his composure and flew off the handle. He stormed over to the officers, who were supposed to be keeping the pedestrians out, and reamed them up and down. When they informed him they had just come on the scene a few minutes before, he eventually calmed down.

"Katie, I need to get the Ident Team over here to dust for prints. They probably wore gloves, but we at least have to check."

"Okay," I said, resigned to the fact that my car was now a crime scene as well.

When Maldonado walked away, it left me to my own devices for a moment. I sat down on the curb and put my head in my hands, going over the events of the day. While I was sitting there, I felt a chill. My gaze-detection radar was going off. Someone was watching me. I looked up and glanced around the area. There was no reason for the sudden discomfort. All I could see were uniformed officers, crime scene techs, and the media, who weren't paying any attention to me at the moment.

Then I saw him; blending in with the other officers: Officer Jimmy Smith. When my eyes connected with his, he stared as if he was trying to read my thoughts. Out of the corner of my eye, I noticed Maldonado coming back in my direction with a tech. I glanced toward him to see if he noticed Smith, but he didn't. When I returned my eyes to Smith, he was gone. I debated whether to bring up my questions to Maldonado, but decided against it for now. He might take exception to accusations against one of his fellow officers. I had questions about the timing of Smith's arrival, but it didn't prove he was guilty of anything. There was just something about him I couldn't put my finger on.

After the tech finished dusting my car, Maldonado followed me so I could drop the car off to be repaired. The doors to the garage were obviously closed, so I parked in the lot. I placed the keys and a note inside a sealed envelope, with the name of my repairman on the front, and dropped it in the mail slot on the front door.

"You interested in hearing what I learned about the crime scene?" Maldonado asked when I returned to his car.

"You know something this soon?"

"It's the initial stages, but I thought you'd like to hear the info."

"Okay," I said, bracing myself.

He glanced at me. "Techs located four slugs."

"Yeah, I knew that already. I heard four shots."

"They came from a 9mm."

That the slugs came from a 9mm helped to support my early suspicion; cops usually carry 9mm, but so do many others. It was clear from his expression that there was more. "What else?"

"They accounted for one slug."

I bristled. "The slug found in Jillian's forehead."

Maldonado nodded. "The shooter took two shots at her. There was a second slug found in the steps, near where her body was."

I thought about that for a moment. "Okay, so what happened to the other two?"

When he looked at me, I could see he was concerned. "Inches away from the location you claimed you were crouched down," he said, letting the information sink in.

My mouth dropped. "So they were shooting at me, too?" I suspected it was a possibility, but hearing it made it real, and it scared me.

"Looks like it."

That sobered me up a great deal. I couldn't help but wonder why the perp could make a direct hit with Jillian's forehead and miss me entirely. Did I have luck on my side? Or were they just trying to scare me?

When Maldonado pulled into the driveway, he glanced at the cottage rebuild and frowned when he looked at the RV. "I'm going to have officers drive by to monitor things for a couple of days."

After debating with him for a couple of minutes, I finally convinced him I'd be fine. Between Bailey and the construction workers that would arrive soon; I had plenty of eyes on me.

His radio squawked at that moment. One tech said they needed him back at the crime scene. That put an end to the conversation and was the only reason he gave up so easily. After I watched him drive off, I walked toward the door while grabbing the RV key from my backpack. My fingers were still trembling from the events of the day, and the news that I, too, could have been a target. When I finally opened the door and walked inside, I was sorry I did. They tore the RV apart too. Somebody was definitely looking for something, and they went through everything to find it. I thought of calling Maldonado to have someone come and dust for prints. Then I freaked: where was Bailey?

"Bailey?" I called out. I stormed down the hall and looked at every one of her hiding places.

I finally found her, shivering, and curled up underneath the nightstand at the head of the bed. It was a spot she discovered once before when there was a storm and she wanted to hide from the thunder and lightning.

"C'mon Bailey," I said, coaxing her out. She slowly crawled on all fours and allowed me to hold her. But it didn't stop her from shivering. I was seething with anger. What I didn't know was whether she hid in that spot before the intruders invaded my space, or if they scared her into it. Either way, they terrified my dog. Unacceptable.

CHAPTER 19

IT TOOK THREE hours to clean, organize and vacuum the RV to get it back to order. Whoever ransacked it; did a very thorough job. Another flash of anger hit when I realized they went through my underwear drawer and made sure I knew it. It was a move that took me back to the time my stalker did the same. That was a personal dig. They also showed their arrogance by sitting down at the kitchen table and helping themselves to my food. That was bad. But my anger exploded when I thought of Bailey shivering and hiding the entire time they were playing their games.

Bailey wouldn't leave my side. Even when I ran the vacuum, she stayed next to me. I took her outside and let her walk around doing her business, but also to reassure her that the bad guys were gone. When it was time for bed, she stretched out beside me, instead of finding a spot at the foot of the bed. I didn't dose off until I confirmed she was sleeping soundly.

I called Derek the minute I woke up in the morning and filled him in on the case; what happened with Jillian and my questions about Officer Jimmy Smith? When I told him that somebody ransacked my car and his RV looking for something, his first concern was Bailey. After hearing that she hid during the invasion, he was genuinely worried about my dog. Then he said I should let her stay with his dogs for the next couple of days. He seemed to sense, as did I, that things were going to get intense. Call it intuition. Within the next twenty minutes, his driver pulled up behind the RV, and Derek stepped out of the backseat. A second driver showed up in another SUV, stepped out of the vehicle, and handed Derek the keys.

When I answered Derek's knock, he dropped the set of keys in my hand. "What's this?"

"You're going to need a vehicle until they repair yours," he said.

"I didn't expect you to supply me with one; I was going to rent one."

He shook his head and gave the thought a dismissive wave. "Nonsense," he said. "How's Bailey?"

Upon hearing her name, she came down the hall to see who was at the door. When she saw it was Derek, she tore out the door to play, her fear of strangers all gone.

"Hey girl," he said, whipping a tennis ball down the sand. When she went bounding after it, he turned to me. "She'll be fine with me and the dogs. You go do what you need to do on the case, and your friend's."

I shook my head in amazement. Bailey felt just as comfortable with him as I did. And he was coming to our rescue again. After a few rounds of throwing and retrieving, Bailey followed him over to talk with the contractors working on the cottage so he could check their progress. After a while, I watched him guide her into the back of his SUV. She didn't even hesitate. I breathed a sigh of relief. I was thankful that he could keep her while I dealt with some things.

"Thank you, Derek!" I said as he stepped into the back passenger seat.

Once they were gone, I went through my notes. Then I called Nauset Bay P.D. and left a message for Maldonado, advising him I'd be at the station in an hour to get my statement out of the way. After I did some stretching to clear my head, I took a hot shower, hoping I could just wash off the horrible events of the previous day. Didn't happen. Before getting dressed, I sent a text to Olivia and Madison and informed them of Jillian's death, and filled them in on what was going on. They suggested they should come down to the Cape early, but I reassured them I was fine, and busy working on the case.

I slipped into a pair of jeans, pulled on a navy-blue sweatshirt, and stepped into my suede cowboy boots. I left my hair down since I didn't have the energy to put it up. After last night, I had no intention of being without my weapon. I put on my gun belt and pulled the sweatshirt down over it. My backpack and keys were sitting on the counter. I grabbed them and my cell phone and headed out the door. Before stepping into Derek's loaner, I retrieved the mail from my box and stuffed it in the backpack to open later at the office.

I was now seated behind the wheel of a white Jeep Cherokee SUV, courtesy of Derek, and headed to Nauset Bay P.D. When I arrived at the station, there was an officer at the desk I didn't recognize. He motioned me to go on back. Detective Maldonado was at his desk. Two other detectives; Al Rosenberg and Stacy Cain sat at a long table with two undercover officers, Ana Lopez and Hank Johnson. They were all engaged in a heated conversation, but the minute they saw me enter, the talking stopped.

Maldonado motioned me over, stood up, and hugged me. "You doing okay this morning?"

I nodded. "I'm okay."

He handed me a statement. "I had it typed up. Read it over, make any changes you feel are necessary, add anything you think you forgot to mention, and then sign it."

I accepted the statement and glanced at the others. They were all seated with their feet propped up on the table, arms folded across their chests, and staring at me as if they could compel me to share some secret they thought I was carrying. Al Rosenberg suddenly got up and poured himself another cup of coffee, added cream and sugar, and then perched himself on the corner of the table in front of me. Psyop mind game, I assumed. He took a sip of coffee and gave me a deadpan stare. "Is there anything you want to tell us about your friend?"

I looked around at the eyes of the men and women staring me down. They were searching for something. "Such as?"

"Such as, why would she want to meet you in a dark alley at midnight?" He placed the mug down on the table and re-folded his arms across his chest, same as the others.

So here I was, a newbie, standing in a room full of trained detectives and cops, purposely trying to psyche me out. "As I told Detective Maldonado, I don't know. I haven't seen her in a while."

"I got that, but it makes little sense. You expect us to believe that she just called you out of the blue, after two decades, and asked you to meet her in the middle of the night?"

I knew how it looked, but that was how it happened. "I expect nothing."

At that moment, I realized he was trying to interrogate me in front of the others; trying to impress them. Maybe it was because someone gunned down my college roommate in front of me, and Finn was still unaccounted for, which had me frazzled, but I couldn't help myself. I laughed, but not out of humor.

Sensing my agitation, Detective Maldonado got out of his seat and crossed the room to stand between us. "Okay, knock it off. Let's try to keep the one-upmanship games out of this case. We're all on the same team."

"She's not one of us," I heard one female say, obviously referencing that I was just a P.I. and not a cop. Not the first time I heard that.

Rosenberg shrugged. "We meant nothing by it, D," he said, referring to Detective Maldonado. "Just confirming information, right Katie?"

I cocked my head to the side but returned his stare. "Just messing with me? Right."

"Right. We good?"

I had more backbone than to let his silly interrogation ruffle my feathers. "Yeah, we're good," I said. Besides, I knew it was nothing personal. I sat down in a vacant chair and read over the statement, made some changes, and added some more. Once I thought it was complete, I signed it and gave it back to Maldonado, who was back at his desk.

"I know I'm probably treading on thin ice here, but what's the possibility of getting a copy of the autopsy report?"

"I see what you're doing there," Maldonado said.

"What?" I said, innocently.

"You're trying to show those bozos that I've got your back. That's why you asked in front of them."

I gave him a slight grin. "Well, do you?"

"What?"

"Have my back?"

He laughed. Meanwhile, he weighed the pros and cons of passing me department information.

"She was my friend," I added when I noticed his hesitancy.

"Call me later today."

"Thanks."

You could see the others shaking their heads because he gave in so easily, but at least they were smiling when I walked out of the room.

CHAPTER 20

WHEN I PULLED out of the parking lot of the police station, I noticed the gray Ford Interceptor SUV, carrying two of Nauset Bay's finest, that exited soon after. They blended in with the traffic, traveling in the same direction a few cars back. Looking through the rear-view mirror, I could tell it was Lopez and Johnson. I already learned a lot about the cops at Nauset Bay from hanging around Derek and being friendly with Detective Maldonado. Lopez was no taller than me and always wore her baseball cap turned backward when undercover.

Johnson was an easy one to figure out. He and Lopez were partners, so expected that they'd be together. But more than that, he had a unique shape from his wrestling years during high school. He was tall and thin, except for his upper body, which he overcompensated for by lifting heavy weights. Sitting shotgun clearly outlined his massive shoulders in the front seat. I knew most of the men and women at Nauset Bay by now, so I shrugged it off when they messed with me. Except for a few, they were all good people. Wonder who gave the order?

Feigning ignorance, I headed towards the Moore residence. If he was home, I planned to pretend I was there to get information on the funeral arrangements for Jillian. If he wasn't, and I hoped that was the case, then I wanted to speak with Jose and Isabella. I was hoping they could shed some light on why Jillian left home. They might not know anything or tell me if they did, since their loyalty was to their employer, but I had to take a shot. Maybe Jillian being killed had something to do with why she left home.

The minute I turned onto Beachwood Drive, I noticed the media had swarmed the area. News finally broke that the murdered woman was the daughter of a prominent attorney with political ties. That the daughter hadn't seen the father in a while only made the story more intriguing for the tabloids. The press had their vans and camera equipment set up so that anyone visiting or leaving the Moore residence couldn't do so without dealing with them.

Not to be dissuaded, I pulled into the circular drive and watched the reporters flock like vultures out for their first kill. A medley of questions came my way as soon as I stepped out of the vehicle. But having Nauset Bay's finest tailing me proved to be beneficial. As soon as I mentioned I was meeting the lead investigators on the case and pointed toward the unmarked car, the media headed in their direction. When they shoved the microphones in their faces, I waved a finger at them and smiled, letting them know I knew they were behind me all along. From the look on their faces, I knew there'd be payback, someday. Games people play. Guess I'll be watching my back for a while.

I rang the doorbell several times before Jose opened the door a couple of inches and peaked out.

"Oh, it's you," he said, appearing anxious. He pulled me through the door in a rush, hoping the media wouldn't notice.

"What's going on, Jose?" I said, seeing his demeanor.

"It's been crazy all morning." He seemed to be in a state of panic. He was probably worried about the exposure; some of his family members could be in the country illegally. "Between the phone and the news media pounding on the door, there's been no peace."

"Is Mr. Moore home, Jose?"

"No, he left early this morning."

We walked down the hall, passing a large and elaborately decorated room. I didn't get a good view, but enough to know they had remodeled it since my last visit. Jillian used to refer to it as The Green Room. She always mimicked putting her finger down her throat when mentioning it. Entering the kitchen, I saw Isabella sitting on a stool at the island countertop, having a cup of tea. She had a tissue in her hand, wiping bloodshot and swollen eyes. It was obvious she had been crying through the night. I was sorry to see her sad, but it was good to know someone in this house showed emotion over Jillian's death. When Isabella noticed me, she got hysterical and rambled words in Spanish. She was speaking so fast I couldn't understand her. I looked in Jose's direction for interpretation.

"Jillian was like a daughter to us," Jose said. "Isabella is taking it especially hard. Would you like a cup of tea, Katie?"

"No, thank you, Jose," I said. I walked toward the island, pulled a stool out, and sat down next to Isabella.

"Jose, what is Mr. Moore doing about the funeral arrangements?"

Isabella's cries intensified and Jose looked at me in despair. "There are no funeral arrangements."

"What?" I said, confused. Maybe I was just misunderstanding. "You mean Mr. Moore hasn't made arrangements yet?"

Jose looked on the verge of tears himself, but his pride wouldn't allow him to give in. His culture demanded that he remain strong. "Mr. Moore took his lawyers to the police station this morning to demand the body. He's having her cremated."

My eyes went wide, stunned.

Releasing his anger, Jose slammed his hands down on the counter. Sighing in frustration, he slumped down onto the stool next to us.

"I don't understand," I said, trying to make sense of it all. "Why would he have her cremated? How could he? That's not what Jillian would want."

Isabella, who had always been a sweet woman and never spoke ill of anyone, was out of her seat, yelling in an angry outburst. "He never cared for her!"

"Calm down, Isa," Jose said, using his nickname for her.

Isabella ignored him and paced the room, yelling in her native language. She finally stopped and looked at Jose as if she was imploring him to do something. "Jose, she was like a daughter to us."

My heart went out to them because I knew that to be true. Jillian told me many times that it was Jose and Isabella who took care of her, while her father pursued his career and political aspirations. What those aspirations were, I never knew, only that he was often involved in throwing fundraisers for certain politicians.

I knew this was a bad time, but if Isabella was up to talking, I needed answers. Maybe she would divulge something that could help, even if she wasn't aware of it.

"Isabella," I said, treading lightly. "Do you know what happened between Jillian and her father? What made her leave home?"

I was sorry for heading down that road the minute I noticed the horrified look on both of their faces. Jose's eyes were glaring at Isabella, willing her not to speak, but she just couldn't help herself.

"It was The Teacher," Isabella said, the anger in her voice unmistakable. "He made her leave."

Jose's body tensed up the minute she said that. He willed her not to say more. He didn't want her to tell me more than she already had.

But even though I knew it was causing them pain, I couldn't stop. I needed to know more. "Who is The Teacher?"

"Isa... stop!" Jose yelled in a fierce tone.

This time I didn't see anger on his face, but outright fear.

He paced the room, checking the hallway and peering out the window, terrified somebody was going to hear.

Isabella walked in front of her husband, trying to plead with him. "Jose, you know we should have done something a long time ago. Our girl would still be here."

"Isa, I beg you," Jose said, his voice sounding desperate. "The same thing that happened to Jillian could happen to us, to a member of our family."

That was all he said, leaving Isabella to think about it, and me to wonder what they knew, yet were afraid to tell.

Isabella uttered another round of Spanish while her hands flailed in the air. After a moment, she slumped back down on the stool, looking as if she lost all hope.

Jose looked at me with sorrow. "I'm sorry, Katie," he said, trying to make me understand. "Nothing we say will bring our

Jillian back. We are leaving and taking our family back home to keep them safe. Please, just keep us out of it."

It was then that I noticed the bags packed and sitting by the back door. I felt terrible for them, for Jillian, and for anyone involved with Howard Moore. I wanted answers to my questions, but I didn't want to be the one to make them suffer. I didn't know what they were afraid of, probably the same thing that made Jillian leave home. The only thing I knew with certainty was that their fear was real if they had to go back to Mexico.

"I understand," I said, even though I didn't. How could I? Someone murdered Jillian, and somebody at this house knew something. Knowing there was nothing more I could do or say, I headed back to the front door. I gave them one last look, knowing I would never see them again. Isabella was crying as if she had just lost her own child.

As I walked back towards the jeep, I expected to see cameras and microphones in my path, but they were still hounding Lopez and Johnson. I smiled. By the time they noticed I was leaving and could get past reporters, I would be on the way to my next destination with them too far behind to catch me. While en route, I punched in the number for Detective Maldonado.

"I understand you had a visitor," I said when he answered.

He chuckled. "Oh, you mean Moore and his three minions?" I could hear the sarcasm in his voice.

"Three?"

"Yeah—his tag team, Manny, Moe, and Jack."

I laughed. "Manny, Moe & Jack, don't they run an auto parts store?"

"These guys couldn't run a lemonade stand. Manny did the talking. Moe listened. Jack took notes. And Howard Moore ignored everything they said."

"And the result."

"Gibberish."

"I was worried he'd show up with a slew of attorneys," I said. "Did you get anything out of him at all?"

"Enough to put him at the top of my suspect list, but only because I didn't like the man."

"Do you think he could have been responsible for having his daughter killed?"

"What do you think, Katie? You knew the man."

I thought about it for a minute. "His behavior is suspicious, but it's hard to imagine any father being involved with their daughter's death. I just don't know. I haven't seen them in so long. It's hard to know what transpired in that household, and Jillian would never tell me."

"I had to release the body, Katie. They completed the autopsy, so I had no choice."

"He's having her cremated."

"How do you know?"

"I just spoke with the butler and nanny."

"The man is a piece of work," he said. "How are you holding up?"

"I'm okay."

"Well, stay that way, Katie," he said. "Remember what I told you about the crime scene?"

"You mean bullets inches away from my head? Yeah, I remember."

"I want you to be careful," he ordered. "Keep your gun with you at all times."

"I will."

Of course, it's difficult to be careful when you don't know what the hell is going on.

CHAPTER 21 - THE TEACHER

Sometime ago

AGAIN THE TEACHER was out hunting for another victim. This time, he stayed close to home. This time, he had help.

Every day after school, and again on the weekends, teens flocked like pigeons to the Cape Cod Mall. Several of them went to work in the retail stores and kiosks. Some would hang out at the food court, and others shopped for the latest fads in jeans and miscellaneous gifts.

Nineteen-year-old Laney Rogers was a sweet and innocent young woman from the suburbs with long legs and a golden tan. Her mother passed away several years ago from a long bout with cancer, and her father a year later from a broken heart. Since then, Laney has been putting in long hours at a clothing store at the mall with dreams of bigger things.

After signing on to be an extra for a movie that was filming nearby, she was hooked. She wanted to be just like the actress getting all the attention on the set. In pursuit of her goal, she applied to a school offering modeling and acting classes. Now, she just needed money to pay the fee.

The man and woman spotted her at The Millennial, a new popular clothing store for young men and women.

They watched her.

Stalked her.

On a Saturday afternoon, when kids and teens crowded the mall, Laney was stacking jeans onto the shelves. That's when the couple strolled into the store. Laney couldn't help but notice them. They looked like models from the cover of a Vogue Magazine. They wore designer clothes and sunglasses—the kind she always noticed celebrities wearing on the cover of her favorite tabloids. An expensive brand she hoped to wear someday. This was the first time Laney saw them. But it wasn't the first time they saw Laney. They had been watching her for some time.

After browsing the store for a few minutes, the woman put on a fake smile and approached Laney. "I hope you don't mind me saying you're beautiful."

Laney blushed. "Thank you." She couldn't believe someone like *that* had noticed her.

"Has anyone ever told you what a unique look you have?"

"What do you mean?"

The Teacher suddenly approached her from the right. "She's hot, isn't she?"

The woman motioned toward Laney's face. "Your eyes come alive when you smile. And your bone structure…"

While looking her up and down in admiration, The Teacher said, "I think she'd be perfect."

"Perfect for what?" Laney inquired, curious. She glanced back and forth at them. She couldn't help it. The attention more than flattered her. Nobody paid that much attention to her, since, well, since her parents died. And they were so beautiful, the man so distinguished.

The woman handed Laney a card. "We're looking for potential models to do a commercial for a major client that might play during the Super Bowl next year."

Laney's face lit up with a smile. "The Super Bowl? Really?"

"You just have that look," he said, "Wholesome. Girl next door. We'd love it if you would join us for dinner some evening, so we could talk more about it. Is modeling something you would ever be interested in?"

"Oh my, yes. It's been a dream," Laney said with more enthusiasm than even they expected. "Are you for real?"

The woman tilted her head to the side and smiled. "Of course we are. Trust me."

"Tell you what," he said, as he pulled an expensive cell phone out of his pocket. "Let me get the client on the phone and see if he is free to meet us for dinner soon." He took a few steps away and pretended to make a phone call. After he disconnected from the call, he walked back over to Laney. "How is Monday? Does that work for you?"

Laney's eyes lit up.

After chatting for a few more minutes, the couple offered to pick Laney up Monday evening after she got off of work. They told her they would make reservations for a restaurant at the waterfront. When they walked out of the store, Laney was smiling from ear to ear, believing this could be her big break.

"I'm on my way," she giggled to herself.

The following Monday evening, at the designated time, The Teacher and woman pulled up to the entrance of the mall in a dark SUV. Laney slipped into the back seat without question. The expensive car impressed her, and she admired the good-looking couple she was now associating with. She was on her way to bigger things. Or so she thought.

They never made it to the restaurant.

They never met with a client.

Laney was blindfolded and escorted into a building, ushered down a set of stairs, and locked in a room with several others. The following day, the woman called the answering machine at The Millennial and left the message Laney accepted another job, and would not be returning.

There wouldn't be anyone looking for Laney.

There wasn't anyone who cared.

Soon, she would no longer matter.

Now she belonged to him.

CHAPTER 22

IT SEEMED LIKE a lifetime ago since I was at the office. In reality, it was just yesterday, only a lot has happened. After I parked and walked across the street, I braced myself for what I might find. I expected they would toss the office the same as the RV and my SUV. When I opened the door, I breathed a sigh of relief. They didn't touch it. The installation of an elaborate alarm system could be the reason. After switching on the lights, I checked the thermostat, grabbed a bottle of water from the refrigerator in the back, and then sat down at the desk to check my emails.

My friend Connie sent me a note that she was free for dinner next Wednesday. She added she was giving up the dating game. Sparks were flying with the new guy. And I could have her hand-me-downs. I laughed, and noted the dinner on the calendar.

The next email was Roger giving me a background on The Miles Modeling Agency. He already informed me that Sarah was the only owner, but this report was more in-depth. He attached a portion of last year's tax filing, showing her business made millions. Clearly, there was a reason Thomas threatened to go after her business. He also provided information from the credit bureau. Reading through it, there didn't seem to be anything out of the ordinary, just the usual for any corporation in good standing. There were a lot of creditors, but they paid the bills on time, and there were no large-term loans listed on the document as being outstanding. Conclusion: the agency didn't have any money issues, and they did not list Thomas Miles on any document. He had no right to the business.

The next email was the hardest. Maldonado forwarded me a copy of Jillian's autopsy. The medical terms were foreign to me, so I scrolled through most of them. There were only two pieces of information I was looking for. I needed to confirm the initial report that the slug found was from a 9mm. The report confirmed it. When the cops learned more, or I supplied them with more, they could use that to confirm the killer. I also wanted to know if there were any traces of drugs in Jillian's system at the time of her death. For years, I tried to come up with an excuse for why she disappeared from my life so abruptly. Drugs were the only thing I could come up with. But the autopsy showed no signs of them in her system. In the early morning hours when she called me, she sounded scared, but there was nothing in her voice to show she was erratic. If she was involved with drugs, would they disappear from her system if she hadn't taken them a couple of days before her death? I might need to follow up on that?

While at the desk, I pulled the mail out of my backpack to see if any bills needed attention. There were the usual; cell phone and electric, credit card statements, and the same miscellaneous junk I received every month. There was also a yellow slip from the post office, telling me I had a piece of mail waiting that needed a signature. I was waiting for a draft script from the producers developing the TV series pilot, and assumed it was probably that. I put it in my wallet for the moment and then went online to pay bills; so much easier than sending checks.

Once that was done, I pulled out a yellow notepad and grabbed a pen to outline questions I had regarding Jillian's death. Thomas Miles would be at his office, so there was no chance to catch him in the act, though I shouldn't say that. Just two weeks ago, I caught a stockbroker in the act while at work. The wife hired me to find out if he was cheating. He claimed he had to work on a Saturday afternoon, which was abnormal, according to the wife.

I studied the building; the routine of the security guard, the cleaning crew, and noted the floor of the office. On Saturday morning when the security guard was walking the perimeter, I rushed inside the building and slipped inside the elevator. Went up to the correct floor, and entered while the cleaning crew was vacuuming. I hid inside the office supply storeroom, keeping the door ajar until my target showed up with his secretary.

A few days later, the husband responded to questions at his deposition. When asked about his infidelity, he claimed it was his wife who was cheating, and that she shouldn't receive alimony or full custody of the children. He was stunned when the wife's attorney presented a video showing his secretary spread-eagle on his office desk and him butt-naked in front of the camera.

Knowing how that case turned out, I scrutinized Molly, Thomas Miles' secretary, early on. She was too smart to hook up with the likes of him.

Getting back to my notes, I still wanted to know why Jillian left home. Where did she go when she left? I narrated everything in my head and wrote the questions I came up with. She asked me about a package before asking to meet. And someone had the balls to search my car, even though there were a dozen cops around at the crime scene. How did they know they'd have time with no one catching them? And how did they know I wasn't at the RV when they searched there?

Mentally exhausted, I put the pen down and rubbed my temples. It felt like I'd been there for hours. Glancing at the clock, it surprised me it was less than an hour. I rummaged through my phone and scrolled through my contacts. I called everyone who knew Jillian during college to see if they had seen or heard from her in the last few years.

The only person who admitted to seeing her was a guy named Lenny Franks. He ran into her some time ago at a private party in Hyannis. He said she had changed so much that he barely recognized her. He couldn't recall whose house it was, or who she was with. He seemed vague. He was sad to hear about her death, but admitted he wrote her off a long time ago. It horrified me to hear that. I couldn't imagine anyone writing Jillian off. What would make him say something like that?

I suddenly felt the need for a break and walked to a local café for something to drink. I opened my wallet to grab some money. Seeing the yellow slip from the post office, a flash went off inside my brain. I slapped myself on the forehead.

Shit, Katie… the package.

CHAPTER 23

BY THE TIME I reached the post office, I was sweating, only not because of the weather. It was mild for December, but I still had to wear a jacket. It was just the fear of what I was going to find. There were three lines of people waiting, so I chose one and tried to calm my nerves. The female clerk working the counter was not a local. Every time she uttered the word next, I could hear the distinct accent that told me she was a New Yorker. When my turn came, I handed her the slip of paper and waited while she went in the back. She returned with a large manila envelope and handed the yellow slip back to me: "Sign here, please".

Once I gave her the signed slip, she handed over the envelope. Before I even looked at the front to see if there was a return address, she said: "Next."

As I walked away, I knew it was the package. I rushed outside and ripped through the sealed end. Inside, there was a letter, along with several photographs, and an even smaller envelope. First, I looked at the letter to see who signed it and my eyes watered. It was Jillian's signature, dated two days before her death.

The package.

I read the letter, trying to force back the emotions:

Katie,

I'm so sorry for disappearing and not keeping in touch. Someday, I hope you understand and forgive me.

I need your help. I got involved in something and it's way out of control. I want no more innocents to get hurt.

The smaller envelope contains a key to a safe-deposit box at a local bank. You'll know what to do once you view the contents, along with the photographs in this package.

Katie, I hope you can find it in your heart to forgive me and look into it.

Friends forever, Jillian

By the time I finished reading, tears were pouring down my face. If she mailed the letter sooner, maybe I would have been able to stop what happened to her. When I realized I was getting some weird looks from people going into the post office, I wiped the tears and hurried back to the jeep.

I immediately pulled the photographs out of the envelope. The minute I got a glimpse of what they were about, I freaked and looked around to make sure nobody was walking by. Relieved to know I was alone, I stuffed them back into the envelope and sped back to the office.

Back at my desk, I pulled out six 5x7 photographs and scattered them across the flat surface. The first two photos were blurry, but I could still make out some faces. They depicted men and women dressed in fancy attire at some type of party.

There was nothing necessarily peculiar about them, except for who the individuals were. The party was being held in an elaborately decorated room. The men and women were standing in groups having conversations.

In one group, there were public officials. I couldn't swear it, but one of them looked like one man I just witnessed going into The Tapestry. They were standing with very attractive and provocatively dressed women, and I knew they weren't their wives. In the second group, there were four men; one was a senator for the State of Massachusetts, and Howard Moore, Jillian's father. I didn't know the other two men. At the sight of Howard Moore, I assumed the party was one of his political fundraisers. And now that I thought about it, the room they were standing in looked like a room I had recently seen: The Green Room.

The next two photographs were more of the same, just not as clear. I would need Roger to work his magic on them.

It was the last two that had me bothered. They were photographs of teenagers and young women. They dressed them to look like China dolls in a pageant. My imagination went into overdrive at why they were dressed that way.

Jillian said she was involved with something that was out of control, so how did the pictures fall into it? Did she witness someone engaging in explicit behavior with the young women? Was someone harming them? Could it be about blackmail? Some men in the photos were high profile. If the thoughts in my imagination were on target, they might not be happy having these photos floating around.

I kept going back to the images of the teenagers. I couldn't pull myself away. In the letter, Jillian said she wanted no more innocents to be hurt. Were they being hurt? I desperately wanted to know more.

Who were they?

Where were they?

Then reality hit me. The photos were probably the reason somebody broke into my car, trashed the RV, and scared Bailey. If they were looking for the photos, then somebody knew Jillian contacted me. But how would they know that? The only people who knew were the police, and Jillian's father, and that was after the fact.

Unless somebody was following her, which would explain how they knew we were meeting at the coffee shop. When she called, she asked me to meet her at our old meeting place. She didn't say the name of the place. Yet, somebody found out we were meeting there.

Well, the photos were in my possession now. If they wanted them, they would have to go through me. That was going to make for some sleepless nights.

CHAPTER 24

MY NEXT MOVE would be to check out the safe-deposit box and find out what Jillian put inside. The photos showed some high-profile individuals with women who weren't their wives, but was that enough to murder somebody? And how did the young girls fit into the scenario? I just hoped it wasn't what I was imagining, and fearing.

I put the photos back in the envelope and tucked them in my backpack, which would remain with me from now on. I put everything else away and double-locked the office on the way out. If that sounded paranoid—you bet I was paranoid.

Now that I was in a hurry, the traffic was heavy. She chose the Cape Cod bank. They have several branches throughout the area, but the one she used was just beyond the rotary, after the bridge.

When I walked inside, I spotted a brunette woman wearing a navy-blue suit at a new accounts desk talking on the phone. I headed in her direction.

"I'll be just a moment," she said, placing her hand over the phone.

"No problem." I remained standing, but casually looking around.

"How can I help you?" the woman said, after finishing the call. "Would you like to open a new account?"

"No, thank you," I said. "Can you direct

me to the safe-deposit boxes?"

"Do you have a box here?"

"Yes, ma'am."

"Can I see the key?"

I gave her the key.

She examined it to make sure it was one of theirs and then stood up and motioned me to follow. We went down a long hallway and stepped into a private room. There were several rows of metal boxes built into the walls. "Your box is over here," she said, looking at me as if I should know.

I followed her to the corner and watched as she put the key into a box that matched the number on the key. She pulled it out, placed it down on a table with chairs behind us, and then dropped the key back in my hand.

"I'll give you some privacy," she said. She walked out and closed the door behind her.

I sat there for a moment, bracing myself for what else I was going to find. When I opened the box, there were two large envelopes and two DVDs, without cases, wrapped in a plastic baggie. I took the items out of the box, closed the box, and locked it back up. I opened the envelopes before leaving the bank.

The first one contained four more photographs. I assumed from the same party. Three photographs had some of the same individuals that were in the ones I viewed at the office. But these photos were graphic, which explained the need to put them in a safe-deposit box. They depicted individuals engaging in explicit sexual behavior with young women. Looking at the photos made me sick to my stomach.

The fourth photo showed some of the young women. Their long hair was loose down their back and they wore skimpy dresses, but they had strange looks on their face. It took me a few moments of studying the photo to realize they were not women, but teenagers, dressed to look like women. Anger surged through me at where my mind was taking me.

What the hell was happening to these girls?

I couldn't explain it, but I got the sense that time was an important factor here. I needed to find out about these girls, and find out where they were? I couldn't fathom that anyone would photograph the girls like this, and then send them home without worrying about parents asking questions. Were the girls isolated somewhere? How did they come to be photographed? And just how many innocent victims were involved?

The label on the second envelope said: personal. Jillian wanted me to view the contents, or she wouldn't have sent the key. Opening it, I learned Jillian knew something was going to happen to her, and she took measures to prepare for it.

She knew she was going to die.

The thought made me shiver. There were documents inside. The first one was a will, signed and filed. I took a deep breath, then put it to the side and viewed the rest. There was a lease for an apartment where she had been living. It was only a few miles from my home. She had been so close to me all this time. The remaining document was a real estate deed for a residential property on Casper Island. That brought my head up. Casper Island was where The Tapestry was located. I don't believe in coincidences.

I knew there was enormous wealth in Jillian's family, but her owning property on Casper Island raised even more questions, especially when noting the value. She always told me she'd accept nothing from her father. Did she give in, or did she purchase the property on her own? And if so, how? What was she doing for the past twenty years?

I was feeling guilty looking over her personal affairs, but I had to. It was the only way to figure out what the hell was going on. While I was at the bank, I needed to decide if I should read Jillian's Will without the presence of her father. To hell with it, I concluded, and started reading.

Since the will is a legal document, it was very thorough and precise, outlining things specifically. Because of that, I almost fell off the chair. It said Jillian was leaving her personal real estate property on Casper Island to me.

Jillian left her home to me?

I was in shock. I haven't seen her for years. Why the hell would she do that? There was a final clause, however. She requested I pursue an investigation into the photographs and find the individuals responsible for her death.

Jillian knew she was going to die, and possibly, by whose hands.

The will had the name and address of her attorney, and there was a note advising me to contact him. It horrified me to know Jillian suspected something was going to happen to her. I couldn't imagine what it must have been like for her. How long had she been running? When did she take the photographs?

I sat at that table for quite some time. The tears kept falling and I couldn't stop them. I tried to make sense of everything, but I couldn't. I wanted to know why she left everything to me. The only explanation; she knew what she was asking me to do was dangerous. She was repaying me because she was putting my life in jeopardy. She knew I'd see it through.

It took me a while to compose myself, but I finally summoned the strength. When I was back in the car, I didn't even realize that I was driving to Jillian's apartment.

CHAPTER 25

WHILE ON THE way, I placed a call to the law firm of Calloway & Calloway; the firm listed on Jillian's Will.

"May I speak with Joe Calloway, please?" I said to the male receptionist.

"Who's calling please?"

"My name is Katie Parker."

"One moment, please."

He placed me on hold.

Another male voice picked up. "This is Joe Calloway."

"Hello, Mr. Calloway," I said. "My name is Katie Parker."

I thought I heard him gasp. "Hello, Ms. Parker. How are you?"

"You know who I am?"

"Yes, of course. But I pray the fact that you're calling doesn't mean something happened to Jillian Moore."

"I'm afraid it has Mr. Calloway."

"Oh no," he said, sincerely. "Can I ask what happened?"

"Somebody murdered her."

"Murdered? I'm so sorry."

I didn't know the man, but I could hear the sadness in his voice.

"I didn't take her seriously when she said something might happen to her. I thought… hoped she was just overreacting."

"I wish that were the case." If only I'd known she was in trouble, I could have helped her. I would have believed her. "Mr. Calloway, I have to check out Jillian's apartment, and then I'd like to come and see you. Do you have the time?"

"Of course, just tell me when."

"How about in an hour? Would that be good?"

"That's fine. Do you know where the office is?"

"Jillian gave me a copy of the will with your address on it. I'll see you in an hour."

"Katie, I'm very sorry about Jillian."

"Yeah, me too."

The apartment building where Jillian had been living was on Cherry Avenue, directly across the street from the park where I take kickboxing lessons. Again, I realized just how close we were all this time, only I didn't know.

There was a garage in the back of the apartment building for each unit, but I parked on the street. I put the photos and Jillian's personal information inside my backpack, opened the tailgate, and placed the backpack inside the spare tire compartment.

As I headed up the walkway to the front of the building, I studied the surroundings. The owner did a good job with maintenance. Cape Cod shingles, tile roofing, and shutters were on the exterior. The grounds were immaculate and professionally landscaped. There were four units inside the building, and Jillian's apartment was on the second floor to the right.

As I approached the door, I could see it was slightly ajar. After what happened to Jillian, I needed to be prepared. I pulled my gun and pointed it forward. I put my toes against the door and pushed it open, as slowly and quietly as I could. Splintered wood was noticeable on the frame of the door, which revealed someone forced their way in. They didn't have a key.

With the gun out front, I stepped into the room. They tore the apartment apart too, but whoever did it was malicious. They knocked everything that was standing down. There were glass-framed pictures broken. Glass was everywhere. The cushions on the furniture were slit open. And there was a putrid smell emanating from the room. As I moved further into the living room, I could see where the smell was coming from. They tossed the food from the refrigerator all over the floor. The milk had soured.

There was a hall leading to other rooms. I swept the room with the gun, and moved down the narrow hall, watching for anything. When I approached the first room, I stopped at the sight of a shadow on the door. Someone was moving inside the room. My heart started pounding as I inched closer to the door and peeked around the corner. I saw the shape of a man dressed in black, wearing gloves and a baseball hat, and even sunglasses to hide his appearance.

He was searching through the belongings in the room. He didn't know I was there, so I had the element of surprise, but my move had to be quick and flawless.

I rounded the corner and kept my gun steady. "Don't move."

As soon as the words came out of my mouth, a second figure came out of a room at the end of the hall. He moved towards me, catching me off guard. Keeping the gun trained on the first guy, I used my left leg and made a high kick to the temple at the guy in the hall. Even with the cowboy boots, it only dazed him. I kicked him again, this time aiming for his groin. My kick landed in the right spot. He doubled over in pain. Expletives were flying. While I was busy with him, I took my eyes off the first guy. He took advantage of the situation by plowing into me and knocking me off balance. While I was down, he bolted toward the door.

As I tried to pick myself up; the second guy was regaining his composure and pissed off. Before I was completely stable, he ran headfirst towards me, hitting me in the stomach and knocking the wind out of me as he tackled me to the ground. I was still holding my gun, but I couldn't get it into position to use it as a weapon. I was lucky I didn't shoot without meaning to.

With him now on top of me, I mentally prepared myself for the blows that were coming my way. I tried to get my hands free to stop him.

The first blow came fast, right across the bridge of my nose. It wasn't a direct hit because of the lack of elbow room in the hall. The next two hits lacked the power of the first blow. Except for the blood from my nose, it wasn't too serious. He was preparing to land another jab when the first guy yelled from the living room: "Somebody's coming, let's get the hell out of here."

The guy on top of me hissed into my ear. "Stay out of it, bitch." Then he punched me in the gut before jumping up and running down the hall.

As I tried to pull myself up, the pain on my face was immediate. The throbbing of my head was coming on slow and dramatic. I positioned myself against the wall with my gun on my lap, in case they returned. Several seconds went by before I accepted they weren't. I pushed myself up and slipped the gun back into my belt. I needed to spit up the blood that was spilling into my mouth and assess the damage to my face. I walked down the hall in search of a bathroom.

The sight that was before me in the mirror wasn't a pretty one. It was hard to see through the blood, but I could tell one of my eyes was going to have some serious color. And my left cheek was already swelling. Those I could handle with some makeup. But the throbbing pain was getting worse by the minute. I just didn't have time for that right now.

I rummaged through a linen closet looking for a washcloth and turned the water on until it was lukewarm. Then I wet the cloth and attempted to clean off the blood. After that, I reached for another cloth and headed out to the kitchen to see if there was any ice in the freezer. There was no ice, but I found a frozen steak. I sat down on what they left of the sofa cushion and put the steak on my face, to keep the swelling at a minimum.

CHAPTER 26

EITHER I DOZED off or had a slight concussion, because the next thing I knew, a roguishly handsome man was leaning over me and preparing to kiss me. I felt a surge of sexual heat but tried to fight it off. This had to be wrong. It must be a dream. When his familiar blue eyes met mine, I lost all control. My lips parted, and his tongue slipped inside as his lips devoured mine. Damn, it hurt, and felt euphoric at the same time.

Seconds later, the moment of pleasure got interrupted when I heard sirens. Then, feet stormed the hall of the building and uniformed officers breached the door with their guns drawn. Maldonado followed.

"Stand down," I heard a voice say above me. "She's okay."

Radios squawked and there was another order to stand down.

I blinked. I saw and felt Finn's presence when I was out, but now there was no Finn. Yet, the kiss felt so real. I ran my tongue over my lips. There was the taste of dried blood, but something else, as well; cinnamon. Finn's cinnamon gum. When I allowed myself to look up, Maldonado stood over me with a worried frown on his face.

"Just what I always wanted," I said to Maldonado, "a knight in shining armor to come in and rescue me when I have a swollen face the color of a plum."

"Keep talking," Maldonado said. "I need to know that you're okay and don't have a concussion."

Maybe I *did* have a concussion. The fantasy of Finn felt so real and my lips tasted like the cinnamon from his gum. "How'd you know I was here?" I asked Maldonado.

Maldonado examined my face and sat down next to me. "We received a call from an attorney by the name of Joe Calloway. He said you were supposed to be there an hour ago. Under the circumstances, he got concerned."

I attempted to sit up. "Wow, is it that late? I was supposed to meet Calloway after I stopped by here. But, as you can see, I got delayed. I'm okay, though."

Maldonado wandered the apartment, assessing the damage. When he returned, he got another look at my face now that I was sitting up. "Damn girl, we can't leave you alone for a minute."

"You should see the other guy," I quipped.

Maldonado frowned. He grabbed the cloth lying on the arm of the sofa and walked out to the freezer. Discovering there was no ice, he brought me another frozen steak. "Seriously, are you okay?"

I nodded numbly.

"What happened here?" he said, as he

looked around the ransacked apartment.

"Cleaning lady failed to show," I said, trying to borrow their cop humor, but the minute I said it, I wanted to take it back. What can you do without humor? Truth was, I didn't know how much to say.

He looked at me and frowned. "Cop humor only works if you're a seasoned cop. You're new to this crazy world. You haven't seen enough to be jaded."

"Sorry," I said. I took a deep breath. "This was Jillian's apartment. I came to check it out. When I got here, two men were ransacking the place. They got the better of me. But I got a couple of kicks in first."

Maldonado said, "Did you get a look at them?"

"Male, white, about six feet, physically fit, wearing black clothing with gloves, baseball hats, and sunglasses." I attempted to rub my temples to keep the pain to a minimum, but it didn't help. I had a killer headache.

Maldonado immediately got on the radio and ordered an officer to tape off the scene, and instructed the Ident tech to dust the entire place for prints, even though he didn't expect to get any. Then he barked out orders to scour the building and neighborhood for witnesses.

"Got any idea what these guys were looking for?" Maldonado said.

I nodded. "Yeah, I got an idea."

Maldonado looked at me with interest.

"You got something to share?"

"Yeah, actually I do, but I need to meet with Joe Calloway first. I can meet you after that and give you what I've got. I'm not sure where it all leads, but I have a feeling this thing is going to be pretty messy."

"Doesn't get much messier than murder," he said.

I forced myself to stand up, fighting through the throbbing pain. "Wanna bet?" I didn't say it, but I had the feeling this case was going to take us to places we didn't want to go, and it would be hard to come back from.

Maldonado said, "Do you want me to come with you to Calloway's office to make sure you have no more trouble?" I could see he was concerned, but it felt good.

"I'll be okay," I said. "He's reading Jillian's will. I think I should do that alone."

He looked at me and seemed to have more questions, but refrained from asking them. We agreed to meet up at the station later. I was hesitant to leave Jillian's apartment the way it was, especially with the broken lock, but they considered it a crime scene, so what could I do?

CHAPTER 27

I RETRIEVED THE backpack out of the trunk before heading to Calloway's office. It was probably ten minutes away, in a small building near the new grocery store. I pulled into the lot and parked right outside the stairs of the entrance, grabbed the backpack, and headed into the building.

Working hours were over, but he told Detective Maldonado that he would wait at the office. When the security guard got a look at my bruised and battered face; he probably assumed I was an abused woman coming to consult with an attorney.

I came to a cherry wood door with the title Calloway & Calloway engraved on it. When I opened the door, an older, distinguished-looking gentleman stood just inside, anxiously waiting for me to arrive. He had a slim physique that looked like he achieved it by being a runner or a cyclist. He introduced himself as Mac Calloway, Joe Calloway's brother.

The minute he got a look at my face, he was immediately concerned and acted like a caring father. "Oh dear," he said. "The officers called and told us you were on your way, but they didn't mention your condition."

"I'm okay," I said, even though my head was throbbing with pain. "I could use an aspirin though, I have a killer headache."

"Follow me," Mac said. "Joe should have some in his office." He led me down the corridor to a corner office. Do all partners have corner offices?

Mac lightly tapped on the door; then turned the knob and entered. It was a large office with windows on the outer walls giving off a spectacular view of trees, and if you go to the other side, you see even more. The office was neat, but not overly decorated. They took more of an effort to display their antique model sailboats than the normal bookcases and wingback chairs in most attorney offices.

A younger version of Mac was sitting behind a maple wood desk going over some paperwork and looked up when we entered. When he saw us, he immediately stood up and greeted me in the same warm manner as his brother; while Mac went into a separate room to retrieve some aspirin.

"Joe Calloway," he said, as he offered his hand in introduction. "I got very concerned when you didn't arrive. I hope I didn't scare you by contacting the police." Standing next to me, he could see the damage that was done to my face. "I guess I did the right thing by calling."

Just then, Mac walked back in with a glass of water and a bottle of Advil. "This is all we have. I hope it will suffice." He handed me the water and opened the Advil for me.

"This is fine, thank you. Mr. Calloway,

I'd like to get started if you don't mind. I'm expected at the police station, and I know I'm going to be feeling some pain pretty soon."

"Of course." Joe politely pulled out the seat opposite his desk for me to sit down and went behind the desk to take a seat. Mac sat in the seat next to me.

"We're very sorry about what happened to Jillian," Joe said, with Mac listening and nodding his head. "How did it happen?"

"Somebody shot her in the back of an alley where she and I were supposed to meet."

Joe looked sincere and saddened by the news, and was shaking his head like he couldn't believe such a thing could happen. He opened a file on his desk.

"Jillian came to this office and requested we put together a will immediately. She informed us her life was in danger and she didn't have time to wait. No matter how hard we tried; she wouldn't tell us what she was afraid of, only that you were the only person she could trust."

I stared at Joe and frowned. "She couldn't go to the police or her father?"

Mac said, "She was afraid of the police, and said she couldn't trust her father. She said under no circumstances were we to contact him. You were the only person we should speak with regarding anything she told us."

I was even more baffled. "I haven't seen

Jillian in years. I don't understand why I'm the one she trusts?"

It was obvious their concern for Jillian was sincere. They were trying to fulfill her wishes now that she was gone.

"All I can tell you is what she told us," Joe said. "She said you were like a sister to her during college, and you continued to check up on her through the years."

Mac continued where Joe left off. "She also told us that whatever she was asking you to do, you would see it through, and bring the guilty to justice." They both looked at me, letting me know the impact of what they said, how Jillian felt.

"Wait a minute, back up," I said, confused about something he just said. "The part about me checking up on her... she knew I had been calling and checking on her?"

Joe and Mac looked at each other and nodded. "She said you continued to call the house to see if she was okay." He didn't understand where I was going with this.

"For her to know I had been checking on her, someone from the house had to tell her. Right?" At least she knew I cared. But, it proved that someone from the house had spoken to her, even after she left, even though they insisted to me they hadn't.

"I guess that's right. Does that help?"

"Yes, it helps a great deal."

Out of the blue, Mac looked at his watch and rose out of his seat. "I'm sorry Katie," he said. "I have to get going. I have a house full of teenagers that I have to get home to. My wife works the night shift. It was nice meeting you. I hope everything works out. And again, I'm sorry about Jillian." He offered his hand in a warm handshake.

"Thank you. It was nice to meet you as well."

"If you need anything, please call one of us here at the office," he said, before exiting the room.

When he was gone, I looked back at Joe. "Mr. Calloway, there are some things I don't understand."

"Please call me Joe."

"Joe," I said. "I haven't seen Jillian in such a long time. How could she afford to buy a property on Casper Island? She refused to work at her father's law firm and she told me she would accept nothing from him."

Joe put his elbows on his desk and clasped his fingers together as if in thought. "I guess you don't know." He looked as if he was debating whether it was okay to continue. "Well, I guess it won't matter now. Our firm represented Ramona, Jillian's mother."

"Oh," I said, clearly in shock.

"Ramona came to this office when she was dying of cancer. We also put together her will. When she died some time ago, we contacted Jillian to let her know."

"So Jillian didn't see her mother before

she died?"

"I'm afraid not."

"And now they're both gone." I don't know why, but it just made me sad that Jillian and her mother never reconciled.

Joe gave me a serious look. "Katie; I have to tell you, Jillian and Ramona both insisted that Mr. Moore not know anything about the property on Casper Island."

I nodded, though it was all so confusing. "What are my responsibilities with the property?"

"Jillian owned the home. The only fee was the property taxes each year, which are paid out of the trust my firm set up for the property. The trust was the best way to keep it out of Howard Moore's sleazy investigations to keep control. You'd need to file the paperwork to change the ownership, which I can do for you if you like. Then the property is yours to do with as you please. Live in it; sell it, whatever you desire."

"It's just so surreal. I haven't been a part of Jillian's life for so long."

"Katie, I didn't know Jillian very long. But I can tell you she loved you and trusted you. In her words; the two of you had a bond that even the absence didn't break. Just as I can tell you, Ramona loved Jillian and regretted every day of not standing up to Howard Moore."

It helped to hear what he was saying. He also confirmed what I suspected all along:

Howard Moore was the one responsible for Jillian's mother leaving. I should have gone with my gut instincts years ago and looked her up so they could reunite. With what Joe just told me, I knew he was involved in what happened to her, and that thought made me shudder. Jillian was right, though. I would not rest until I found out.

CHAPTER 28

BEFORE I LEFT Calloway's office, I signed several documents. He handed me the copies and several keys. In just a few weeks, I would be the owner of a piece of prime real estate, but at what cost? I would give it back just to have Jillian alive, hanging out on the beach, debating the plots of our favorite books, just as we did all those years ago. We daydreamed about our futures; she wanted to go to law school and become a hot-shot attorney. I thought of criminal justice but didn't know to what capacity. Back then, it was Jillian who recommended I become a P.I. and work with her firm. I laughed it off as a joke. She even mapped out a plan for the two of us. She always said the two of us working together, we'd be unstoppable.

That was a lifetime ago. Now, I was walking out of her attorney's office because she was gone. I must have looked like the weight of the world was on my shoulders back in the lobby. This time, the security guard showed his sympathy. He even made sure I made it safely to my car. It was obvious Mac Calloway filled him in when he left the office.

I sat in the driver's seat for a moment, trying to gather my thoughts. I wiped away the tears. Getting emotional had to be put on hold. Maldonado was expecting me back at the station, but first I had to see if Roger could do something with the photos. While he worked, I could view the DVDs. The prospect of viewing them alone was not something I wanted to do, even though I didn't know what was on them. I hoped they'd shed more light on what was going on.

Roger, and his wife and baby, personified the perfect family with the white picket fence. They literally had a white picket fence. Their home was in a cute little cul-de-sac community of three-bedroom ranch homes with two-car garages. There were two American-made SUVs in the driveway. The homeowner's association meticulously maintained the properties. The grass was green, with no weeds or dandelions. The perennials were colorful, but not overly done. There was a slight incline on the street, which meant they had a breathtaking view from their back decks.

Roger was waiting for me at the garage door when I arrived. He kept his work space separate from his family life. When he got a look at my face, he rushed me inside, so his wife wouldn't see. He renovated one side of the garage and turned it into an office. He had an expensive mahogany desk and leather chair up against the back wall. The rest of the room housed camera equipment, two PCs, laptops, and three flat-screen TVs, which he used as monitors when needed. Two black leather recliners sat opposite the

TVs. I also noticed a DVR so he could record shows and a gaming system. He also hung a dart board and had a ping-pong table. I smiled... the man cave.

"Looks like you forgot to duck," he joked, reminding me he still had his former cop humor.

I stuck my tongue out at him.

"Rough day at the office?"

"I've had better." I sat down in the chair next to him. "I had the strangest dream after getting pummeled. Finn showed up to rescue me. It was so real; I could taste his cinnamon gum on my lips. Have you heard anything more about him? "

"No, but I'm sure he's fine. I'm sorry I worried you."

He averted his eyes when he spoke, and I noticed a strange expression on his face. Something was going on with Finn that he wasn't sharing, though I could also tell he was no longer worried. I had bigger fish to fry at the moment, so I put it out of my head. I retrieved the photographs and handed them to him. "Can you try to enlarge these and bring them into focus?"

He glanced at them for a moment and his jaws clenched. "I'm guessing this is a 911 emergency."

"I'm meeting Maldonado after I leave here to discuss them."

He walked toward his desk to get to work.

"Thanks," I said. "Mind if I use one of your laptops?" I held up the DVDs.

"Anything I might be interested in seeing?"

"I'll let you know, you sicko," I said jokingly. I never understood their sarcastic humor until recently.

"Use the black laptop," he said. "It's one of my spares and not password protected to get in."

I grabbed the laptop he suggested and sat down in the recliner. I opened it and waited for it to load, then slipped one of the DVDs into the slot and hit play. At first, what I saw on the screen made little sense to me. When I hit rewind to watch it again, the horror of what was playing out in front of me became clear. I immediately wanted to hit the eject button, but I forced myself to sit through it.

Several prominent figures sat in comfortable chairs positioned around a platform. At the sound of a voice from somewhere off-screen, a female host ushered a young woman into the room. Studying her, I realized she was trembling and looked scared. She walked up the steps and onto the platform that was used as a stage. In robotic mode, she stood in front of the men while they leered at her as if she was a specimen on display. They dressed her up as if she was going to a nightclub… a china doll. Hair and makeup were perfect. The provocative dress and stilettos she had trouble walking in couldn't hide the fact that she was probably sixteen or seventeen. After an appropriate amount of time, a male in a tuxedo carried a silver tray around to the men. Those interested placed a bid on the tray. With a nod from the tuxedoed host, the one who placed the highest offer stood up from his seat and escorted the terrified girl out of the room. That's when I heard the host say: "you have an hour in a private room, without interruption."

I thought I was going to throw up right then.

Seconds later, a second female walked up the steps and onto the platform for another round of bidding.

I didn't have enough information yet, but what I just witnessed reminded me of the *Jeffrey Epstein* and *Ghislaine Maxwell* case. Prosecutors alleged that *Ghislaine* groomed young women for him, and possibly others. Sex trafficking.

My hands balled into fists as the anger surged through me. It felt like I was watching illegal sexual transactions right here on Cape Cod. Only the men were prominent citizens, and the females might not be willing participants. I couldn't watch another female being purchased, so I switched videos, hoping the second one wasn't more of the same. It was so much worse. Roger was standing over me now.

At first, several exotic resort-style images flashed onto the screen like a flipbook. Only the title was in Spanish: Las Islas Santuario. "What does it mean?"

"It looks like a travel brochure," Roger said. "Does it have something to do with your case?"

"I don't know?"

Then a large room appeared on the screen. There was a bed in the center. As the film played, a teenager walked into view. She was pretty, dressed like the typical teenage girl: shorts, a t-shirt, converse shoes, and her hair in a ponytail. There was a look of innocence about her. She was fidgety and nervous as her eyes roamed around the room. When they faced the camera, I physically saw the terror when I heard a male voice in the background issuing instructions.

"Get on the bed," he said with a slight accent.

"Oh, no!" My body shook, and I covered my mouth with my hand to stop myself from screaming. I feared what was about to happen, knowing I couldn't stop it. It horrified me to see the tears as she reluctantly did as instructed.

Then the man slowly came onto the screen. He walked over to where she was now sitting on the bed. He only allowed himself to be viewed from behind and kept his face hidden from the camera. I also couldn't tell how old he was. All I could tell was that he had dark hair and tanned skin. Standing next to her, he used his hands to guide her and helped her to remove her clothing.

"I'm The Teacher," he kept saying. "I'll show you how it's done."

"Ohmigod!" It was exactly like Epstein. The scumbag was teaching her... grooming her. He continued, taking it slow, making sure she followed directions. She didn't scream, yell, or even say no. I wondered if they drugged her. When he went to get onto the bed, that's when I lost it. This time I did scream, but what came out was a terrified: "No!"

Roger placed his hand on my shoulder. I averted my eyes, but I was afraid to shut them off, fearing I'd lose sight of the girl. I could still hear him speaking: "I'm The Teacher."

Seeing my anguish, Roger hit the stop button and ejected the DVD. I walked into the bathroom, sat down on the toilet, and put my head in my hands. I thought about what happened to Jillian, the innocent teenagers and young women being used and abused. And all I could do was cry. Dealing with my ex-husband's betrayal and a diabolical stalker was a cakewalk compared to this.

Each moment I spent thinking about the situation, with every morbid piece of information I learned, my anger intensified. It scared me to know just how much. I looked at my reflection in the mirror, horrified by what I was seeing.

Get a grip, Katie, I told myself. Jillian needs you. These girls need you.

I looked in the cabinet for some toothpaste, put some on my finger to clean my teeth, and splashed some cold water on my face. When I rejoined Roger, he was viewing one image with a photo magnifier, talking to himself.

When he heard me, he studied my face. "You okay?"

I nodded, even though I wasn't okay. But I had to get my act together.

"There are some pretty heavy hitters in these photos, Katie."

"Yeah?" As a former cop, he knew more than I did. He motioned me to his side and put the magnifier over some faces.

"See these guys here in the center. What do they look like to you?"

I studied the men he pointed out. "Cops," I said because I recognized one of them: Officer Jimmy Smith.

Roger nodded. "Officers Jimmy Smith and Larry Foley," he said. "They're both plainclothes."

"Do you know them personally?"

He shrugged. "Not enough to make an opinion."

Since my father was a cop, it always disturbed me when one of them crossed the line. It gave the department a poor reputation and dirtied the good cops in the department.

"If Jillian knew some of them were cops; that would explain why she didn't trust them with her evidence."

"Katie, you can't just assume they're bad guys because they're in the photo. You need more proof."

"I know, but it's sure suspicious."

He moved the magnifier over to another group. "What about these guys?"

"Sicilian wannabes?" I joked, though I couldn't tell what their nationality was. They could have been Italian, Hispanic, or even Portuguese. Cape Cod had a mix of cultures. But the men looked familiar to me. And then I realized. They looked like the men who went into The Tapestry, only the photograph wasn't clear enough to be one-hundred percent sure. "I wasn't aware of any mob connections on Cape Cod?"

"Who says they're from Cape Cod?"

"New York, possibly," I said, remembering that I took down the license plate when the three goons entered the so-called exclusive dating service.

I thought about it for a moment. "Let's say you're right. Then what have I got going on here?"

I took the magnifier and showed him the other men I recognized. "These guys are public officials. And in this photo here, we have a state senator with a high-profile attorney, Howard Moore. I can connect the senator with the attorney because he represents high-profile clients and is heavily involved in politics. Not to mention, he throws huge fundraisers. But how would cop and mob-like figures fit in?"

Roger shrugged. "From these photos, all you know is that they're all together at some fancy party and some are getting their rocks off."

"Yeah, and somebody is grooming teenagers. Unfortunately, I can't see his face."

I used the magnifier to scroll through the teenagers and young women. A few of them looked innocent, like the girl I just saw in the video. In others, they dressed them more provocatively. Obviously, that was to parade them in front of the leering men.

"Last night, somebody gunned down the last person who saw these photos."

Roger's head whipped around and his demeanor looked serious. "They do that to your face, too?"

"That'd be my guess."

We were both quiet for a minute, and then I scrolled over the images he enlarged. As I did, I came across another face I recognized, and it just blew the case wide open, at least for me.

"Well, what do you know?"

"What?"

"This guy here...," I placed the magnifier over the image I was looking at. "It's the case I'm currently working on. His name is Thomas Miles. He's also an attorney."

"He's your client?"

"His wife hired me. She wanted me to prove he was cheating on her."

Roger smirked. "I'd say he's been doing a little more than cheating."

"She said investigate anything suspicious."

I realized right then that there was a connection between the two cases. How else would Jillian have a photo of Thomas Miles? But what was the relationship between Thomas Miles and Howard Moore?

Roger asked, "Any ideas on who took the photos?"

"The woman killed was my college roommate," I said. "She sent me the photos. I'm guessing she took them. I just don't know. But, you want to know the clincher?"

"What's that?"

"Her father is the attorney in the photos."

Roger shook his head. "Not likely to get the father of the year." Then he gave me a look of concern. "You know you're dealing with some heavy shit here?"

I sat down in a chair. "It seems rather similar to Epstein, wouldn't you say?"

"Epstein got off easy," Roger said, gritting his teeth. "But you're dealing with the same sick mindset here."

I knew it would take him a few more minutes to finish the photos, so I went over to collect the DVDs. I needed to collect myself. Jillian was dead, and there was no time for self-pity. The puzzle pieces were coming together. I just had to put it together, find out who killed her, and how that might involve Thomas Miles and all the other players.

CHAPTER 29

AS I WALKED to my car, the thought of how far into the darkness I was going to have to go to find out who killed Jillian overwhelmed me. And what other horrible things was I going to find along the way? Roger must have been thinking the same thing. He stood at the door of the garage and watched until I was safely inside and pulling out of his driveway. He saw the determined look in my eyes and knew I would not stop until I had the answers.

On the way to my next stop, I called Sarah Miles at her office. I was hoping she could tell me how her husband knew Howard Moore. The photos showed he attended a party at Moore's home. Was she there as well? I didn't see her in any of the images, but there might have been others at the party who didn't make it into the photos.

Sarah's secretary answered, which was odd at the late hour. When I asked to speak to Sarah, she informed me Sarah wouldn't be in until morning. I left a message for her to call, and then tried her cell phone, and left another on her voicemail.

Next, I called Maldonado and asked if he could meet me at El Torito's Restaurant instead of at the station. Food was a priority.

The décor inside El Torito has a warm and cozy feel and always makes me feel at home. They covered the walls with a soft gold textured paint, matching the multi-colored floor tiles, and the dining area had rustic tables and chairs, as opposed to the booths with vinyl benches that you normally saw in Mexican Restaurants.

When I arrived, there was a new hostess on duty. She glanced at my bruised and battered face, but tried to look away before I caught her. I had to get used to that. It made me feel self-conscious, but nothing I could do about it. I asked to be seated in a private area and told her I was waiting for another party. She escorted me to a table in the back and placed two menus down on the table.

"Carlos will be your waiter this evening," she said, trying hard not to stare.

Carlos has worked at the restaurant since the day it opened and knew all the regulars. He also knew not to pry. Before I even asked, he brought me a tall glass of water with two lemons. As he passed the busboy, he told him to rush over with a fresh batch of chips and salsa. Even though I had a swollen face, I still devoured them. Not long after, Carlos brought a fresh batch. While he was there, I placed an order for a taco salad and a side order of guacamole.

Another twenty minutes went by before Maldonado walked in, showing physical signs that the case wasn't so easy. He looked like I felt. There were dark circles under his eyes and his hair was an unruly mess. Murder doesn't phone it in.

He sauntered over to where I was sitting.

When he stood next to me, he studied my face and frowned. "Margie would kick my ass if she knew I allowed you to keep working. How do you feel?"

"I'll live." Even though it hurt like hell.

"I'm glad you're safe."

"Maldonado, I hate to ask, but I have to… do you know anything about Finn? Derek and Roger told me he lost contact with his team."

He averted his eyes and massaged the back of his neck, showing the stress. "They shouldn't have worried you. He's on a unique assignment. But that's all I can say."

I nodded. "But he's not in danger."

"Katie," he warned. "That's all I can say."

I knew to let it go, so I tried a different tack. "How's his son, David?" David was Finn's seven-year-old son from his first marriage.

"He's good. Finn's mom is at the house for a couple of days."

I couldn't help but smile. "That must be interesting." Since we've only dated a short time, it was too soon for me to meet David, but I met Finn's Mother. She was far removed from the typical grandmother. I could describe her as the Irish version of Joan Rivers. She talks a mile a minute and the discussion usually involved her latest fling. According to Finn, she dates men half her age.

"Interesting is putting it mildly," Maldonado said with a laugh. "I stopped by to check up on them. David is the adult in the house."

That got me to smile. "So, have you found out anything about Jillian's murder yet?" I had to ask, but I knew he wouldn't share anything with me, even if he did.

He gave me one of those looks. "Did you ask me here to bust my chops about the case?" He rubbed his face in his hands, showing just how exhausted he was. Carlos approached, carrying a frozen mug of Maldonado's favorite beer, which meant he was technically off duty. Maldonado thanked him, and they exchanged pleasantries.

"I know we have to keep our friendship separate from work, but Jillian was my friend." I reminded him once we were alone again.

He gave me a look of sympathy. "That father of hers is some piece of work."

"More than you know."

He raised his eyebrows. "What have you got?"

I shook my head at him and smiled. "Typical cop," I teased. "You want everything I have, but you won't tell me squat."

He shrugged good-naturedly. "You don't have to worry about brass jumping down your throat."

Unfortunately, I had to give him that one.

Watching my dad work through the ranks of the police department when I was a kid, I learned all about the bureaucracy within the departments.

I nodded. "You're right. I work better without a bunch of shadows lurking overhead."

Maldonado tipped his glass of beer to me in agreement.

The corner where we were sitting was private; so I reached into my backpack, retrieved the envelope, and handed it to him.

He opened the envelope and viewed the photos. One by one, he examined them with a keen eye. When his jaw clenched, I knew he came to the photos of the teenagers and young women. The expression that followed scared the life out of me. He dropped them down on the table and raked his hand through his hair. "Damn!"

Seeing his reaction, I was hesitant to tell him about what else I had, but I knew I had to. "I also have two DVDs which are more graphic."

It must have dawned on him that somebody could walk by and see them. He picked them back and up and slipped them back inside the envelope. "Where the hell did these come from?"

"Jillian sent them to me," I said, wishing I knew about them earlier. "I picked them up at the mailbox this morning. She sent them to me asking for my help. I can't let her down. If only I received them earlier."

He studied my face and realized I felt responsible. "It's not your fault she's dead, Katie."

"I know," I said, wiping away a tear. "But there's something very sick going on."

"Well, that's for damn sure," he said, taking another long swig of his beer. When he set the glass back down, he looked at me. "Let's go over everything again, now that we're away from the crime scene. Maybe there's something I missed. You said you haven't seen your friend for some time. What happened?"

"We were inseparable during college. Like sisters, we clicked. I thought we told each other everything, but I guess not. She led me to believe there were issues between her and her father, but she never said what they were. After college, she went back to live with him. During that time, something must have happened. She unexpectedly moved out and didn't tell anyone where she was going."

"Not even you?"

"Not even me."

"What do you think happened?

"I honestly don't know, but with these photographs, my mind is not going to a good place."

Maldonado tossed the information around in his head. "Tell me about the phone call again."

"She mailed this package to me before

they killed her because when she called, she asked if I received it. She said she was involved in something, was in trouble, and needed my help. Then she asked me to meet her in the alley behind Rosie's at midnight. When I arrived, someone fired shots, and she was dead."

"And they shot at you, too," he reminded me.

I nodded. "You and I leave the scene to inform her father. While we were gone, someone broke into my car. When you dropped me at the RV, I discovered they tossed it, too."

He wasn't happy to hear about this new revelation, and the look on his face said so. "You didn't tell me about the RV being ransacked."

I shrugged. "I didn't see the need. They probably wore gloves anyway."

"You should have told me, Katie."

I nodded, but continued. "The following morning, I found a slip of paper in my mailbox and picked up the photos." I didn't have to ask what he was thinking. It was all over his face.

"Somebody knows she sent you the photos, and they want them back."

I nodded. "That's my guess."

"It also tells me whoever tossed the car and RV, might have been at the scene and knew you left the area, or they were watching you."

He had a strange look on his face when mentioning the revelation. I wanted him to focus on the fact that they might have been at the scene. I didn't want to push him into thinking a cop might be involved. He needed to get there on his own. Cops don't take kindly to an outsider pointing the finger at another officer, even if they don't like that officer. It's still one of their own.

"You want to hear something even more peculiar?"

He looked at me and frowned. "More peculiar than what you already divulged?"

I pulled the photos out again and pointed to Thomas Miles. "This guy here, he's an attorney. His wife hired me to prove he's been cheating on her."

"That's a little coincidental." He sat back in his seat, taking sips of his beer while he ran things through his mind.

While it was quiet, I went back to working on my taco salad, never really eating much of it. Then Maldonado's cell phone buzzed, drawing his attention away from the discussion. He looked at the screen and frowned. "Shit, I have to go," he said, grabbing some cash from his wallet as he stood up.

"I've got this, just go ahead," I said.

He ignored me and dropped the money down on the table. "Margie taught me better than that. You okay to go home?"

"I'm good," I said, waving him off.

"Come by the station first thing in the morning so we can go over what you've got. And Katie, we need to keep this close to the vest and not discuss it with anyone; just me, you, and Finn when you see him." With that, he hugged me and practically ran out of the restaurant, making another phone call as he did.

I didn't know what his call was about, but I also found it odd that he mentioned Finn. Something was going on.

CHAPTER 30

WHEN I PULLED into the driveway, the hair on my arms was standing up, but I didn't know why. I looked around. There was nothing amiss. The RV was dark. The construction site for the cottage looked as it usually did. There were no signs, or any bad guys running away from the RV, leading me to believe I had visitors. It was just my woman's intuition. After everything I learned in the last two days, it was going into overdrive. I parked the Jeep in my spot, grabbed the backpack, and headed toward the RV door.

No sooner had I put the key in the lock, when the door pushed open, making me unsteady on my feet. Two men in dark clothing, baseball caps, and goggles—that looked like night vision—jumped down the RV steps and knocked me to the ground.

While I scrambled to get up, I saw a third man running toward me from the street—and I swear he looked like Finn.

"What the hell?" I said, confused. "Finn?"

"It's me," he said, calmly. "Stay here."

And he took off running after the intruders. They ran in the opposite direction of the street, forcing them into the backyard behind the cottage. They were the same guys I ran into at Jillian's house. Boy, would I like to catch up with them? Once I confirmed it was Finn chasing after them, I slipped the backpack over my shoulder, reached for my gun, and followed.

The perps were running through the seagrass and headed toward the path in between mine and Olivia's cottage, headed toward a vehicle that was parked on the street. When Finn noticed their getaway car, he pulled out his gun and yelled, "Freeze, police!"

They ignored the warning and continued. Finn followed suit, hoping to catch up with them before they reached the car. I wasn't far behind Finn when I noticed a dark SUV coming down the street from the entrance of the community. Through the glare of the streetlights and headlights from the first vehicle, I could see the driver. There was a man in the passenger seat as well, but he sat at an odd angle. And then I discovered why: he was holding the barrel of a shotgun and pointed it out the passenger window. These maniacs wanted to take us out.

Finn was too busy chasing the two perps to notice the second vehicle or the gun.

"Finn, gun!" I yelled as loud as I could. "Get down." With all the noise and commotion, he didn't hear me.

"Shit!" I pushed myself to move, sprinting as fast as I could. Before I realized what I was doing, I jumped and tackled him to the ground. We rolled into a protective area of seagrass, just as several rounds of gunfire came our way. We scrambled to get out of the line of fire, rolling onto our stomachs and aiming our guns to return fire. The SUV made a U-turn at the cul-de-sac and hauled ass back the way they came. The two perps were now safely inside the first vehicle and followed.

Finn immediately radioed in the call; advising dispatch of the direction the two cars were heading

We both waited a few minutes until we could verify they wouldn't return. Once we knew it was all clear, we stood up and tried to catch our breath.

Finn looked me up and down to see if I had any injuries. His jaw clenched. "Are you okay?"

I nodded, finding it hard to speak. "Close call," I said when I could find my voice. I was shaking so badly that I put my gun back in my belt so I didn't accidentally shoot myself. Finn caught on and wrapped his arms around me. For the first time in a few days, I felt safe and didn't want him to let go. We stood like that until we noticed the patrol cars rolling toward us.

Finn was immediately all business when the officers arrived. He filled them in on the events that occurred, with me standing on the sidelines until they needed information about the car with the shotgun. I informed them of what I saw and showed them the area where bullets were flying. That would help the crime scene techs narrow down the type of gun used.

I kept quiet about the fact that I had seen the SUV before, which only added to the proof that there was a connection between Jillian's death and my case. Maldonado was right. We needed to be careful who we shared information with. Somebody knew Jillian contacted me. I couldn't shake the feeling that it was someone from the police department or Jillian's father. Until I knew, I wouldn't be disclosing anything unless I had to.

Finn nudged me and guided me toward the RV. "You know we have to check to see what damage they did inside."

I nodded, dreading what we'd see. The first time around, the damage wasn't severe, just time-consuming. But recalling what they did to Jillian's apartment was brutal.

"I'll grab the tech," Finn said.

CHAPTER 31

AT THE DOOR of the RV, Finn motioned me to wait outside while he and the tech did the initial walk-through. It surprised me when they waved me inside less than a minute later. The intruders didn't trash the place as I expected. Other than a couple of drawers being left open, it was difficult to know that someone was even inside. That had me wondering what was up. I walked through each space; living area, kitchen, bathroom, and bedroom, two times. I still couldn't see what they had done.

"They must have known I had the evidence with me," I said. "The place is virtually untouched."

"First things first," he said, walking toward me. His eyes held mine as he leaned in close. My body reacted when his fingers laced through my hair. I instantly felt the butterflies. Then my lips parted the minute his lips brushed mine. I tasted the sweet cinnamon.

When he pulled free, I looked into his eyes. "That was you at the apartment, wasn't it?"

He pulled me close. "I couldn't let anyone know, other than Maldonado. I'm still undercover."

"Then what are you doing here now?"

"I can't say too much," he said.

"That's what Maldonado said." Their evasive comments were making me even more suspicious.

He dropped the subject and looked from one end of the RV to the other. "These guys weren't here for the evidence. They were here for another reason."

"What do you mean?"

He studied the light fixtures and the speaker system on the walls and ceilings. The screws on one speaker were loose, showing the fixture was not secured to the wall.

"Derek just bought this RV recently, didn't he?"

I nodded. "He bought it brand new off the lot, had it delivered to his Boston office, where it sat until my cottage burned down. Why, what are you thinking?"

"I think they had the RV bugged, and these guys came back to retrieve them. That's the reason the place doesn't look tossed."

"Oh, hell no," I said. "I just dealt with my privacy being invaded during Lexy's stalking antics."

He pulled me close. "I know, and I'm sorry."

I studied him. "How much do you know about what's been going on?"

He shrugged, sheepishly. "Maldonado filled me in. I'm sorry about your friend."

I got quiet for a minute. That suspicion crept up again. If he was undercover, how did Maldonado fill him in? And then something occurred to me, but I couldn't say it out loud.

"So they've been listening to me for quite some time? That's how they knew I was meeting Jillian," I said. I pulled away from his embrace so I could see his face. His expression confirmed there was more, only I knew not to push.

"No way to know when they put the bugs in place. I'll have the tech sweep the place to verify they're all gone."

I couldn't put my finger on it, but his expression made me believe there was a lot more. When I was about to ask, he took a seat on the sofa and motioned toward the TV.

"I need to see those photos and DVDs."

I stared at him. "Maldonado told you about the evidence?"

He nodded, and that's when I knew. The undercover case he was involved with had something to do with this one.

I handed him the photographs from my backpack and carried the DVDs toward the entertainment center built into one of the inner walls. I slipped one of them into the machine, grabbed the remote, and sat down next to him. I turned on the TV, switched the HDMI to the DVD player, and hit play once it loaded. For several minutes, we sat still, neither of us uttering a sound while the DVD played. The tech paused what he was doing and watched as well.

After it finished, I could visibly see the inner volcano of anger that Finn was ready to unleash. He got up off the sofa and paced in front of me while raking his hands through his hair. "All this bullshit is about sex and drugs!" he shouted after a few seconds.

"People have been killed for less."

"There are some well-known faces on that DVD," he said, resuming his seat. "That tells me whoever recorded it did so without them knowing, or they assumed it would never go public."

"Maybe one of these guys started worrying about their career, or their marriage, and when they found out Jillian had the photos and DVDs, they killed her?"

"Had to be more than that," Finn said.

"Think of the scandal that would come out if the information became public," I added. "Heads would roll."

"They should have thought of that before getting involved in this shit. I don't care how it hurts their reputation if they have anything to do with the murder. I'll bring each one of them down."

"Not if I get to them first," I said in a whisper. I didn't want to get into a competition with Finn, a man I was just getting to know, romantically. Jillian's murder was personal for me. His allegiance was to his job, mine was to my friend.

"Is the next one more of the same?"

I shook my head. "You think you're

pissed off now? The next one will have you enraged."

I removed the first DVD and added the second one to the machine. Then I sat back and braced myself for the Irish temper I was sure would follow.

It wouldn't have surprised me if Finn started throwing things, but his silence unnerved me. I pitied whoever ended up on the receiving end of his fury. He sat on the edge of the sofa, keeping his emotions on the surface, but not expounding on them. Neither of us wanted to watch it to its conclusion, and definitely not in front of each other. It was just too sick.

As angry as Finn was, the crime scene tech was visibly despondent. I think I even caught a tear in his eye. He went back to dusting for prints as if his work was the key to finding the perpetrators.

"Any idea who the teacher is?" Finn asked, breaking the silence.

"Not yet."

"There's also something that's not right about the teenage girl," he said. He grabbed the remote and hit rewind to take another look. "She seems afraid, but she complied without a fight."

"I thought the same thing the first time I viewed the tape, but then something occurred to me."

"What's that?"

"You want my gut instincts?"

"Try me."

"I think teenagers and young women are being trafficked."

Finn looked at me with uncertainty. Not because he didn't believe it could happen. *Jeffrey Epstein* and *Ghislaine Maxwell* proved it could, and did. Drugs and sex trafficking are billion-dollar industries. He wanted details.

"I think somebody is abducting young girls and women who have had a hard life or they're runaways on the streets, and nobody is out looking for them, or even purchased. I think she doesn't fight back because they drugged her. Look at her eyes, how glazed-over they are."

"Katie, are you inferring the parents sold the kids to these assholes?"

"I'm just postulating right now, but you know it happens, Finn. Just recently, we heard about the Afghani parents who sold their kids because they had no money to feed themselves or the rest of their family? You know it happens here, too. They could have been a poor family who was desperate and someone approached them with pretenses. Maybe they promised a better life for the kids and provided funds for the families. They even solicit teenagers in chat rooms."

"What about the teacher?"

"I think the scumbag is helping to run the operation. Maybe she didn't fight back because she had formed a relationship with him already. Maybe she felt indebted to him. Who knows how long she was in his possession or under his control?"

"And someone brainwashed them into believing they had a debt to repay," he said, disgusted.

"It's a possibility. Sex trafficking was happening long before the public heard the names of *Jeffrey Epstein* and *Ghislaine Maxwell*."

"Yeah... whatever is going on, we need to find out."

"It would help if we knew where they came from."

"I'll tell Maldonado to check with Interpol, to see what he can dig up on missing girls. If it's as you say, though, there won't be a missing person report."

"They're innocent victims who think nobody cares," I said, feeling morose.

I didn't have to ask Finn what he was thinking. It was clear from his expression he was thinking about what he'd like to do to the people who were running the operation.

"You can't stay in the RV alone tonight?" he said, unexpectedly.

The minute he said it, images of the two of us sprawled out on the leather sofa flashed through my eyes, causing butterflies in my stomach.

Finn must have been reading my thoughts. He had a smart-ass grin on his face when he looked at me. "Worried I might take advantage of you while you're feeling vulnerable?"

"N–no," I said, stuttering. We just started dating before his undercover gig and hadn't slept together yet. Not because we didn't want to. Our passionate phone calls revealed that. But after being betrayed by a husband of two decades, Finn wanted to take it slow, to make sure I was ready.

"Liar," he teased. "I don't want you staying alone right now, but I won't push. If I stay, I'll sleep on the sofa."

I nodded, but I admit it was disappointing. There was a part of me that hoped he would take advantage of my vulnerability.

The tech finished up with the prints and motioned for Finn, bringing us back to the present. He had the tracking device to check for bugs. Finn got back to business.

Left to my own devices, I pulled the DVD out of the machine and stored both of them in the bedroom. With all the break-ins lately, the thought occurred to me I should probably have Roger make a copy of the evidence just in case something happens to the originals. I would also like him to do some digital enhancement on the DVD to see if we can get a look at the man who called himself The Teacher.

While Finn and the tech were busy, I decided it might be a good time to relax in a hot bubble bath to relieve some of the tension. That was one luxury about Derek's RV. Most of them had small tubs that were not large enough for an adult. This one had a full-size Jacuzzi tub and a separate walk-in shower. I was going to miss them when I returned to my cottage.

While waiting for the water to fill up, I searched through a drawer for a pair of boxer shorts and a tank top, and a new thong that I was sure the intruders hadn't touched. Once the tub was ready, I piled my hair on top of my head and slipped into the scented bubbles, letting the heat of the water soothe my aching muscles. Until now, I hadn't realized just how much the tension was impacting me. I gave in to the relaxation and laid my head back against the tub.

It was a good half-hour before Finn invaded my privacy, and burst into the room without knocking. I suddenly felt shy and vulnerable.

"Sorry," he said with his mischievous grin on his face. "Need to sweep this room for bugs."

I gave him a sideways glance. "Would they put a bug in the bathroom?"

He shrugged, but his goofy grin remained.

"Okay, just let me get out first."

"I'll wait," he said, his handsome face looking unusually devilish at the moment. Instead of leaving the room to give me privacy, he leaned against the doorframe. He crossed his arms and his intense blue eyes watched my every move.

I found myself in somewhat of a

dilemma because I didn't want him to get the better of me. I forced myself to be bold and shrugged off my inner shyness. I mustered up the courage to rise out of the tub, with only the left-over bubbles to shield me. Finn's eyes locked on mine. But as I stood there, completely exposed, they roamed the length of my body. When he came to my breasts, he hesitated, and then his penetrating eyes slowly continued until he devoured me from head to toe. Those eyes were suddenly dark with passion.

When I knew my bravado had succeeded, I reached for a towel and slowly wrapped it around me. I smiled and purposely brushed up against him as I walked out the bathroom door. The look on his face and his physical reaction gave me all the ammunition I needed to know I got to him more than he got to me. But boy, it felt good to bring a little flirtatious levity to a horrible situation.

CHAPTER 32

FINN WAS OUTSIDE, finishing up with the tech, when I summoned the courage to emerge from the bedroom. As I glanced around, I realized the RV looked worse now that they dusted for prints. At least the perps didn't leave a mess behind for me to clean up. It had been a long day, and I was exhausted, but I was still hungry since I only picked through the taco salad. I opened the refrigerator to see if there was anything worth eating.

"Sonofa—" I yelled, louder than I meant to.

Finn heard me and rushed back inside, ready for action. When he saw me standing in front of the refrigerator in one piece, he reached for a dishtowel and threw it at me in frustration. "What the hell?"

"The jerks finished my coffee cake," I said, embarrassed but chuckling at the same time for his daring valor.

"Damn girl; from the sound of your voice, I thought you found a dead body or something."

"Sorry." I closed the refrigerator door and slumped down into one of the dining chairs.

Finn walked over and nuzzled my neck, obviously feeling a little amorous after seeing a naked body in the bathtub. "If you're nice to me…" he said, letting the statement linger, "I can whip up one of my special omelets David can't live without."

"Hmmm," I said. "I do like omelets."

He kissed me on the lips and left me hungry for more, as he walked to the refrigerator and rummaged through it. While he mixed ingredients, I looked for a pad of paper and pen and began organizing my thoughts. Normally, when I worked out a plot for one of my books, I typed my thoughts on index cards in the writing software on my laptop. My laptop and PC were torched when the cottage burned down. I bought a new computer, but I haven't had time to load all my old software yet. Paper and pen would have to do. It helps to put the pieces of the puzzle together.

When Finn finished with the omelets, he searched through the cabinets, trying not to disturb my concentration. He grabbed two plates and placed a gourmet-style omelet, along with two orange slices, down in front of me. Then he sat down next to me with a plate of his own.

"This is sooo good," I said, after taking a few bites.

"Glad you like it," he teased. "But you're not getting the recipe."

I laughed.

We got quiet for a few moments, both of us enjoying the savory food. Then, out of the blue, Finn said, "Is there anything about this investigation you neglected to tell me?"

The question put me in a difficult situation. Finn suspected there was a possibility. And truth be told, I was keeping something from him. It was a dilemma because I wasn't ready to give up the information until I had more proof. "I've told you everything I'm prepared to," I said, hoping that would suffice.

"Katie, if you have information that has something to do with this investigation, you can't keep it from me or Maldonado. In case you've forgotten, that's obstruction of justice."

My eyes met his. I knew at some point his being a cop could interfere. But I knew he had to answer to the bureaucracy and the pressure of solving cases. Still, until he came out and said so; this wasn't his case.

I stood up, picked up both plates, and placed them in the sink for the time being. I was trying to put space between us for a few seconds while I took the time to think. Then I turned around and faced him. "I'm not obstructing anything," I said calmly. "I showed you and Maldonado what Jillian sent me, and I let you view the DVDs, which I didn't have to do."

"Funny, I don't remember you telling me what happened at Calloway's office."

How did he know I went to Calloway's office? Was he watching me, too?

"I didn't think the reading of Jillian's

will had anything to do with the investigation."

"Really? Another department might not look at it that way. She wants to meet you, she's killed and everything's left to you. How do you think that looks?"

"How do you know what was in her will?"

"That's a silly question; Maldonado checked the court records."

Shit, I thought to myself. I didn't think they'd get to it that fast. "If you read it, then you know why she left me the property."

"What I read is that she doesn't like her father much, and she doesn't trust the police. Her father, I can understand. After talking to Detective Maldonado about their meeting, I don't like him much myself. But why mistrust the police?"

"You saw the pictures," I reminded him. "There were cops in the photographs."

"There are other cops she could have gone to."

"C'mon Finn, you know outsiders believe there's a Code of Blue. She could have assumed you guys would defend each other."

Finn looked at me sideways, as if he was trying to discern if that's how I felt too. "Not all of us."

I had trust where he was concerned, but that didn't mean I had a blanket trust. So I kept my opinion to myself. It would be easy for him to say he wouldn't defend them. But if they put him in a position to work against one of his fellow officers, would he be able to? I had questions about Officer Smith and his early arrival at the crime scene. I also had questions about Officer Foley, but I wasn't sure if Finn and Maldonado were ready to hear my reservations.

He was still studying me, trying to discern my feelings.

"I *can* tell you this; some of the photographs were taken in Jillian's father's house."

"Why do you say that?"

"Something happened between Jillian and her father that made her leave home. Maybe she suspected something and needed proof. I think she went back recently. I recognized the layout of the room, only it looked different. On the night Maldonado took me to make her death notification, they had renovated the room. She used to refer to it as The Green Room."

"And you're just now sharing this?" I knew he wouldn't be happy, but that's not all I was withholding. How could I tell him I think someone from his department might be involved? I couldn't just blurt out my suspicions. I needed something to back it up. You can't just go around accusing police officers.

He would have continued to challenge me if his cell phone didn't start buzzing. It gave me a temporary reprieve while he went to answer it. When the call ended, it was clear there was an emergency, and he had to go. A lot of emergencies going on tonight, I thought to myself.

Before he left, he walked toward me and the look in his eyes was unmistakable. It was payback time for my bathtub antics. He gently picked me up and set me on top of the counter, pressing his body between my legs. I immediately felt his rising attraction. His eyes, level with mine, held my gaze. A finger traced the outline of my cheek, getting my senses aroused, and then traveled down my neck and into the outline of my tank top. And suddenly, his lips were on mine, welcoming me into a sensual and sweet kiss.

He pulled away and whispered in my ear, "I have to go."

"I know," I responded, my body wishing he would stay to continue what he started.

With him pressed up against me, sexual heat surged through me, sending sensations to my vagina and leaving my thong damp. He grabbed my wrists and raised my arms above my head, holding them against the cabinet door. Our eyes locked again, and we felt it at the same time. His lips covered mine in a frenzy of passion, and our tongues devoured the insides of each other's mouths.

When his phone buzzed again, he slowly pulled away. He knew he had to leave, but his body wanted to stay. He kept his eyes on me as he walked toward the door. When he was gone, I felt a longing to be touched that

I hadn't felt in a while.

On the one hand, I was happy to have a reprieve from answering more questions. On the other, I was alone again, and apprehensive. I needed noise. The silence was unnerving. The only way to make it through the night and get any sleep would be to camp out on the sofa. I grabbed a blanket from the bed, put my gun on the coffee table, and turned on the TV to low volume. It didn't work. I still tossed and turned through the night, waking up every time I saw a vision of Jillian lying in a pool of blood. I would have felt better if Bailey was with me.

When morning rolled around, I chastised myself for allowing the dirtbags to have power over me. I pushed myself to go out for a run and felt a lot better when I returned, so I completed my quota of sit-ups and push-ups.

I needed energy for the busy day I had planned. I poured a cup of water and ice into the blender. I added a half-cup of freshly squeezed orange juice, some blueberries, a banana, sugar-free yogurt, a raw egg for protein, and some leafy spinach for energy. After I finished my drink, I cleaned the kitchen mess from the night before and went to take a hot shower to prepare for the hectic day.

I had no intention of wasting my day doing surveillance. Today, I was ready to take some aggressive action to get answers.

Howard Moore was on my list. Maldonado could wait; Finn would fill him in on what he viewed.

CHAPTER 33 – THE TEACHER

AGAIN, THE TEACHER was searching for a new victim. This time, he didn't have to go far. All he had to do was turn on his PC and chat.

Carolyn was an innocent fifteen-year-old teenager when her mother's boyfriend started waking her in the middle of the night. The smell of alcohol was overwhelming as he attempted to fondle and have his way with the girl. She screamed, but no one was listening. Her mother passed out in the next room.

Carolyn was angry with herself for not leaving before now. She knew she was the only one who could get herself out of the disgusting situation. She kicked, punched, and tried to fend off his advances, but he was too big for her. She didn't stand a chance. In the end, her only alternative to get out of the repulsive life she was living was to let him do what he wanted, and wait until he passed out. She knew he would. It happened so many times before. After this time, she would escape. Even if it meant ending up on the streets, she had to leave. Anything would be better than this.

When he finally passed out, Carolyn shoved his disgusting body off of her, snuck out of the room, and cleaned herself raw in the bathroom. She made a list of friends in her head and tried to think who would help her. Her school friend, Lacy, would let her stay at her house, but if her mom found out, she'd send her back home. JT said she could sleep in his basement, but he was working the next three nights, so that was out. She couldn't stay here another night.

Then she remembered a new chat friend who offered to hang out. That would get her out of the house, and then she could think of what to do after. She finished up in the bathroom and signed into her Facebook Messenger account under the screen name: coolcarolyn.

coolcarolyn: "*He did it again,*" she wrote to her online chat buddy.

hope1234: "*No way. That sucks. You gotta get outta there.*"

coolcarolyn: "*I know. I can't take it anymore.*"

hope1234: "*Yeah, I get that. I'd want to leave too. That's all kinds of wrong?*"

coolcarolyn: "*His grimy hands were all over me and that alcoholic mother of mine was passed out in the next room. She doesn't care.*"

hope1234: "*I'm so sorry, coolcarolyn. What can I do to help?*"

coolcarolyn: "*Is your offer still good?*"

hope1234: "*Which one? I offered a few.*"

coolcarolyn: "*You said we could hang out, and you'd show me a place where I could stay?*"

hope1234: "*Oh that, yeah, I mean for sure we can hang. When?*"

coolcarolyn: "*The sooner the better. If he wakes up, he'll do it again.*"

Hope1234: "*You shouldn't have to deal with that. Let me check something out. Hang on.*"

Carolyn kept checking the door for a surprise visitor while waiting for the response. She grabbed the gym bag under the bed, reached for the money she'd been hiding in the heating vent, and waited.

Nearly twenty minutes later, her computer signaled she had a message.

hope1234: "*I can meet you at the park down the street. By the swings. I'll be wearing a black hooded sweatshirt. Don't diss me.*"

coolcarolyn: "*Cool. I won't diss you. Leaving now.*"

Carolyn deleted all the messages and then her entire account. She didn't want her mother and her disgusting boyfriend to track her down. When she walked out the door, she knew she was never coming back.

It was dark, but she tried to stay in the shadows and away from the streetlights. She ran away before. The last time she ran into a cop. When she told him what happened, he bought her home and believed her mother's lies when she said it was all made up to get attention. Carolyn knew the same thing would happen again, so she did her best to avoid being seen.

When she reached the park, she hid behind a set of trees and waited until she saw her friend in the black hooded sweatshirt sit down on a swing. She smiled, thinking she was finally free. The minute she stepped out into the open. Someone grabbed her from behind and placed a foul-smelling substance over her nose and mouth. As she started to zone out, she saw the hooded figure walking toward her. When the hood was removed, their identity was revealed. At that time, Carolyn knew that someone had set her up. It wasn't the teenager she thought she'd been chatting with, after all. It was a predator. When she lost the fight and slumped into her captor's arms, he picked her up and carried her to a nearby car.

There wouldn't be anyone looking for Carolyn.

There wasn't anyone who cared.

Soon, she would no longer matter.

Now she belonged to him.

CHAPTER 34

JILLIAN TOOK ME to Howard Moore's office once during college, so I knew I could make it to his floor without a problem with security. Walking at the same steady pace as the flow of men and women arriving for their workday, I headed toward the elevator. The law office was inside a building that used to be a hotel. Some years ago, Howard Moore and his named partners purchased the building, renovated it, and turned it into offices. I stood out in my jeans and cowboy boots, amongst the others dressed in conservative suits and dresses. When I entered the elevator, I pushed the button for the fifth floor and waited for the last-minute arrivals in a hurry to reach their designated floors.

Howard Moore's firm takes up the entire floor, but there was only one entrance. When I walked through the door, the receptionist wasn't at her desk, assuming it was a woman. These days there were just as many men applying to be receptionists and secretaries as women were applying to be firefighters and police officers. I contemplated rushing down the hall toward Howard's office before anyone noticed me, but a woman walked around the corner, foiling my plan.

She was a middle-aged woman, but she had no intention of letting her age get the better of her. She had long gray hair pulled back into a ponytail and she wore a conservative business suit, but kept it hip by wearing a pair of red ankle boots.

"I'm sorry for making you wait," the woman said when she returned to her desk. "It's my job to make the coffee around here, and as usual, someone left an empty container in the coffeemaker. God forbid, they take the time to open another bag and push the stupid button."

"I know what you mean," I said, sympathetic to her plight.

"Sorry, I didn't mean to ramble on."

"No problem."

"Can I help you?"

"I'm here to see Mr. Moore, but I was hoping to surprise him. I'm an old friend of the family and haven't seen him in a long time."

This is where things get tricky; if she announces me, I don't know if Mr. Moore will see me. I was hoping I could persuade her otherwise.

"I'm sorry," she said, though she looked disappointed. "I can't let visitors in unannounced. The last time I did, they sent me home for the day."

I looked at her and thought she was joking, but the look on her face said she wasn't. "Please tell me you're kidding. That's grade school mentality."

She chuckled. "You're right, of course, but they're neurotic around here. Somebody has to hold their hand."

"And I guess that person always has to be you?"

"Yes, I'm the lucky one, but they pay well, so I don't complain."

"I understand. If you have to announce me, then go ahead. I was just hoping to surprise him, that's all. He's like a second father to me." Oh, he's like a second father all right, I mused. Just call him Big Daddy.

She looked at me sympathetically. I could tell she was debating whether to give in. "Do you know where his office is located?" She was testing me to see if I really was a friend.

I nodded. "I used to come here with Jillian."

Her eyes softened at the mention of Jillian, and I could see she was caving. After another moment, she looked around to see if anyone was listening, and then leaned forward. "If he asks; just tell him I was away from my desk."

"You can count on me." After I was through with Howard Moore, I doubt he'd want anyone to know he even had a visitor.

I walked around several cubicles, pretending I knew where I was going. I caught the look of a nosey legal secretary who gave me the once over and then turned to gossip with her neighbor, only to be ignored. Every office has one.

I continued down the corridor until I came to a corner office with Howard

Moore's name engraved on the door. I braced myself for Howard Moore's wrath, opened the door without knocking, and then shut the door behind me.

The minute he looked up from his desk and saw me, he was grappling with ways to have me removed without causing a scene. After seeing his reaction, there was no doubt he was involved up to his neck.

"What's the matter, Mr. Moore?" I said sarcastically. "Aren't you happy to see me?"

When he reached for his phone, I crossed the room in a flash and knocked it out of his hand. Then I grabbed the first available weapon I could find on his desk: his letter opener. I didn't want to pull my gun right away. With the anger and repulsion I felt for the man, I was afraid I'd shoot him, and then where would I be? That wouldn't help me get the information I needed.

I held the letter opener in my right hand and the damaging photos in the other. "Are your law partners aware of your extra-curricular activities, Mr. Moore?"

"What do you want?" He maintained his arrogant demeanor, which pissed me off even further.

"I want to know who killed your daughter."

"How do I know who killed her? Who knows what she got involved in? It could have been anyone."

I placed the photos down on his desk,

making sure the enlarged version of the one showing him and the Senator was on top. He cringed. He didn't know I had photographs of him and his despicable behavior. I got a little satisfaction at seeing his sudden discomfort. "Now, you want to try again."

"I swear... I do not know who killed her."

"Then tell me what you know and don't waste my time."

"Get that thing away from me." He tried to grab the letter opener out of my hand.

"Would you prefer I use my gun?"

"You're not going to hurt anyone," he mocked, talking to me as if I was a child.

I leaned over the desk and got in his face, moving the letter opener closer to his throat. "Don't confuse me with your daughter. I'm not intimidated by you like she was."

He smacked my hand away, making me drop the letter opener, so I grabbed my gun and aimed it at him instead.

"Like that better?"

The look of surprise in his eyes emboldened me. "I'd just as soon cap your ass right here and now. You're involved in this mess and I guarantee you, you're going down. I suggest you give me some answers."

He shifted in his seat, but he wasn't changing his tune. He didn't believe I'd follow through. "You have nothing on me but a photograph with a bunch of whores.

There's nothing wrong with a man deriving pleasure out of a woman. That's what they're good for, isn't it?"

He glared at me with a perverted smile on his face. At that moment, I realized he actually believed the garbage coming out of his mouth. He had no respect for women. That's why he treated his wife and daughter so poorly. I wanted to smack that smirk right off his face. But I knew that wouldn't impact him. I came up with a better idea. With people like Howard Moore, you had to hit them where it hurt.

"Okay then, let's see how you like this," I said. "If these photos are useless, why don't we see if your partners want to have a look at them? I wonder how they'd feel to know women are just pieces of meat, made to be used and abused. How would that impact your partnership?"

After gathering up the photos, I walked toward the door to give him time to realize what I was going to do. "I wonder what they'll have to say; you, a so-called prestigious attorney, pretending to be a morally righteous man. You're right, there's not much to worry about. I'm sure your partners and clients, most of whom are upstanding conservative citizens, will fully understand the implications of them to the law firm."

My hand was on the doorknob, ready to show the goods. I observed Howard Moore out of the corner of my eye and noticed the pathetic indecision he battled within himself. When I saw him shrivel up in his seat like a cornered little rabbit, I knew I had him.

"Wait!"

I half turned back around to face him, waiting to see what he offered, but still prepared to walk out if he didn't cough up something useful.

"I don't know who killed my daughter," he said. "But I think someone killed her because of something she saw." He paused for a moment, trying to gather the resolve to continue talking.

I turned the knob, opening the door just enough to let him know I was serious about getting everything. He knew I wasn't leaving him any choice.

"I had a fundraiser at the house. Some big players attended. I didn't expect Jillian to be there. An associate of mine lined up the entertainment for the evening, and things just sort of got out of hand."

"By entertainment, I assume you're talking about the women and drugs," I said, easy to assume, since I had the photographs to prove it and the women were definitely drugged. I also already knew the party was at Howard Moore's house. So far, he didn't tell me anything new. I wanted more.

"What types of drugs are we talking about?"

He looked at me as if I were a young, naïve fool, but refused to say.

"Sounds like drugs are common in your world."

He glared at me.

"Who's the drug connection?"

"Don't do this to me."

I reached for the knob again.

A heavy sigh escaped his mouth, aggravated that I wasn't giving him a way out. "The men came in from New York. My associate lined them up."

New York. What a coincidence, those goons at The Tapestry came from New York. "With lots of drugs and plenty of women to satisfy your guests, I bet you made a lot of money for your political fundraiser. I'm curious; do all the politicians you represent have the same desires as you?"

He ignored my derision. "Do you want me to continue or not?"

"This should be interesting. Go on."

His face contorted. "Later in the evening, I found out that Jillian had been there during the party."

All I could do was shake my head in disgust. He was her father, for god's sake; could have been a grandfather to her children.

"How did you find out about the photos?"

"Someone informed me."

"Who?"

"An associate."

"How did your associate know Jillian

had the photos?"

"Someone at the party saw her taking them."

"So why didn't they just stop her at the party?"

"They tried and failed. They wanted me to contact her and get them back."

I didn't believe him. "Which one has the sick fetish for teenage girls?" Just hearing the words made my stomach turn over. I had to force myself not to strike out at Howard Moore in retaliation.

"What are you talking about?" The look on his face led me to believe he practiced his reaction. I let that part go for the moment.

"Who is your associate?"

"I can't tell you that. That could get me killed."

"It could have been your associate that had Jillian killed," I shouted. "Doesn't that bother you?"

"He couldn't have done it."

"Then who could?"

"I don't know."

What was it about this man that made me not believe him? "I want a list of names of who attended the party that night."

The panic on his face was unmistakable. "I won't do it. You don't know these people."

I shrugged. I didn't care what happened to him. "You should have thought of the danger before you got involved."

"I can't," he whined.

"Look, I already know some of their names. I have the photos, remember. It wouldn't take me too long to find out the others. So either you help me, or…"

He knew he had no alternative. He could see it in my eyes. If he didn't give me the information, I'd bring him down, which I planned to do anyway, but he didn't need to know that right now. It didn't take too long for him to decide. He reached for a pen and paper and took a few minutes to write the information. Then he handed me the list without making eye contact.

I briefly glanced at it. "Which one is your associate?"

"If you force me to give you that information, it could force them to get rid of me."

"Yeah, you already said that," I said, showing no mercy. "Give me his name."

He had a strange expression on his face when he finally responded. "His name is Thomas Miles."

I was stunned, but only for a minute. After everything I'd learned in the last few days, there wasn't anything that would surprise me. "I don't believe in coincidences."

"What?"

"You wouldn't understand," I said, shaking my head.

"What happens now?"

"That will depend on where the

investigation leads. I have no control over what the police do with you. They're working on that now."

I didn't believe he told the whole truth or gave me the full list; just enough to get me out, but it was a place to start. I walked out of his office without looking back. Let him worry about what the cops know. I hope they nail him and need my help to do it.

CHAPTER 35

WHEN I WAS leaving the law office, I noticed a Ford SUV with tinted windows pull in two cars behind me. Nauset Bay's finest was at it again. I knew it was one of their unmarked cars. I smiled to myself; I guess the two officers drew the short straw.

Following me must be important. Maldonado and Finn keep sending their best.

I headed toward the shop where the windows and door panels were being repaired after the break-in. At the same time, I was grappling with ideas on how to lose the tail. I pulled into the parking lot, parked the jeep in a spot out front, and walked inside to pay for the repairs. I watched the Ford through the reflection in the glass door. It parked in a spot down the street, but within a distance, where the officers could still observe me.

While I was inside, I called Derek's office to let his employees know they could pick up the jeep, as previously planned. When I inquired about Derek, they said he was on the golf course with some out-of-town visitors. Next, I solicited the help of Javier, the young mechanic who repaired my car. Together, we devised a plan to help me distract my two followers. I conveniently left out the detail that they were police officers. Javier wouldn't be as eager to help if he knew. I led him to believe they were competitors of my P.I. investigation, so he was happy to oblige in my fun.

Javier nonchalantly stepped into the shop's tow truck, drove around the block, and pulled in front of the Ford, blocking them in. Ignoring the men inside, he pretended he had papers to tow the vehicle, and went about hooking the crane to the front.

Immediately, the officer in the passenger seat jumped out, yelling obscenities. From where I stood, I could see it was Lopez, which meant Johnson was driving. The same partners following me when I had the reporters hound them at Howard Moore's house.

While Javier argued with Lopez, I was able to jump into my car and drive away. In the rearview mirror, I saw Javier pump his fist in the air in a congratulatory manner, but Lopez wasn't too happy. I felt a moment of regret, but it didn't last. I wouldn't want to be the one who had to explain to Maldonado and Finn that they lost me again.

This P.I. gig was getting fun.

On the way to my next destination, I placed another call to Sarah Miles. It was curious that she hadn't returned my call from the previous day. When her secretary answered, she informed me that Sarah left word that she wouldn't be in the office for a couple of days. I left word again, and then immediately dialed her cell phone. It went to voicemail again. As I disconnected, I wondered if the walls were closing in on Thomas Miles, and wondered if he would harm his wife.

It did not surprise Roger when I showed up at his garage unannounced, but he looked at me funny. "You're wearing makeup?"

I shrugged. "I had to hide the bruises."

"It looks good," he said. "I bet I can guess why you're here."

"I bet you can." I pulled the photos and DVDs out of the backpack and handed them to him. "I need an extra copy of everything. And I need to know if there's anything you can do with the DVD to bring the identity of the individual to light."

He thought about it. "I can try some digital enhancement, but I can't guarantee anything."

"Just do what you can.

"You got it."

"Just call me when you've finished with the copies, and I'll come by and pick up the originals."

He nodded.

"Can you keep the copies here just in case the originals turn up missing?"

"Not a problem."

"Thanks."

"You can stop by later today to pick them up."

"That's quick, but you don't need to

rush."

He waved his hand in the air. "Making copies is a piece of cake."

"Thanks, I appreciate it."

When I arrived in front of The Tapestry, it was still quiet. It wasn't time for the noontime specials just yet; I said to myself. First, I drove through the alley to see if the Mini Cooper and Corvette were in their respective parking spots. This morning, I intended to get inside, at least to look around.

Obviously, I couldn't just go in and ask questions as Katie Parker, the private investigator. Instead, I put on a pair of wire-framed readers that looked like eyeglasses and clipped a fake badge to my jacket. If anyone stopped me inside, the guise would be that I was a building inspector checking the site for a permit requested for a renovation. After I chatted with Howard Moore, I was going on the assumption that Thomas Miles had something to do with this fine establishment, so I'd use his name if necessary.

Since it was nearing the lunch hour, which appeared to be the beginning of the workday for the joint, I suspected the door would be open. I was right. When I entered, it would be an understatement to say I was stunned. The décor was impressive. The interior was like the exterior; it resembled an expensive designer home. They painted the front room in a light blue color that was warm and inviting. A large white sectional sofa sat near a far wall, facing a beautiful mural of the ocean with sailboats of various sizes. Oversized chairs sat opposite, and a round glass-top table sat in the center, with an expensive vase of fresh flowers on top. As I continued down the hall, I noticed a reception area near a door painted in a unique color of gold. There wasn't anyone around at the moment, which was odd. But that allowed me to be nosey. Maybe there was another floor? Since the entire first floor had carpet, I could move about undetected, so far. Past the reception desk, I realized there were several doors along the hall, each one painted a different color, and each one locked.

As I walked further along, I heard voices and tried to figure out where they were coming from. My assumption was they were somewhere in the back of the building. They locked all the doors in the hallway. When I put my ear up to each door, I didn't hear any noise. I suspected that would change when noontime rolled around. I assumed the further down the hall I walked; the closer it would bring me to identifying the voices. That wasn't the case.

I wound up in an elaborate kitchen that looked like it belonged in a mansion. That was strange. I also noticed the back door that Tracy Donavon had entered the day before. Despite that, there were still no bodies to go with the voices, even though I could still hear them. It sounded like I was in an echo chamber. There was no second floor, so there had to be a basement. But where was the door leading to it?

Viewing the kitchen, it surprised me at the amount of money that was spent on the design and decor. The room was larger than my kitchen and family room put together. The appliances were top of the line and the cabinets looked custom-made to match the Italian marble countertops. They must have events and parties for their high-profile clientele to validate such an expense.

Feeling confident I made it this far with nobody stopping me, I walked through the entire kitchen to find where the voices were coming from. There was a set of French doors on the far side of the kitchen that opened to a private patio. Nobody was there. A floor-to-ceiling wine cooler was built into another wall, and there was another door adjacent. It surprised me when I turned the knob and the door opened.

I stepped into a fully stocked walk-in pantry, probably as large as a small bedroom. Standing inside, the voices were stronger, which encouraged me to search for another door. The amount of food stunned me. Obviously, there was a lot of entertaining going on at The Tapestry. At the end of the pantry, I noticed a seam in the wall that looked odd; a hidden door? If so, it had to be the door to a basement. The voices were definitely louder, and coming from down below.

I placed my hand on the wall and felt around for something that might open it. I couldn't find anything on the wall in front of me, so I moved my hands along the wall behind the food. At one point, I felt something metal. I pushed some food to the side and noticed a raised metal button. I was just about to push it to see what happened when I heard several female voices come inside the building. Damn, I thought. The working women arrived.

Shit!

I put the food back as it was to hide the fact that somebody was looking. Then I hurried out of the pantry, closed the door as quietly as I could, and snuck out the back door to the alley. Once I was back in the safety of my car, I stuck around to see if anything new happened. While I observed, I pulled out the list of names Howard Moore gave me. The first row I recognized, but he knew that because they were in the photos: his pal, Senator Lawrence Sanders, the two public officials, Darryl Finson and Jake Haloran, and then Thomas Miles. Out of the remaining names on the list, there were only two others I recognized, but they had me pounding the steering wheel: Officers Jimmy Smith and Larry Foley.

Was it a coincidence that Smith attended the party and was the first officer to arrive on the scene of Jillian's murder? Fat chance.

He was involved, but did he kill Jillian? What about Larry Foley? Where was he at the time? Could he have been the one running away from the scene, seconds before Smith rolled onto the scene? Circumstances looked that way, but I needed proof and I didn't have that yet. But I was getting close.

CHAPTER 36

AFTER A FEW hours of watching, I determined the same routine was taking place at The Tapestry. The females that arrived the day before also made their appearance, and the men continued to show up and exit at hourly intervals. Since there wasn't anything new to be learned, it was time to focus my attention elsewhere.

I was concerned for Sarah Miles. I put in a call to make sure her husband was at his office. When the receptionist patched me through to his secretary, Molly, I had to think fast. I went into a long technical rendition to give the impression I was a prospective client. She couldn't make sense of what I was saying, so she put me through, as I hoped. Once he identified himself, I hung up. I reached my objective, which was to confirm his location. Now, he wouldn't get in my way when I checked their house. I needed to make sure nothing happened to Sarah; her not returning my calls seemed rather odd, considering.

The Miles's home was about two miles away from their respective offices. I turned left onto a street just off MA-28 and followed a winding road with trees on both sides. A right-hand turn and the Miles home sat at the end of the street with a long driveway to their three-car garage.

The house was impressive but felt cold. There was no landscaping around the property, to give the home a feeling of warmth. There was no car parked in the driveway, and no way to see if anyone was home. I stepped out of my vehicle and looked through the garage window. It was dark, but I could make out what looked like a black SUV. I couldn't tell the make and model or see the license plate.

I knocked at the door on the off chance there was a maid or butler, but there was no answer. I tried the knob; it was locked, as it would be. I went around to the back of the house. There was a set of French doors off the back patio, but I couldn't get to them because of the eight-foot wrought iron fencing around the backyard. After verifying all the windows within reach were secure and impossible to enter, I knew the only way to gain entry would be to pick the lock on the front door and do so without a nosey neighbor calling the police.

A voice in my head, which was probably Maldonado, reminded me that picking a lock to gain entry into someone's home was breaking and entering. It was the other voice that eventually won out. If anything happened to Sarah Miles, and I didn't at least check it out, I'd feel responsible. I could call the police and let them do a wellness check. But if everything was fine, I'd look like a fool, and they'd be pissed I wasted their time. With what I learned, I knew Thomas Miles was erratic. Sarah told him of her suspicions. Was he erratic enough to do something to her? I just needed to verify that she was not inside injured, or worse.

Since I've only been at this P.I. gig a few weeks, picking locks was not a natural skill. Derek and Roger showed me how to do it, but I needed practice to become an expert. It took longer than I hoped because there was a sophisticated deadbolt system on the door. When I finally got inside, I was thankful an alarm didn't go off, or a vicious dog didn't attack me at the door. Remembering Sarah's reaction to Bailey, I knew a pet was not her idea of security.

As I stood in the entryway, I looked around at the surroundings and called out Sarah's name. Like the exterior, the home lacked décor and felt cold. There were artifacts from different parts of the world on the wall, which made me conclude they traveled. During better times, I guess. I didn't know how much time I had to check around, so I moved quickly through each room. I searched for any signs of a struggle or indications that anything happened to Sarah.

I came to a room with a desk, a computer and printer on a stand to its left, and bookcases up against the other walls. The same artifacts I noticed in the other rooms adorned the walls in this one, too. I entered and looked at the documents stacked on the desk. They had Sarah's company's address on them, so I surmised she used it as a second office. There were real estate documents next to the computer. I gave them a cursory glance and couldn't help but notice there was a different corporate business name listed, and not her Modeling Agency corporation. That told me Sarah kept her personal properties in legal corporations and trusts. If she knew how to protect them, legally, why did she hire me? I put the question in the back of my mind to revisit later. I put the papers back the way I found them and proceeded with my search.

As I walked upstairs to the second floor, I was thinking I overreacted. I'd probably get a good laugh when Sarah confirmed she took a couple of days off to enjoy the nice weather. The first room looked to be a guest bedroom, possibly where Thomas Miles slept during their difficult times; an unmade bed, shirts, suits, and ties were thrown around the room. Messy, but nothing suspicious.

I heard a noise and stopped to listen. It sounded like someone was banging against a piece of metal down the hall. I continued and approached the second room. The racket was coming from inside. On impulse, I reached for my gun. Something I've been doing a lot lately. I stood to the side of the door and slowly turned the knob. If someone was inside, they weren't getting past me. I pushed the door open with my foot and firmly planted myself in the center of the door frame. I expected to be jumped by the same two thugs I ran into at Jillian's and breathed a sigh of relief when it didn't happen. I nearly wet my pants when an exotic bird jumped inside his cage in a corner of the room and scared the life out of me. Damn.

I took a minute to get my heart rate back to normal. Then I closed the door and walked towards the last room at the end of the hall, which was the master bedroom. When I opened the door, I braced myself for anything else that could scare me and chastised myself for being such a wimp. This room was the only one in the house that had any kind of decor. The room was large with a king-size poster bed covered with a lace comforter and pillows in various colors. There was a set of French doors that led to an outdoor patio. A tea set sat atop a bistro table outside. A throw blanket was thrown across the love seat in front of a large window with a stack of books on top. One of them had its page saved by a bookmark. A look at the title told me Sarah Miles liked exotic locations. This book was about islands in Mexico. The room was full of color from several exotic plants situated around the room. A walk-in closet showed off her designer attire and led to an enormous master bath. She probably spent most of her time in this room.

There was no Sarah or any signs that anything happened to her. I checked through her belongings, like makeup, shampoo, and conditioner, inside the shower. Everything seemed to be in its place. If she was leaving for a couple of days, as her secretary said, you would think she'd take some personal items with her. With her wealth, maybe she just purchased new items? After making sure everything was the same as I found it, I left the house, reassured that I didn't find a body or signs of injury. I still didn't know her whereabouts, but couldn't dwell on it. She hired me to find proof her husband was cheating, so I decided it was time to fulfill that part of the investigation.

I could continue to tail him and hope I'd catch him in the act, or go on offense, like I did with Howard Moore. Offense, it is. I only had a couple of hours before he left the office. I learned he was a man of repetition. Now, I just needed to dangle the bait and wait for him to bite.

Roger wasn't in his office when I arrived to pick up the photos, but he left a note. He wasn't successful with the DVD, but the copies were made, and he left the key next door with the neighbor.

I'd met the homeowner before. He was a short, but proud oriental man, who seemed to understand the English language, but maintained he couldn't speak it. I joked with Roger that it was just his way of pretending ignorance if he didn't like the conversation. I retrieved the key, opened the garage door, and verified the contents of the envelope he left for me. Then I returned the key to the neighbor. The entire exchange took place with no words exchanged, only heads shaking up and down.

Once I arrived at the RV, I checked through everything to make sure I had no more visitors while I was out. The cell phone vibrated a few times while I was inside Sarah's, so I checked the voicemail messages. Detective Maldonado called to say he had the information I was waiting for, which meant he finally got around to running the license plates. Bravo.

The next message was from Finn. He said he spent some time with his son David and now he was working his case and wouldn't be available. That was for the best. I had something important to do for the evening that couldn't wait. If I called Finn and told him I was busy, he'd question me until I told him what I was up to. Then he would immediately put a stop to it. I decided not to return the call.

The last call was from Loretta. She called to tell me Bailey was doing great. That she was having fun hanging out with Derek's two dogs, enjoying the beach. She also confirmed that Derek had visitors in from out of town, and would get in touch after they'd gone. After the call, I was relieved to hear Bailey was doing okay. We had never been separated before.

I had an hour to get ready for my charade with Thomas Miles. I looked through my closet for something to wear. After trying on several outfits, I settled on one I thought was fitting. Then, I went to take a shower, blow-dried my hair, and added curls with the iron to flow down my back. I dabbed on makeup to hide the bruises and added color to my eyes. I threw away most of my lingerie after learning the thugs were in my drawer, but I still had a new lace set I purchased from Victoria's Secret. I hated to waste it on a scumbag like Thomas Miles, but what could I do? Now, for the important part of the ensemble; I secured a small recording device to my stomach and hooked the mouthpiece inside my bra.

For the evening's charade, I chose a black sleeveless tuxedo blouse, a mid-length black fitted skirt, showing tanned legs, and a pair of black heels with ankle straps. I added a set of hoop earrings and looked in the mirror at the finished product. Not bad. It was conservative and simple, but sexy at the same time. No need to be too obvious. The darkness in the pub and the makeup would hide my bruised face.

I hate carrying a purse, but tonight I had no choice. After rummaging through the bottom of the closet, I found a black one large enough to hold the items I needed. I reached for a bottle of perfume and lip gloss, grabbed some cash and a pair of latex gloves, and put them inside. Then I retrieved the camera from my backpack and placed it, and my gun and cell phone inside, too.

Even though Roger had a copy of the photos and DVDs, I still needed to keep the originals secure. I walked out to my car, opened the tailgate, and placed my backpack in the tire compartment. With that done, I headed on my way and hoped I could pull off the charade.

CHAPTER 37

WHEN I WALKED into Pier 25, I searched for my target, hoping he was true to form. He was already at the bar with an empty Martini glass in front of him. No way to know if it was his first, or third. He dressed the same; conservative suit, but no tie. I would bet he had suspenders underneath his jacket to complete his conservative illusion. Most of the attorneys I used to work for always wore suspenders. I assumed it was a standard accessory for most of them. There were two seats available next to him. If I sat down next to him, he could get suspicious, so I settled on two seats away. I just hoped my ploy worked.

"Excuse me, is this seat taken?" I said.

Thomas turned in my direction and gave me an appreciative smile. He liked what he was seeing, though I wasn't flattered by that. I glanced at his left hand. He wasn't wearing his wedding band. Did he ever?

"No, please sit down. Can I get you a drink?"

"You don't have to do that."

He smiled. "I insist."

"That would be nice, thank you. I'll have blueberry vodka on the rocks with a twist. My name is Selena." I slid the purse over my shoulder to keep my gun close and sat down so I was facing him.

"Thomas." He offered his hand in introduction, but let his fingers linger a little longer than necessary. "Joe, bring the lady blueberry vodka with a twist and I'll have another one for myself," he said to the bartender.

"This place is nice." I glanced around, pretending to be interested in the scenery. In reality, I was surveying the surroundings and looking for any familiar faces, like Connie with her new beau. The last thing I needed was someone to approach and blow the charade. "Do you come here often?"

"Once in a while after a long day at the office," he said. "What about you?"

Funny, my surveillance showed him here like clockwork.

"This is my first time. Some friends told me there was a friendly crowd for happy hour."

"What kind of work do you do, Thomas?"

"I'm an attorney."

"Oh, really? What kind of law do you practice?"

"I dabble in various forms."

"Impressive." I had to keep reminding myself to stay in character, which meant satisfying his ego. Otherwise, I wouldn't be able to pull it off.

"I bet I can guess what you do," he teased.

"Really?" This should be good, I thought

Without an invitation, he jumped onto the seat next to me and studied my physique. "You couldn't be a nurse, because you wouldn't want to hide that figure in those scrubs."

I raised my eyebrows. "Scrubs are very comfortable."

"I don't peg you as a teacher, either."

"Why is that?"

"You're too sexy to sit behind a desk dealing with kids every day."

This guy turned into the sleaze I knew he was without me even trying.

After another short period of back and forth, the happy hour picked up, making it hard to hear. I prayed the recording device was catching both sides of the conversation.

"Would you like another drink?" he said, noticing his martini glass was empty.

I was hoping he wouldn't notice I hadn't even touched the first one of mine.

He waved to the bartender and asked him to bring another round, then he boldly placed his right hand on my thigh, leaving it to linger.

"Are you married, Thomas?"

"Nope, no attachments here. I am completely at your disposal."

"Really; how could an attractive and successful man like you still be available?" Picture me with my finger in my mouth, trying to keep myself from gagging. I didn't like it, but I knew this was the quickest way to get the goods and end this investigation, by manipulating him to act.

"I was too busy with work to worry about a relationship," he said with a smirk.

I was thinking maybe he was too busy with the women at The Tapestry to have time for a relationship.

The bartender brought over another round of drinks. I pushed the first drink forward, locking eyes with the bartender, hoping he wouldn't mention the glass was still full. Thomas Miles was oblivious. The bartender slyly took the drink away and winked, letting me know my secret was safe with him. Oh good, I had an ally.

Thomas reached for his Martini and downed it in one shot. He was feeling his oats. "What do you say we go somewhere a little less crowded?"

I intended to catch him in the act, but I didn't expect him to move so fast. I thought I'd have to work at it. What a snake.

"Where did you have in mind?" I wanted him to say The Tapestry. That way, I'd get another look inside. But then again, I could get myself jammed up. Handling a guy like Thomas Miles was one thing. If I had to butt heads with the goons, then I'd be in trouble.

"We could go back to my office. It's only up the street. There's a mini-bar, then we can talk and get to know each other better, without all the noise."

Talking was not what he had in mind, but how else was I going to get the goods? "Would we be alone?"

"We'll be alone," he said, his eyes filled with mischief.

Something in the way he said we'd be alone sent a chill up and down my spine.

Thomas stood to go and left some cash on the bar. He called the bartender over and placed a twenty-dollar bill in his hands, thanking him for the prompt service. The bartender gave me another wink. I got the impression he knew exactly what I was up to.

I grabbed my purse off the bar. "Do you mind if I freshen up first?"

"Fine," he said, a little impatient. "I'll meet you out front."

In the bathroom, I readjusted the recording device in my bra to make sure he wouldn't notice it if he tried to touch me. The thought made me want to gag, but it was the best way to put a quick end to this case. I freshened up my hair and added some lip gloss, then talked myself into game mode for what was sure to be an eventful evening.

When I walked into the lobby, I noticed he was agitated. He didn't like to be kept waiting. "Thank you for being patient," I said, as politely as I could muster.

"We'll take my car," he said rather brusquely. "I'll bring you back to your car later."

Before I could comment, he put his arm around my waist to guide me out the door.

This wasn't exactly what I had planned,

but he'd get suspicious if I complained. Hopefully, I could grab a cab after I've accomplished my mission. When we walked outside, he led me to the corvette that I had seen in the alley behind The Tapestry.

He sped out of the parking lot and headed toward his office. I had to hang onto the door each time he took a turn. When he pulled into the circular drive in front of the building, he made small talk as we exited the vehicle and walked through a set of glass doors.

There were four floors. He entered the elevator and took me up to the top one. When we stepped out, it was a typical law office. The attorneys' offices were on the outer walls with window views. The secretary cubicles, filing cabinets, and a conference room with law books were all in the center. We walked past four cubicles until we reached an office in a corner with his name on the door. It was a modern design with a glass-top and leather chair in front of the large windows showing views of Nauset Bay. A sectional l-shaped leather futon sat in the opposite corner, with pillows added for comfort, and large plants sat atop two glass-top end tables. The only other décor was the artifacts from different parts of the world. It reminded me that Thomas and Sarah Miles traveled during better times. He walked toward a two-door closet on the opposite side of the room and pulled it open. There was a bar inside. He offered to make us both a drink and motioned for me to have a seat on the futon.

My eyes remained on him as I complied. When he had his back to me, I put my purse on the other section and opened it, pulling the camera to the edge so it had a full view of the room, and made sure it was on. Then I positioned the pillow to keep it from being seen.

After he made the drinks, he handed me one and sat down next to me. He looked at his drink and swished the liquid around for a moment, glaring at it, like the liquid was going to reveal his future. In one gulp, he downed the drink and slammed the empty glass on the end table, so hard I thought the glass would shatter. I tried to act cool and pretended to take a sip of my own. I had no intention of drinking it, knowing he probably slipped something inside.

In less than a minute, his own eyes looked droopy and his movements sloppy. Damn, I thought, did he put something in his own drink? Then, without warning, he grabbed the drink out of my hand and set it on the table. He maneuvered me so that my back was up against his chest.

"What are you doing?" I asked, trying to keep the anger out of my voice and just act surprised.

"You're so tense," he said, sexually massaging my neck and shoulders. "You need to relax."

The last thing I wanted to do was relax

with this asshole, but I needed to put on a good show if I want to succeed. "I'm just a little nervous," I said, trying to slow him down. I was concerned about the sudden aggressive behavior.

He nibbled my ear and then lowered down to my neck. "No need to be nervous with me. It's not like this is the first time you've had sex."

"Sex?" I turned around to look at him as if shocked by the words. "What made you think we were going to have sex?"

"You did honey." He leered at me with menacing eyes. "You came to the bar looking for it. You got fuck me written all over you. What'd you think was going to happen when you came here?"

"I was flirting, but…"

Suddenly, his left arm wrapped around me and pulled me close, while his other hand started fondling my breast. I secretly prayed my shirt blocked him from noticing the microphone. His breathing was heavy and his body was shaking, more than if he were just turned on. When I tried to pull loose, he held me tighter. I was seriously going to gag.

I finally pulled free from him and was up on my feet, grabbing my purse. At the same time, I tried to make sure the camera was still filming, and he wasn't aware of what I was up to.

"I shouldn't be here," I said, as I started toward the door.

"Get back here!"

Now I could see his anger. Within minutes of me coming to his office, he was losing control. Then I realized whatever he took was making him behave this way. I had to make a move, and fast. This was getting out of hand.

"You're not going anywhere. You came here to tease, so you're going to finish what you started."

He was up and headed in my direction, cutting me off from getting to the door. He lunged at me and pulled me back with both hands. I lost my balance and fell to the ground. He jumped on top of me and held me down with his weight. We were fully clothed, but he humped like a clumsy puppy in heat that didn't know what he was doing. I couldn't help but laugh. It was the only way I could escape the reality of the situation. His hands tried to reach underneath my top.

I kept telling myself not to panic. But if I didn't do something and quick, I was going to get sick all over the bastard. Of course, right about now, that wouldn't be so bad.

Think, Katie, think. What could I do to get myself out of this mess? I tried to push a knee into his groin, but I could not connect. My gun was in my purse, so I tried to open it while keeping his hands from getting under my clothing. I didn't want him touching my skin.

I finally had my purse open and reached inside, but he unexpectedly stopped.

Oh shit! He found the wire.

"What the fuck is this?" He shouted, staring at it, stunned.

Taking advantage of the moment, I reached for the gun. I had my hand on it and was ready to pull it out when there was a knock at the door.

"Fuck!" He muttered under his breath, covering my mouth to keep me from yelling out.

"Thomas, are you in there?" a woman's voice said from the other side of the door. "It's Molly."

"What the hell is she doing here?" he whispered in an angry voice. He glanced towards the bathroom. It looked as though he was struggling with how to get me in there and keep me quiet at the same time. He stood up, pulling me with him, while keeping his hand over my mouth, and attempted to drag me towards the room.

On my feet, my hands had more freedom. I pulled the gun out, ready to regain control. My left knee came up and connected with his groin. He doubled over. I brought my right leg around and kicked the back of his knees. His legs buckled. He was falling forward, but I gave him a push backward so he landed on his ass. To get that smug look off his face, I straddled him and pointed my gun at his face.

"Keep your grimy hands where they are,

you piece of slime." I was back in charge.

There was no more knocking, so I assumed Molly had left. It was time to make this scumbag weep. There was enough evidence on the camera for Sarah to be satisfied, but he pissed me off.

I confirmed he was the associate who provided the entertainment for Howard Moore's party. Now was not the time to get into that. I would deal with that later. Now, it was personal payback time.

"Take off your suit, you disgusting animal," I said, nudging the gun at him to let him know I was serious. I didn't know my plan; I was acting on emotions, not my brain. But the loser actually trembled.

"Who are you? Did my partner send you?"

Good. The guy was too stupid to catch on that his wife hired me. I wondered about his partner, though. That might be something to analyze later. What did he do to his partner?

"I said take off your suit." I pointed the gun toward his crotch and watched him jump in fear.

He awkwardly disrobed, fumbling with his buttons as he did. While doing so, he looked around the office for a weapon or means of escape.

Meanwhile, I was trying to figure out how I was going to finish this little charade. Once he was standing in front of me in a pair of boxers, he didn't look so much like a powerful attorney. He wasn't much older than me, but his skin was flabby and sagged. Looking at him now; he reminded me of a weasel.

"Get over there behind the desk." An idea was forming. I just hoped what I needed to complete the task was inside his desk. I reached into the purse and pulled out the latex gloves. When I put them on, you could visibly see him panic. He didn't know who sent me, or what I was up to.

"Sit down," I ordered. I motioned to the chair behind his desk. Then I rifled through his desk drawers and took a pair of scissors and duct tape from the one with office supplies. Keeping the gun trained on him, I grabbed his tie and suspenders. Using the tie, I secured his wrists together. Then I cut the suspenders in half and used them to wrap his ankles around the chair legs. Since I couldn't find anything else, I wrapped duct tape around him and the chair until he couldn't get loose. He wasn't very cooperative. He bucked and kicked through the entire ordeal. Losing control was something he didn't like.

I pulled the camera out of my purse, sat it on the desk so that it had him in perfect view, and double-checked to make sure it was still on.

"You still want to have sex, Mr. Miles?" I taunted. He glared at the camera.

"Fuck you."

I laughed. "I'll take that as a no."

When I heard a commotion out in the hall, I decided I'd had enough fun for the evening, and wrapped things up. "Say goodbye to the camera."

"Fuck you."

I laughed again. "I must be off."

"You'll regret the day you walked into Pier 25," he said, feeling emboldened now that I was leaving and he was still alive. "I know people."

I wanted to say, yeah, I know. Instead, I bent down to his feet, took off one of his socks, and stuffed it in his mouth.

"Suck on that, you slime."

I turned the camera off and placed it, and my gun, back in the purse. I picked up the drink he made for me and dumped the contents into the sink. Then I wrapped the glass with a paper towel and stuffed it into my purse as well. Then I found some paper towels and wiped everything down. I wanted to remove any trace of me. If he wanted to track me down, I didn't see any need to make it easy for him to check my fingerprints. Let him work for it. Glancing in his direction one more time before leaving, I gave him one last wink and said, "I'll be back."

I flipped off the lights on the way out the door.

Standing in the hall, I heard a female voice. I assumed it was Molly. She was further down the hall and not in an area where she could see me. I headed back the way he brought me in earlier and exited out the front door. Nearly two blocks away, I heard footsteps and feared someone was following me. When I turned around, I saw two men in leather jackets enter the building through the glass doors, though I couldn't see their faces.

I spotted a restaurant down the street and went inside. Once the hostess escorted me to a table, I sat down and ordered an iced tea. While waiting, I called for an Uber to take me back to my car. After being alone with my thoughts for several minutes, I thought of calling Thomas Miles' office to have them cut him loose. But then I talked myself out of it. Molly would rescue him soon enough.

When I finally made it home, I grabbed my backpack from the tire compartment and made sure I had no unwanted visitors. I removed the contents of the purse and placed them back into the backpack. Then, I removed the wire taped to my stomach and dropped it inside as well.

Before doing anything else, I turned the water on in the shower, leaving it to run long enough to make the bathroom hot and steamy. After a couple of minutes, I stripped down, entered and stood underneath the *PowerPulse* shower head, and let the therapeutic massage do its job. The heat and pulsating stream of water soothed my aching muscles. I grabbed the loofah sponge and soap and scrubbed my body until it was raw.

The scene at Thomas Miles' office didn't go as I hoped. I was so wrong to think it would. I shivered at the thought of what could have happened if he got the upper hand. If Maldonado or Finn knew what I was up to, they would have locked me up in a jail cell for the night. It was common practice for a female P.I. to act as bait to catch a slimy cheater, but I took it too far. After the betrayal of my ex-husband, a stalker trying to ruin my life, the torching of my cottage, and everything surrounding Jillian's death; my anger just exploded. I didn't realize how much I had been holding it in.

Finally cleansed of the evening's events, I put on boxer shorts and a tank top and then called *Domino's* to order pizza. The goal was to relax for a couple of hours, not think about anything, and get some needed sleep. I turned on the TV and got comfortable on the sofa. When I heard the knock at the door twenty minutes later, I grabbed the cash and headed to the door. When I was just about to answer, something made me stop. I retrieved my gun from the backpack, held it at my side, and looked through the blinds. When I saw my regular delivery guy, I breathed a sigh of relief. After paying for the pizza, I grabbed a bottle of water from the refrigerator and planted myself on the sofa.

I settled on continuing with episodes of *The Good Wife*. I devoured the first slice of pizza and reached for a second when there was another knock on the door. Again, I was on alert. I walked to the door to check through the blinds. All I could see was a shadow. They didn't want me to see who it was. My first thought was that Finn was just playing around. But with all that was going on, would he do that about now?

I had a decision to make. Should I open the door? If I did and the two perps were on the other side, would I be able to handle them, or would they overpower me? If I had my boots on, I'd be in my comfort zone. I could at least count on them for a power kick. But my feet were bare. What if it was the perps, and they tried to bust through the door? Thankfully, there was only one door in the RV. There was a window to use for emergencies, but it could only be opened from the inside. Was I prepared to shoot my way out of this situation?

I stepped back away from the door and planted my feet firmly on the floor with the gun pointed forward, ready to shoot.

"Who is it?" I yelled.

Silence.

I was sweating from the adrenaline surging through me, the feeling of the unknown.

"Who is it?" I yelled one more time.

Again, silence.

I walked to the door again and looked.

This time, the shadow was gone and there was nobody there. I pushed the curtain aside above the console and looked out at the driveway. I couldn't see anyone. Since my cottage was under construction, there were no walls yet, so I could see the street. I couldn't see anything. No vehicle or men in black. Whoever was there, toying with me, was gone now.

I shook my head and returned to the sofa to settle in again. I grabbed another slice of pizza and hit the rewind on the episode I was watching. Musing how the main character went through a similar experience to mine with my ex. It was getting good, but another knock on the door interrupted it.

"C'mon," I said to myself.

This was getting ridiculous. I went to the door and peered out. Again, there was nobody there. Seriously? I didn't just imagine somebody knocking at the door. It occurred to me they were trying to torment me psychologically, or scare me off. Frustrated, I yelled at the door. I swear I heard laughter outside the door.

CHAPTER 38

WHEN I WOKE the following morning, it amazed me I got a few hours of sleep. After the jerks started messing with me, I wound up checking the doors and windows every half-hour, just to see if anyone was there. I'm sure that was their intention. It was probably three a.m. before I closed my eyes. The TV remained on and my gun remained at my side. It was also the first time I slept without seeing the vision of Jillian in a pool of blood.

I forced myself up at seven, drank a cup of green tea, and took a quick shower to wake myself up. I had a pre-arranged appointment with Roger for kickboxing training at a local park. Once I got the P.I. gig, Derek thought it wise to have other forms of defensive skills. Running into the two thugs at Jillian's and last night with Thomas Miles, I put some of that training to use. After jumping into a pair of sweatpants, a t-shirt, and cross-trainers, I headed out the door.

I purposely arrived twenty minutes early so I could get in my warm-up exercises. I started with some stretches, sit-ups, and push-ups, and finished up with four laps around the park. By the time Roger arrived, I was ready, fueled by the anger and stress over the last few days.

Roger picked up various defensive skills

before he joined the force and wound up training several of his fellow officers; Finn too. Kickboxing was only one aspect of his training, but it was the one that worked best for me. I knew his training could ultimately keep me alive.

"Hey Katie," he said when he approached.

"Hey, yourself," I said. I could call him good-looking, but his wife would probably have my hide. He reminded me of a young Denzel Washington with a rock-solid physique.

"Looks like you're more than ready for a workout today."

I moved my head to the right and held the position for thirty seconds until I felt my neck stretch, and then to the left. "I'm ready to combust."

He nodded. "Okay then, let's get down to work so you can work off those frustrations and keep your mind on track."

He started me off with shadow boxing, basically using the air to practice the moves. The training forced me to focus on my mental and physical abilities and stamina. After twenty minutes, he pulled out the pads so I could work on perfecting the techniques. The entire time, Roger barked out orders like a drill sergeant, forcing me to push harder; never letting me give up. He worked me relentlessly. He pushed so hard I wanted to kick him, but I knew I'd suffer the consequences.

When he thought I was good and ready, it was time for sparring. Since I was in the middle of an investigation, this part of the training was especially important. It helped with kicks to specific parts of the body, which was good when dealing with thugs.

When sparring with Roger, I wanted to push myself further, even after my body was telling me enough. I was drenched by the time it was over.

Once I returned home, showered, and changed, I called Sarah Miles's office, only to be told she was still out. Where the hell was she? When I finished with the call, I put a label on the video I filmed of Thomas Miles, placed it, along with the recording, inside a manila envelope, and dropped it in my backpack, after removing the other equipment I no longer needed. Then I sat down at the computer and typed out a chronological surveillance report, with full details on the behavior and tracking of Thomas Miles, including his time at The Tapestry. I printed out the report and made myself a copy. The original went into the envelope and the copy was in my files.

Now, all I had to do was track down Sarah Miles, and give her the information with the bill, and this phase of the investigation was complete. Considering the anguish she felt when she came to see me, I would have thought she'd be waiting by the phone. Like everything else going on, I knew something was up, just not what it was, yet.

Even though the Mile's investigation was complete, I still wanted to know the connection between Jillian's murder and why she had a photograph of Thomas Miles. I grabbed the backpack and keys off the counter and headed to Nauset Bay P.D. to pick up the license plate info Maldonado had waiting for me.

They waved me on back the minute I arrived in the lobby. When I entered the detective's bullpen, two uniformed officers were speaking with Maldonado. All three were standing, and the talk looked serious, so I waited before approaching. They kept looking in my direction, which led me to believe I was the subject of their discussion. Oh joy.

A few minutes later, the officers left and Maldonado motioned me over. I could tell from his serious disposition that there was a problem, and I was at the center. He instructed me to take a seat. Instead of sitting himself, he stood opposite me with his arms crossed. Now, I was intimidated.

"What do you know about an attorney named Thomas Miles?"

I gulped. By the look on his face, I didn't think right now would be a good time to joke. "His wife hired me."

"To do what?"

This could get tricky. I'm not required to give information regarding my investigations. If it was anyone else, I wouldn't. But Maldonado was not just a Sergeant and detective. He was a friend. If he needed the information, it was important for him to know.

"She said he was cheating on her and asked me to provide her with proof. Why?"

Maldonado locked eyes with mine. "He's dead."

"Dead?" I was in an immediate state of panic and fear. This couldn't be happening. I assumed Molly would find him tied to the chair. This wasn't good.

"How?"

Maldonado studied my reaction. He could see how anxious I was. Maybe it was because my palms were sweaty and I repeatedly rubbed them on my jeans. It could also be the look of utter fear on my face.

"Somebody shot him; bullet to the center of his forehead. Sound familiar?"

"Whew!" I said, relieved. My hand went to my mouth seconds after I said it.

"Excuse me?"

"Sorry, I didn't mean that the way it sounded." Shot in the center of the forehead, just like Jillian.

"Funny thing though," Maldonado said, after getting over the shock of my reaction. "When officers arrived at the scene, they found Mr. Miles dressed in his underwear, duct-taped to a chair. And whoever was crazy enough to do that kept him quiet by stuffing one of his socks in his mouth."

I know my face turned red because it felt like I was having a hot flash. I was relieved to hear I wasn't responsible for his death. But if I admitted taping him to the chair, I'd be the number one suspect. After weighing the options, I knew I couldn't lie to Maldonado.

"I'm the one who taped him to the chair and put the sock in his mouth." Now, I was concerned about what I had done, even though it felt good. Would he still be alive if I didn't confine him?

Maldonado already knew I was responsible. I don't know how he knew, but he did. I could tell he was relieved to hear me admit it, though.

"You know what girl," he said, giving me one of those looks like I used to receive from my father when I did something stupid. "You've just gone plain crazy."

"So it appears," I said, looking down at my hands, hiding the humiliation in my eyes. I was bothered by Maldonado being upset, more than I was about what I did to Thomas Miles. "But he really pissed me off."

"I know you didn't shoot him," he said, shaking his head and trying to suppress a grin. "But what you did was still stupid."

I nodded in agreement, feeling completely chastised. "Any word on the bullet yet?"

"Too early in the investigation."

"Would I be pushing it if I asked to be

notified when they have that information?"

"Yes, but that won't stop you." At least he was grinning when he said it.

During college, Jillian always said I would be a talented investigator because of my insistence on knowing everything and pushing until I got the information. Relentless, she called me. While I was thinking about it, another thought occurred to me.

"How'd you know about my connection to Thomas Miles?"

He shrugged. "When the officers informed me that someone killed an attorney in his office and mentioned his name, I noticed it on your list of license plates. Besides, when they told me how they found him, I immediately thought of you. You've been through a lot. Sounds like you're fighting back."

Lucky for me, he was smiling when he said it.

"I need to see that list," I said. "I wasn't aware I gave you a license plate number for Thomas Miles." His wife only told me about the Porsche which I had been following. Maybe the corvette that was parked behind The Tapestry was his?

"If the officers know I was in Miles' office, I must be on their list of suspects."

Maldonado shuffled through the papers on his desk until he came up with the information on the plates and handed the sheet to me. "You're lucky. A buddy of mine is in charge of the investigation. When he needs to speak to you, I'll arrange it. He will have questions. He might want to know what you have on the guy. If you write everything down and email it to me, I can get it to him."

"I won't be able to give him everything." The last thing I needed was to give the info to another cop I didn't know. Especially since some of their own were in the photographs. Still, I would have to give them something. Maybe I would be lucky enough to wrap the case up before then; then they could have it all.

"I noticed two men going into the building when I left Thomas Miles."

Maldonado looked at me with interest.

"I didn't get a look at their faces, and I had no way of knowing they were going to his firm," I said. "There are four floors in the building. Thomas Miles' secretary was there. Maybe she got a look at them."

"They have her in the interview room now," he said. "She was the one who phoned it in."

"Oh." Poor Molly, I thought.

"You realize his wife is a suspect."

"Spouse usually is."

"They said they haven't been able to locate her. Do you know where she is?"

"Her secretary said she took a few days off. I haven't been able to reach her either."

That gave him pause. "Think she's good for it?"

I knew Maldonado would keep anything I said confidential, so I didn't hesitate to tell him what I thought. "She has motive and the anger to do so. Her reasons for hiring me were valid, only she seems to be incognito now that I got the goods, which makes me highly suspicious. But she also has a lot to lose with a prestigious modeling agency. Either way, I'm not sure I'd peg her as the shooter."

Maldonado nodded. "Doesn't mean she didn't hire somebody."

We agreed there. I rose out of my seat. "Thanks for getting the plate info for me."

"No problem, but do me a favor."

"What's that?"

"Stay out of trouble," he implored. "Dead bodies keep turning up around you lately."

"Yeah, what's up with that?" I said.

"I'll let you know when you can repay me for the plate numbers."

"I can't wait."

"Oh, and by the way, keep me and Finn up to date on anything new you find."

I nodded, hoping Maldonado wouldn't catch onto the fact that I was already withholding information. I also didn't mention I believed whoever killed Jillian might also be responsible for the death of Thomas Miles. He probably considered that already. It wasn't just because they were both killed with a direct hit to the forehead. There were too many coincidences linking the two cases. We don't believe in coincidences.

Bullet points:

Sarah Miles hired me to investigate her husband.

A day later, someone killed Jillian.

Evidence sent to me by Jillian showed Thomas Miles in a photograph.

They killed Thomas Miles.

Definitely connected; I just need to find the missing link.

CHAPTER 39

AFTER LEAVING MALDONADO'S office, I walked back to the lobby and sat down in one of the guest seats to look through the license plate info. I wanted to compare the list of names Howard Moore gave me of attendees to his party, to the names from the license plate list. It would be interesting to see how many ended up on both.

First thing I noticed: Thomas Miles was the registered owner of the Corvette parked behind The Tapestry. Jessica Carter was the registered driver. Her number was on Sarah's phone bill. Why was he the owner of a car she was driving?

Another thing that piqued my interest and I wondered if Maldonado noticed it as well; the Mach-E that I suspected was an undercover vehicle belonged to Nauset Bay P.D. Why would an unmarked vehicle park at The Tapestry, and the cop go inside? It occurred to me that Finn might know the answer to that question.

The list also showed that the black Range Rover, with the three goons inside, was registered to Mateo Ortiz from New York. Sounded like a Hispanic name. So, what would a group of New Yorkers be doing at The Tapestry on Cape Cod? Two of which took shots at us. Were they branching out into fresh territory?

While looking through the list, a few thoughts went through my mind. On the off-chance I was correct, I grabbed my cell phone. When I started the investigation for Sarah Miles, I had Roger run a background on The Miles Modeling Agency. In retrospect, I should have had him run a check on Thomas Miles, an individual. I remembered him asking if his partner hired me, which led me to believe he was in trouble with his law partnership. Using my intuition, I called Roger.

"Hey Katie, what's up?"

"I need you to run two names for me. I've got a theory I'm trying to follow up on."

"What are they?"

"Thomas Miles, an individual; and also run a check on Callahan, Miller & Miles; a limited partnership."

"When do you need the info?"

"Yesterday," I said, hoping he'd take the hint.

"Do you want me to email it?"

"That would be great. Thanks, Roger."

"You got it."

Next, I placed a call to The Tapestry. When Tracy Donovan answered, I pretended to be an associate of Howard Moore and asked to speak with the owner. Tracy was more than helpful, which proved to me that my suspicion was correct: Howard Moore had clout at the facility. She said the owners were not in, and that she would leave a message for one of them to get back to me. It surprised me to learn there was more than one owner, but all I could do was leave a fictitious name and see who phoned me back.

When I disconnected, my phone pinged, signaling I had an email: the report I asked for from Roger.

The report for Callahan, Miller & Miles showed nothing of significance that would alert me to any financial troubles of the firm. They had several outstanding loans, but they weren't in arrears on any of them, and had an excellent credit rating, until recently. There wasn't any way to verify if there was any cause and effect related to the firm's partnership with Thomas Miles.

His report painted a different picture. He was in debt up to his eyeballs. The Corvette and Porsche were both leased and behind in payments. He defaulted on several credit cards. And several personal loans were outstanding. The document didn't show him owning any real estate, which meant the house belonged to Sarah. The black SUV that was parked in the garage didn't appear on the report, which meant it also belonged to Sarah.

I found myself wondering how many personal loans Thomas Miles had outstanding that originated from someone other than a bank, like maybe a loan shark. That was just speculation, but it could have something to do with why goons from New

York were hanging around. There still had to be more. They wouldn't have killed Jillian because of the debt of Thomas Miles. But why was he in debt? He was a senior partner at a law firm, which meant at least a six-figure income. What was he spending his money on? If it was just about regular bills, he could have gone to his wife for help, unless his reasons for having financial trouble were illegal. If they were, then maybe he didn't want to involve her, which meant he had to find another avenue for money.

According to Howard Moore, he was the associate who supplied the entertainment for his fundraiser. Women being supplied as entertainment would fall under the category of escorts, prostitution, or high-class call girls. If Thomas Miles supplied them for money, it had to be a lot of money. Yet, he was still in debt. And he obviously had a drug problem? Was he just a middle man supplying the entertainment? Seeing Thomas Miles in action, that seemed more likely. He was just the low man on a totem pole.

I went around and around with my thoughts, but still came up with the same answer: something was missing. I just couldn't put my finger on it. By viewing the photographs, it appeared there were a lot of guests who attended the fundraiser at Howard Moore's house. They had to know about the drugs and sexual exploits. So why would somebody kill Jillian because she took some telling photographs? Did something prevent every other person who attended the party from talking about the escapades? Did something happen at the party that only Jillian knew about? Was Jillian the only one who knew about the teenage girls?

Maybe the senator or one of the public officials didn't want photos floating around depicting despicable behavior. Or maybe the answer isn't in the photos, but the DVDs? People did crazy things when they thought they were going to get caught. Maybe one of them thought their career and life as they knew it was going to be ruined. Would they kill to keep that from happening? Should I pay a visit to the Senator or the public officials?

Every time I analyzed the situation, my thoughts returned to The Tapestry. Something told me the answers were there. I needed to get inside the building again and do a more thorough search. How could I do that during normal working hours? I definitely couldn't go in pretending to be a call girl. With my luck, I'd get locked in a room with a John. I would blow my cover when the guy ran out of the room screaming that I shot his balls off.

If getting inside during working hours was out of the question, I'd have to go in after hours. That meant taking a quick drive to city hall. When I walked in, I gave the clerk the address of The Tapestry.

"Can you get me the paperwork on the building, including the floor plan?"

After her search was complete, I pulled out some cash and asked her to make me a copy.

Back in the car, I studied the documents. It showed the original layout of the building and the significant renovations that were added. What I couldn't find was the existence of a basement. That told me the owners didn't want anyone to know it existed. Why not? The document also showed when they purchased the property, the selling price, and how much the owner paid in taxes each year. The only thing the document didn't tell me was the individual identities of the owners; it only listed the name of the LLC. That wasn't unusual. Wealthy individuals placed their real estate in a corporation or trust. It was safe business. Add in all the other circumstances, especially a hidden basement; I couldn't help but take notice.

My phone buzzed during the drive home. I clicked the phone icon. "Hello," I said, surprised when I noticed Sarah Miles' name showed up on the screen.

"Hi Katie, this is Sarah Miles," she said. "I'm sorry for not getting back to you sooner. I had an emergency with my mother and had to go out of town."

"I'm just glad to hear you're okay," I said. "A lot has happened."

"I'm aware. The police notified me about the death of my husband. I just left the station a few moments ago."

"They questioned you?"

"They did. I provided my alibi."

"Good."

"Obviously, you can stop investigating my husband, since the matter is no longer important."

"I already completed the investigation and put together the final report," I informed her. "I can mail it to you if you prefer."

"You can send it to my office," she said, without emotion. "And send the last bill. Thank you for your time, Katie."

"I'll get that right out."

She disconnected without another word. The whole phone call had me puzzled. The woman who was so anxious about her future only a few days before had everything just fall into place. I don't know why, but my gut's intuition ran into overdrive.

CHAPTER 40

SARAH'S CASE WAS wrapped up since somebody killed her husband, but Jillian's was far from over. I was determined to find out who killed her, and why. The police didn't have a clue, yet. If they knew about The Tapestry, they weren't sharing. And I still felt duty-bound to investigate myself.

I made myself a quick meal and read through my notes. After, I cleaned up the mess and went to take a quick shower. Once I finished, I dressed in an old pair of jeans, a long-sleeve black sweatshirt, and a pair of black cross-trainers. I put on my gun belt, added my gun to the holster, and hooked my cell phone to it, but switched it to vibrate to avoid the phone buzzing at an inopportune time. As I headed toward the door, I placed my camera equipment and jackknife inside my backpack and then grabbed the keys off the counter.

When I drove along Casper Road and took a quick pass by The Tapestry, I noticed cars packed the circular drive, the alley, and along the street as well. I recognized some cars; the usual customers were taking care of business inside. Once I found a spot to park that wouldn't draw any attention, I did a little recon by walking the perimeter. I returned to the vehicle an hour later, and prepared myself for the long wait.

It was two a.m. when the last male visitor left the premises, and The Tapestry finally closed for business. Tracy Donovan left hours earlier. Now, I was waiting for Jessica to get into the corvette and leave. On days when I did surveillance, she was the first to arrive. Seeing she was also the last to leave, I assumed she was probably management, allowing the owners to keep a low profile. It could also explain why Thomas Miles was the registered owner of a vehicle she was driving. Another hour later, Jessica left the facility.

I suspected the local P.D. would drive through the area during the night, so I pulled onto a side street, further away from the building. Residents had stickers on the windows of their cars, so my vehicle could get ticketed, but they wouldn't tow it, thinking I was visiting someone. And, my car being further away wouldn't draw unnecessary attention to The Tapestry.

To be incognito to some extent, I pulled my blonde hair back into a ponytail and put on a black baseball hat. Then I slipped into a pair of gloves, grabbed my tools, and walked the streets toward the alley. When I reached the back door, I searched the area to make sure there wasn't anyone lurking nearby. I grabbed my pen light and jackknife and prepared to work the lock when I heard movement. My eyes searched the alley again. That's when I noticed something moving in my peripheral view. A dark figure started toward me. Sensing danger, I reached for my gun. The figure didn't stop.

"Don't come any closer," I ordered, keeping the gun aimed in that direction.

"Katie, it's me," a male voice said.

I looked hard at the figure as it closed in on me. "Finn, what the hell are you doing here? You scared me to death."

He glanced down at the drawn weapon and gave me a sardonic grin. "I can see that."

"What are you doing sneaking around out here?"

His smile unnerved me. "Hmmm, I'm not the one carrying a jackknife. I thought you might need some help."

"Help with what?"

Finn moved me to the side and prepared to pick the lock. "You just going to stand there gawking or help me by shining some light on the door? I can't see the damn thing."

I pulled my penlight out and did as he suggested. "How did you know I was here?"

He gave me another wise-ass grin. "I took over where Lopez and Johnson failed."

"You've been following me?"

"Just today," he said, but his response sounded iffy. "Maldonado was worried about you after your shenanigans with Thomas Miles. That was insane, by the way."

"I don't think he meant for you to join in

my escapades. Won't this get you into trouble?"

"Not if we find something to make him happy."

I heard the distinct click of the lock and verified there was no one around before Finn opened the door.

"And they say police officers never cross the line. Hah," I teased.

With the door slightly ajar, we could see enough using the penlight to guide us. But I realized Finn seemed to know his way around. It dawned on me that his case definitely involved The Tapestry. I kept the knowledge to myself for the moment.

"So, what are you looking for?" he whispered.

"I don't know exactly."

He eyed me with curiosity. "Good to know you have a plan."

"That's kind of the way this P.I. gig has gone from the get-go."

He walked towards the front of the building, while I browsed through the kitchen. Again, I realized how easily he moved through the hall with little light.

"They used the kitchen earlier in the evening," I said. "There are still pans soaking in the sink."

"If you don't know what you're looking for, what's your take on this place?" Finn asked, looking through a receptionist post.

"Easy version; I think it operates as a high-class brothel?"

"And the hard version?"

"I think there are underage teenagers and young women involved against their will."

His head whipped around to glare at me from where he stood. I couldn't see him very well, but I could feel it. "Are you shittin' me?"

I knew that knowledge would strike a chord with Finn, but I gathered he already knew it was a brothel, just not about unwitting victims.

He started opening doors by punching in a combination of numbers instead of picking the locks. How did he know that information? Once he concluded searching through several rooms, he returned to my location. "They've got seven bedrooms off the hall; each one designed like an exotic location."

"Maybe they're fulfilling some sort of fantasy?"

"When we make the arrests, I will ask," he joked.

"Finn, is this joint part of your current investigation?"

Either he didn't hear me, or purposely ignored the question. He opened another door and went inside. "Come check this one out."

I joined him. The room was enormous, and looked like it belonged in a resort, instead of a sex club on Cape Cod. There was a wall-to-wall mahogany bar with mega-bucks liquor. They set a lavish casino up with tables for poker, blackjack, roulette, and slot machines. The large flat-screen TVs were for those interested in gaming opportunities and cages hung from the ceilings that held dancers to entertain the crowd. There was a stone fire-pit built into the center of the room, surrounded by a circular sofa. One section of the room had oversized chairs positioned in front of a platform.

I had an immediate sense of déjà vu and felt nauseous. In the videos I viewed, they forced teenagers to walk the platform like specimens on display to be auctioned off for the evening. Taking it all in, I kept going back to the thought that whoever owned The Tapestry spent an enormous amount of money to design and furnish the facility. Everything was new and top of the line.

"Well, it may be a brothel trafficking victims," I said. "But it sure is a high-class facility that obviously makes huge money."

"No problem, we've got a high-class jail cell waiting for the proprietors."

Cop humor.

"Whoever put up the money to design and decorate this place must have known they'd recoup their losses and profit as well."

"Katie, there's a lot of money to be made in the sex trade and illegal gambling."

"Is that what you're investigating, illegal gambling?"

Finn gave me a deadpan stare. I got the message not to push. The last thing I wanted to do was to interfere with his investigation, as long as he didn't interfere or obstruct me from completing my goal.

"Okay, Katie," he said, looking around the room once more. "We've checked the entire first floor and didn't find any usable evidence. What else you got?"

I stared at him. He knew I had something that he didn't, that's why he's here? "We didn't check the basement."

I thought his eyes were going to pop out of their sockets from the shock. "What basement?"

I cocked my head to the side. "Oh, you didn't know?"

"Show me," he said. He shut the door to the casino room, and I led him back through the kitchen. When I opened the pantry door, I walked inside and let out an audible gasp, disheartened.

"They blocked the door."

Finn stepped into the room. "What do you mean?"

I used my pen light and examined the space where I found the seams earlier.

"They nailed sheets of paneling from floor to ceiling and wall to wall, blocking the door that leads to a basement."

Finn glared at me. "And just how do you know there's a door behind that paneling?"

I averted my eyes. "I found it when I was in here earlier."

Finn shook his head. "So, this isn't your first time breaking in?"

"I pretended to be a building inspector when I came inside earlier."

He shook his head. "We'll talk about your dangerous escapades later. Right now, we need evidence. If you're right about the door, the owner is going to great lengths to hide it. But why now, if you noticed it earlier?"

While he stood there dumbfounded, I went in search of a hammer and went about removing the nails. "Well, are you just going to stand there babbling, or help me remove the nails?"

He looked at me, stunned, probably wondering how I got to be so brazen.

"What do you think they're trying to hide in a basement?"

"Well, if you'd help, we'd find out."

Finn smiled, grabbed the hammer out of my hand, and finished removing the nails. Then, together, we removed the two thick sheets of paneling it took to cover the wall. I placed my hand behind the food and felt along the wall, as I did during my earlier visit. I pressed down when I found the metal button. The door slid open. I pointed the penlight down a spiral staircase that stepped down into a wide hall with closed doors on each side. We looked at each other and headed down.

Once we reached the bottom, we looked at the plush surroundings, stunned.

Imported Italian marble tiles covered the stairs, floor, and walls.

"There was major planning and design preparations when putting this brothel together. These floors are not only exquisite but damned expensive. These guys couldn't be amateurs."

"No shit!"

I studied the floors again; I'd seen them before. They were the same Italian marble floors in Howard Moore's home. The scumbag was in this up to his eyeballs.

I moved toward the first door to the right, turned the knob, and pointed the penlight inside when it opened. It was a huge laundry room. There were six washing machines on one side and six dryers on the other. At the end of the room, they had two ironing boards built into the wall, along with built-in shelves, where they stored the laundry paraphernalia.

"Nothing useful in this room," I said, but wondered if they used the laundry room for more than cleaning the sheets and blankets. Did someone stay on site?

Finn opened the next door and stepped into a second kitchen. It was smaller than the one on the main floor, but they equipped it with similar appliances, with a farmer's table in the center of the room and ten chairs around it. He strode toward the dishwasher and placed his hand on top of it.

"They used this room earlier too," he said. "Dishwasher's still warm."

The next door opened to an oversized, yet modern bathroom with several private stalls and showers.

A door directly across from the bathroom turned out to be an elevator. On impulse, I hit the up arrow. The metal doors opened, and we stepped inside. It was so quiet; we didn't realize it was moving. When the doors opened, Finn pulled a satin curtain aside, showing we were in the casino room again. The surprised look on his face told me he didn't know about the elevator either, even though he'd been here before. We closed the curtain and went back down, ready to resume our evidence search.

There were two doors left. One was locked and bolted. It would take time to pick the locks, so we checked the other one first. The most glaring thing we noticed was the king-size bed and expensive video equipment set up opposite it. Built-in bookcases with doors covered an entire wall. A studio entertainment system and a humongous flat-screen television took up another wall. I entered the room, walked toward the video equipment, and checked to see if there was a video inside. I had another feeling of déjà vu. The two women who had affairs with my ex-husband had the habit of filming their sexual liaisons. The one who stalked me felt the need to share them with me.

"What is this room?"

Finn gave me a look of sympathy. "You don't recognize it?"

I took another look around and it hit me like a punch to the gut. I had seen the room before. "Oh no," I said. "It was the room depicted in the other video Jillian sent me."

Finn nodded.

It horrified me to know I was standing in the same room where they abused a teenage girl. Something else donned on me as I walked toward the bookcase. "Finn, this door has a deadbolt. If they went to the trouble, there has to be something inside they don't want us to see."

He joined me and checked out the lock. "Let's find out." He picked the lock, a move that would have taken me a few minutes.

As soon as he opened the doors, we knew we hit the jackpot. Finn looked at me, but neither of us smiled. This wasn't something to celebrate. The left side of the bookcase had shelves fully stocked with DVD cases of videos, each one of them labeled with the name of a female.

"Must be the female with the starring role," Finn said cynically.

While he was busy looking over the DVDs, I opened the right door. The top section was more shelves of DVDs, but they had male names. Three drawers made up the lower half. I opened the top drawer and started rifling through it, patting the sides for pockets.

"This is bizarre," I said, pulling out a set of papers and reading through them.

"What is it?"

"A set of dummy records." I showed him several pages. "If anyone came in to question the business, and didn't have access to the rooms to know the truth, these records would give the illusion the business was a legitimate dating service. A legal professional could tell they were fake, but not a random Joe."

I put it back where I found it and opened the second drawer. As I searched it and patted the sides, I stumbled upon a secret wall in the back. I pulled the false wall down and retrieved a book that looked like a typical journal one could buy at the local store. Once I opened it and scrolled a few pages, I got so excited I pulled Finn close and planted a deep, passionate kiss on his lips.

"Damn girl," he teased when I stopped. "Don't start what you can't finish."

"This is too good to be real," I said. "These look like the actual records for the company, showing all the transactions. Whoever was in charge was stupid or meticulous. Every transaction that transpired in the last year has been documented."

"They can't be that stupid." Finn viewed the pages over my shoulder. "Wholly shit! Names, dates, type of transaction, and how much? Katie, this is unbelievable. There's enough in here to bring the entire place down. Who would be so foolish?"

I got quiet as a couple of points hit me: to be that foolish almost seemed deliberate, and then there was the reality. "Finn, it doesn't matter if they were stupid. We can't use them. We came in here illegally. You didn't have a warrant."

Finn raked his hands through his hair, frustrated. But then his lips curved into a smile. "No, I can't use them. But now that we know the evidence is here, we can get a warrant. This is not over."

Even before we found the records, I knew what this place was about from my surveillance of Thomas Miles. It was Sarah Miles' phone records that led me here, but how I got here wasn't important. With what we found, there was enough to bring the place down if he came through with the warrant. But that still didn't solve the question of who killed Jillian, and that was important to me. It might not be Finn's priority, but it was mine. I also had a DVD of a teenager being abused. And photos of several others, who I assumed were being abused as well. And possibly still were. So something had to be done. It was critical to find out the identity and whereabouts of the girls, and I was sure that's why Jillian sent me the information, which got me thinking about something else.

Jillian sent me photographs of events that occurred at the fundraiser at her father's house. But they filmed the videos she kept in the safe deposit box at The Tapestry. How did Jillian know about them, figure out what was going on, and then get inside to get the evidence to pass on to me? She didn't have the skills to break in or pick a lock. Hell, the only reason I had the skills was because Derek taught me. What drew her to the location?

An unnerving feeling settled in the pit of my stomach as ugly thoughts whirled back and forth in my head. I glanced toward the shelves of DVDs. They were all labeled in alphabetical order. I followed my intuition and scrolled through the names. My heart sank when I found three of them with Jillian's name on the front. With shaky hands, I forced myself to retrieve one and looked toward the entertainment system.

Finn eyed me with curiosity. "Katie, what are you doing?"

"Following my intuition," I said. I removed the DVD from the case, turned on the TV and DVD player, and slipped the DVD into the machine. Once it loaded, I hit play.

My fists clenched at my sides as I watched Jillian's face fill up the screen. She was a teenage girl, but I knew that face anywhere. She wore jean cut-offs, a t-shirt, and her gorgeous hair fell down the center of her back. I noticed the glassy eyes and droopy lids, which convinced me they drugged her. And just like the video showing the other teenager, Jillian followed the instructions of The Teacher. Again, he wouldn't show his face as he stepped into view. But he appeared younger here and thinner with longer hair. And his voice wasn't as deep as it was in the other video. I suddenly felt a deep sadness like I'd never known. The Teacher had been grooming innocent teenagers for years.

Finn wrapped his arm around me. "Jillian?"

I nodded. "Now I know why she disappeared out of my life. She didn't want me to know this about her."

He stopped the video before it played all the way through and held me to stop me from shaking.

"Finn, I might never find out the truth about Jillian, whether they abducted her or her father allowed her to be trafficked. But she was trying to stop it. That's why she sent me the evidence. She couldn't continue to stand by while teenagers and young women were being abused. Even when she knew her life was in danger, she followed through."

Finn nodded. "She doesn't want others to go through what she did."

I nodded, sobbing and crying into his shoulder as he held tight.

After several minutes, he withdrew his comfort. "You okay? We better wrap things up, we've been inside a long time."

I nodded.

Finn took the DVD out of the machine, slipped it back into the case, and put it in its designated spot on the shelf. I went to put the documents back in the secret compartment. When I tried to close the drawer, something blocked its path. I tried to glide the drawer back and forth, thinking it just got off the track. When that didn't work, I pulled the whole drawer out as far as I could. I heard it catch, which meant it would not come out all the way.

"This is not good," I said, agitated.

"What's going on?"

"Something is blocking the drawer. If I can't get it closed, they'll know somebody was in here."

Finn took over from where I failed, trying to force the drawer closed. When he ran into the same problem, he forced his hand back behind the drawer and felt around.

"There's a damn envelope blocking it," he said, gloating when he pulled it out and handed it to me.

The envelope was laser designed on the front, which made me curious. While he maneuvered the drawer back in place, I opened it and viewed what was inside.

"I don't believe this," I said.

Finn joined me. "What now?"

Gritting my teeth, I said, "There's going to be another party, similar to the one in the photographs."

He looked at me for confirmation. "You mean the big wigs-type?"

"The current owner wants to introduce their new partners," I said.

"And I guess you know who that owner is?" he said, looking at me sideways.

"Only lists the corporation, SJM. The new partners are the Ortiz brothers."

"Who the hell are the Ortiz brothers?"

"The goons who tried to take us out," I said, getting ready to duck from the daggers that were sure to come my way, once he found out I knew.

"What the hell did you say?" Finn said, angry that I kept that info from him.

I ignored his mini outburst while I tried to think things through. The New Yorkers teaming up with the current owners put a new spin on things. That brought up an interesting thought: how did they decide how much the brothel was worth to discuss finances with new partners? How did they decide how much the call girls were worth? I looked through the documents to find out when the party was happening.

"Damn," I said when I found the information I was looking for. "The party is tonight." Inside the laser-designed envelope, there were laser-designed invitations. I grabbed several and waved them in the air at Finn. "And we just got invited."

"What's with the new, living dangerous persona you're adopting?" he said, shaking his head at me.

"They want to welcome the new partners," I said. "We're going to be here when they do. It's invitation-only, and the guests have to wear masks. They won't know who we are."

It still annoyed Finn that I didn't tell him about the three goons. But he saw the upside to us being at The Tapestry during a party with most of the players on the premises. The thought of a legal bust made him cave in and relent. "Guess I'll finally get you out of those jeans," he finally said, leaning in and planting his own kiss. When we parted, I tasted the cinnamon on my lips. I smiled. A possible big bust was about to go down, and Finn's mind instantly went to getting me out of my jeans.

We put everything away as we found it and locked the door. Once we were back in the hall, I glanced at the last door that we didn't check. If we stayed longer, we could get caught. Besides, I didn't think we'd find anything that could top what we already found. I put it to the back of my mind but hoped I could check them out later when everyone was occupied at the party.

Back in the pantry, we put the sheets of paneling back in place. Made sure the rooms were exactly as they were when we arrived and locked up on the way out. Finn and I parted ways once he made sure I made it to my car. He had to get back to the station to work on Maldonado about getting a warrant. I wanted to be a fly on the wall and watch him squirm when he tried to explain how he knew about the evidence and figure out how they could use it as probable cause.

CHAPTER 41

"YOU WANT US to gatecrash a party?" Madison said with a stunned look on her face. She placed an aluminum tray with one of her homemade calzones down on a table I placed in the center of the two leather sofas in the RV.

Olivia followed with paper plates and napkins and handed me one.

The two of them arrived early that morning and I already filled them in on everything that was going on. I smiled at Madison. "Wasn't it you who told me she wanted to be a little more adventurous?"

"You did say that," Olivia said, smiling at her.

The two of them put a cut slice of calzone on their plates, grabbed a napkin, and sat down on the sofa opposite me.

Nervous laughter escaped Madison's lips. "I meant something like enjoying the scenery of exotic men on our upcoming cruise, wearing a daring color and showing more cleavage, or allowing myself to be a little carefree with my money at the casinos. Not in my wildest dreams would I have thought I'd be going to an event at a brothel. I wouldn't know what to wear. What *do you* wear to a brothel?"

That response made me laugh. "Choose a daring color and reveal some cleavage," I teased. "You'll be a hit."

"I have nothing to wear either," Olivia said.

"It's formal," I said. "All three of us will need something. We'll need masks too."

"I like that idea," Olivia said, smiling. "I'm wearing purple." She said the same thing when we discussed the premier for the TV series for my book, Before She Knew, recently purchased and currently in production.

The room was quiet while we devoured the calzone. After we finished eating, I cleaned up the mess, grabbed my backpack, and rejoined them.

"We're not technically going to gatecrash," I said, handing them each a ticket that I confiscated from the basement.

"Sonsabitches," Olivia said, using one of her favorite words. "How did you get your hands on an invitation to a brothel?"

"There might have been a little breaking and entering involved," I said, sheepishly. "But I may have had some help."

Madison raised her eyebrows. "Finn helped you? But he's a police officer?"

I nodded. "Hence the reason for us to go back in using the invitations, and hopefully, Detective Maldonado gets the approval for the warrant. Until then, we'll just have to blend in and act as if we're supposed to be there."

"Oh sure, all three of us know what it's like to be a skilled sex worker in a brothel," Olivia said sarcastically. "We'll fit right in."

"Will it be dangerous?" Madison asked.

"What's an adventure without a little danger?" I teased. "To be frank, I have a purpose for getting inside. But Finn will be there with us."

"He'll be there to protect your body. Who protects ours," Madison said.

"Do you want your own Finn?"

She gave me a devilish smile. "Can I?"

I couldn't tell if she was serious or not.

"Nauset Bay's finest is currently working on a warrant," I said, hoping to put her at ease. "If they're not on the premises when we arrive, they should be shortly after. Though I suspect they'll keep a low profile and not come in guns blazing."

~~~

At seven o'clock that evening, a six-door Cadillac platinum limousine pulled up in the driveway. I stepped out of the RV wearing a fitted silver gown, a matching pair of sandals, and a sequined mask. My eyes and mouth were visible, but my identity was pretty well hidden. Finn stepped out of the back seat, looking roguish and handsome in his tuxedo and matching black mask. If I was the author of a romance novel, I'd put him on the cover.

"Will this suffice?" he teased with his lopsided grin which the mask didn't hide.

I gave him the once over, appraising him from head to toe. "It'll do," I said in return.

Hell yes, it'll do.

He extended his hand and returned the favor; devouring me with his eyes. "You look sensational."

"Thank you." I know I was blushing under the heat of his gaze.

He guided me toward the back seat and helped me inside. "Where's your gun?"

I pulled up the slit of my dress, showing the gun strapped to my upper right thigh, and a view of enough skin to make him sweat.

He smiled. "Nice." He was spending entirely too much time admiring the scenery.

"Finn, try to keep your mind focused on the job, will you?"

"That's going to be tough, the way you look tonight."

"Is Maldonado working on the warrant?"

"As we speak," Finn said, continuing to gaze at me in the dress. "One call from me, and the cavalry should be there."

"Good. Let's hope all the bad guys decide to make an appearance."

"Here, take this." He handed me a nude-colored earpiece, which I stuck inside my ear and draped my hair over it. "If we get separated and you run into trouble, hit the button to talk. Just like if you were answering a cell phone call."

Next, the limo pulled into Olivia's driveway, where she and Madison were also waiting out front. Finn stepped out and escorted them to join us.

"You ladies look magnificent!" I said when they stepped into the back and sat down opposite me.

They were both in long gowns, Olivia in purple, which brought out the color of her eyes, highlighted by the elegant glitter-designed purple and black butterfly mask with laser-cut wings on one side. Her long curls were up in a twist, with ringlets dangling down the sides of her face. She accessorized with her own custom jewelry, a pair of black sandals with thin straps, and a black satin purse.

Madison opted for a daring red satin gown with thin straps and a plunging neckline that nearly showed off her assets, except for the custom piece of jewelry Olivia designed just for this purpose. Her long, dark hair was straight, her bangs swept to the side to accommodate the exquisite black Venetian mask, and she wore a pair of black strapless sandals that matched her satin purse.

"Check out this car," Olivia said. "How'd you manage this?"

Finn rejoined us, opened a bottle of red wine, and poured us each a small amount. "The department is springing for the car, this monkey suit, and the bottle of wine. You don't want to drink too much, so you can keep your wits about you. But it won't hurt to have a little to stop the nerves."

"Is there anything we need to know before going to the party?" Olivia said, accepting the plastic cup of wine and taking a sip.

"Just be yourselves and stick together," I said. "We'll need to blend in and not draw any attention to ourselves."

Finn nodded in agreement. "Don't accept any drinks from strangers. If you order anything at the bar, watch the bartender pour it into the glass. Remember, not everyone that will be in attendance is a criminal or even knows what's going on, but those that do could be watching."

"Will anyone try to solicit us?" Madison asked, looking a little nervous, but looking forward to attending the party just the same.

Finn smiled. "No. Anything like that happening will only occur in private rooms after an auction and bid takes place."

I studied Finn. He seemed to know more about how the brothel operated than I assumed.

When the limo pulled onto Casper Road and we were less than minutes away, all three of us looked outside in stunned silence. It looked like we were arriving at a Hollywood movie premier. We pulled in behind other limousines and expensive cars entering the circular drive for The Tapestry. Men in white shirts, black vests, and pants greeted the guests, helped the women from the vehicles, and escorted them toward the hostess station, where they accepted invitations.

When it was our turn, Finn stepped out of the limo and helped the three of us exit, completely ignoring the hired men in vests there to escort us. He guided us toward the entrance to the building, handing over the four invitations to the hostess who I knew was Tracy Donovan from my surveillance, and led us inside where we were told to sign the guest book. I took a moment to peruse the list while signing an erroneous name and noticed some interesting guests on the list.

The puzzle pieces were coming to me. All I needed were the last pieces to complete it.

"Looks like they're all here," I said to Finn. With the guests that were in attendance, I was pretty sure I was going to complete it tonight. I wasn't sure what pieces Finn was looking for. Call me crazy, but I got the sense that The Tapestry had something to do with him missing in action from his undercover gig.

Olivia and Madison looked fascinated by all the beautiful people. They knew it was a brothel, but I didn't tell them that some players were big wigs. The Senator, Howard Moore, the public officials, the Ortiz brothers, and the cops that I knew were involved. They were all in attendance.

"The men all look so proper in their tuxedoes and smiles," Olivia said.

"And the women look like models," Madison added.

"So do you," Finn said, making Madison blush.

"Anyone that might recognize you?" Finn asked me, knowing I spoke to some players involved with The Tapestry.

"Yeah, quite a few," I said. "Having the mask helps. We should probably separate. It's easier to spot us if we're all together. Olivia, Madison; you two stay together, and try to enjoy yourselves."

As I walked away, Finn said, "Stay alert."

I nodded as I worked my way around the room, paying attention at each point of interest. Gorgeous men and women enjoyed expensive liquor at the bar. Women danced in cages, keeping the men entertained. The gambling was in full swing at the poker tables, blackjack, and the roulette wheel. It made me think of Finn. Did the illegal gambling have something to do with his case? Was that why he was here? Looking back at him, I noticed he was in a serious conversation with a few beautiful women. Studying them, it looked like they all knew each other, which confirmed my suspicion about The Tapestry being part of his case.

I roamed the room again to check up on Olivia and Madison and almost laughed out loud. Madison was drawing upon a few of her inner desires for adventure. One was enjoying the scenery of handsome men and the other was feeling free to spend more money at the casino.

Fulfilling both options; she and Olivia stood at one of the blackjack tables. Handsome men stood behind them, cheering them on. A pile of cash and rows of chips were in front of Madison, showing she was preparing to go big. From where I stood, I could see they were having a good time, despite where we were, and Olivia was acting as security for Madison's future winnings.

With my friends preoccupied, I got down to business and worked the crowd to get a feel for where the introduction of new partners was taking place.

When I made my way into the kitchen, I noticed Mateo Ortiz and his two brothers. Mateo was talking to someone, so I stood out of view and observed him for a few moments. There was something familiar about him. Yet, the only time I saw him was the day the three brothers paid a visit to the Tapestry, looking like they were there for a shakedown. The two brothers were alone when they took shots at me and Finn at the RV. So what was it about Mateo? After another minute, he made his way toward the pantry and motioned for his brothers to keep watch. That told me something was going down. Great! How was I going to get past the two goons?

I returned to where I last saw Finn, but he was gone now. I checked on Olivia and

Madison one more time. Madison was on a winning streak and enjoying the attention. I took a deep breath and headed back to the kitchen, trying to figure out how I was going to get past the goons.

CHAPTER 42

SOMEBODY TOOK CARE of the problem for me. A couple of scantily clad women had their full attention. I picked up on some of their conversation. Apparently, the women just recently had their breast implants put in, and they were eager to show them off, inviting anyone who was interested to verify they were as hard as they maintained. The Ortiz brothers were more than happy to comply as I watched from the sidelines. Since they were preoccupied, I secretly slipped into the pantry and down into the basement, with no one being the wiser.

All was quiet as I tip-toed through the hall. I bypassed the laundry room and crept toward the room with the video equipment. The door was closed, but as I approached, I heard talking inside. I couldn't distinguish between voices; didn't know who they were or what they were saying. Maybe they were having their own private party. While they were taking care of business, I chose that time to check out the last room that Finn and I had failed to open. I tucked my jackknife inside my bra before arriving at the party, so I retrieved it and went about picking the door lock and deadbolt. It took some time, and I was dripping in sweat by the time I heard the click.

I put the jackknife back in place and

cautiously opened the door. What I saw stopped me in my tracks. "Oh dear God," I said, immediately distraught.

The wall had a light switch, so I turned it on and removed my mask. I needed to verify what I was seeing and make sure I didn't just step into the middle of a nightmare. My imagination was conjuring up images. At the same time, I instinctively pulled my gun out of the thigh strap and closed the door behind me. My hands shook and my heart was pounding a mile a minute. I stood there frozen with fear and dread, and other things that I wasn't even aware I could feel.

There were several cots set up in the room, but they weren't empty. I forced my body to move, wanting to get a closer look at who was on the cots. I couldn't see their faces, but I knew who they were. And all I could think about was this stuff couldn't possibly be happening. Some things went on that everyone liked to keep quiet on Cape Cod, secrets and sin, but not this. It was just too sick. Standing next to the cots, I wanted to throttle the people who did this. There were eight victims; some teenagers, others young adults. Blankets covered them to keep them warm. The perpetrators secured them to the cots by handcuffing an ankle. And they covered their mouths with a strip of duct tape to keep them quiet during the night's event.

Tears were streaming down my face at

the horrific sight. The thought of the girls being held captive, and who knows for how long, kept the rage surging through me. The people who did this had to be held accountable. When I came to The Tapestry tonight, I hoped to find the last piece of the puzzle, but I didn't expect to find the girls. But it all made sense. Where else could they keep them?

While I struggled to get over the shock of seeing them defenseless and handcuffed, I noticed one of them opened her eyes. She looked at me with a look of fear, but curiosity at the same time. When she saw the gun in my hands, her body trembled and my heart broke, seeing the pure terror on her face.

"It's okay," I said as gently as I could. "I'm not here to hurt you."

I immediately put the gun back into the strap on my thigh to ease her fear. She looked to be about fifteen years old, with long brown hair and brown eyes. For a moment, I thought she was the girl I viewed in the video, but even though there were similarities, it wasn't the same girl. I did a cursory inspection of her. Except for being bound to a bed—and god knows what else she suffered physically—she still appeared to be in good health.

"I'm going to remove the tape from your mouth. Is that okay?"

She slowly nodded.

As gently as I could, I pulled the duct tape off and watched her move her lips.

I whispered, "What's your name?" I stroked her hair to reassure her she was safe from me.

When she spoke, her voice was so soft that I had to bend over to hear her, and I detected an accent. "Svetlana."

"Are you hurt?"

She looked like the tears were going to fall, but she shook her head no.

"Where are you from?"

"New York."

New York? How the hell did these scumbags get a child here from New York? They couldn't get her on a commercial plane? Did they drive? I hated to put her through this, but I needed to know. "Who brought you here, Svetlana?"

Her body trembled. "The teacher," she said, visibly crying now.

I put my arms around her to let her know she'd soon be safe. "You're okay now. I won't let anyone hurt you again."

"They said they bought me," she uttered through muffled cries, "and I had to pay back the money."

It was exactly what I had feared. I'd heard stories about children being purchased, and then trafficked and made to do despicable things to pay off their debt. There was no debt, it was just brainwashing and grooming. But never in a million years would I think it would be a part of my world. "Do you know the teacher's name?"

Even though I had my suspicions.

She shook her head no. "We were told to always call him the teacher."

"Do you know how long you've been here?"

She was shaking her head. "I don't know."

"Okay, I'm going to get someone to help me, and then I'll get all of you out of here."

She nodded, but kept her eyes on me, hoping I wouldn't walk back out the door, leaving them here once again.

"Finn, I hope you're listening," I said, tapping on the earpiece in my ear. "I need your help down in the basement." I had no way of knowing if he could hear me.

She kept her eyes on me and must have assumed I was talking to myself. I checked the other girls and young women for injuries. They were all still asleep, which I found odd that they didn't wake from the noise. Maybe the scumbags forced them to take a tranquilizer? So how did Svetlana wake up? I turned around to ask when I noticed her expression changed and her eyes went wide. She pulled the blanket up and I could instantly see the fear. I cautiously turned around to see what was making her terrified, and that's when it happened.

It was instantaneous, leaving me with no chance to react. A rag with a foul-smelling substance covered my nose and mouth.

Another arm wrapped around me, holding my arms in place.

"You think you're so smart?" a male voice hissed into my ear. "Trying to take us on was a mistake, Katie Parker—a big mistake. One more day, and we would have been out of it. You couldn't just wait one more day."

If I waited one more day, you would have gotten away, I thought to myself as my mind became fuddled. I tried to fight him off, using my feet. I slammed my heel down on his foot several times. Kicked his shins and knees, and tried to punch his groin. But my hands were immobile, and the smell was too intense and overpowering. It made me drowsy. I was losing the fight. My body was becoming limp and I couldn't control my limbs. I feared what would happen to the girls if I didn't get out of this. My body kept falling, with only this evil man to hold on to me. I looked at Svetlana, hoping to hang on and set her free, as I promised. I willed myself to keep fighting, but then everything went dark.

CHAPTER 43

I DON'T KNOW how long I was out, but my body felt like it went through a major trauma. I opened my eyes and looked around. It was dark, but the light from under the door let me see. It took me a moment to focus. My mind was murky. I was lying down, so I forced myself to sit up. When I did, the pain was immediate. My head was spinning. It felt like a time bomb was going to explode, or already did. They cuffed my hands in front of me. I realized I was on a cot in the same room with the girls. How long was I out?

I heard voices from somewhere outside the room. I couldn't hear everything they said, but I could tell they were trying to decide what to do with me. One person said they should just eliminate me. Another said they needed to know what I did with the evidence so they could tie up loose ends before leaving the country. The voices were muffled, but it sounded like three different males and one female.

I looked over at Svetlana. She was awake and watching me, terrified of what they were going to do. They recovered her mouth with the tape to keep her from speaking. They did the same to my ankles, but I could still move my legs. Odd that they didn't cover my mouth. They must need me to answer questions. My upper thigh felt bare.

Shit, they found my gun. I brought my hands up and felt my chest. Good, they didn't find the jackknife.

I started to speak to Svetlana, to let her know I was okay, when I heard the knob turning on the door. It opened and two men walked in: Officers Jimmy Smith and Larry Foley, both in plainclothes. My suspicions became a reality when I noticed Foley gloating over my capture.

The two officers had been friends for a few years. I did my research on them. Couldn't find much on Smith, but learned that Foley was a disgruntled cop after being turned down repeatedly for promotions. Derek told me about him. He met Foley when a former employee kidnapped and murdered his wife. Back then, there were rumors Foley discussed the ransom details with someone who ultimately got the info back to the kidnapper. Derek couldn't prove it, but he warned me to keep my distance. Other than Smith saying he didn't think I was qualified to be a P.I. I knew little about him.

"You killed Jillian," I said, fueled by anger I've never felt before as I glared back and forth at Smith and Foley. That was how Smith was on the scene so soon after the shots were fired. They did the deed.

When he smirked, I realized pure evil was looking back at me. He shrugged, as if Jillian's life had been meaningless. "She became an inconvenience," he said with absolutely no emotion in his voice.

I looked over at the teenagers and young women handcuffed to the cots next to me. "That's because she knew what you were doing, and she wanted it stopped!"

Foley stared at me with pure hatred. "It doesn't matter what you know. You won't survive this to talk about it."

"Why couldn't you just get rid of the evidence? Why did you have to kill her?"

"She sent you the evidence!" Foley barked so loud, that it made me jump.

I thought about all the evidence in my possession. Surely, what I had wouldn't be enough to bring them down? Not without the rest of what Finn and I found.

"She wanted to meet with you and tell you what she knew. She wouldn't shut up. She left us no alternative."

Was there something in the evidence she sent I didn't catch? Something so detrimental they had to kill her to keep it quiet? Something that they're now worried about that they need to know what I did with it? That's why the secrecy when she called me. She knew they were following her. That's how she knew she was going to die.

"Why did you have to kidnap and groom teenagers and innocent young women? You already had willing participants? Weren't there enough women to satisfy the clients?"

Foley smirked. "How do you think they

became willing? They didn't start that way. Besides, some of the well-paying clients had a fetish for the young and exotic."

"You have no soul or no regard for their lives," I spit at him. "You're talking about them as if they're nothing but slabs of meat."

Foley's laugh was menacing. "You know the saying," he said with a shrug that showed his narcissism, "money talks. There's big money to be made from innocence."

"You're sick."

This time, both men laughed, but it was maniacal.

Smith looked at me, his eyes roaming from head to toe, studying me as if he noticed me for the first time. "You still have a touch of innocence. I bet we could make a big money maker out of you, too."

Foley nodded. "Maybe we should keep her alive and put her to good use. Pay us back for all the trouble she caused."

Smith looked at me, long and hard. "As much as I'd enjoy that, we've got our orders. Besides, she'd just turn into another Jillian."

I bristled at what they were saying, and the thought that they stole the innocence of all their victims. But my reaction only encouraged them.

Foley gloated. "We gave these girls a better life than what they were living. They were destitute."

"You're drugging them, confining them to cots in a dungeon, and turning them into prostitutes, against their will."

They both shrugged and smirked. "They can earn their freedom, just like the others."

These people were pure evil. "And Thomas Miles; was he an inconvenience as well?"

Smith looked at Foley. "You could say he was collateral damage. His drug and sex addictions were interfering with the owners' plans."

"So you murdered Jillian because she knew what you were doing and Thomas Miles because he might disrupt the business?" I didn't know if I'd make it out of this, but I wanted as much information as I could get on the off-chance I did.

"You just don't get it," Smith mocked. "You really are a novice at this investigating gig."

"So enlighten me."

"When we showed up to off Miles, it didn't surprise us to see you leaving his office." Smith looked at Foley again, and they both laughed, but it was an evil laugh. "Seeing him tied up with duct tape and a sock stuffed in his mouth... let's just say that gave us a good laugh. It pleased our client as well."

So it was the two of them entering Thomas Miles' building when I was leaving it. "Your client?"

"How do you think we got involved in

this business?" Smith said, as if I should know the answer.

Foley smirked. "You think we took the girls? We had nothing to do with that. We're not predators. We're in it for the money. Who the hell can afford to retire on a cop's pension these days?"

"So you're the clean-up crew, paid thugs? It was you trashing Jillian's apartment?"

They didn't deny it.

"What were you hoping to gain by bugging the RV?"

"You ask too many questions!"

"So if I'm going to die, humor me." Although talking about my impending death didn't sit well with me.

"The owner knew Jillian would contact you. We were told to be there when she did."

"Why would the owner assume she'd contact me?" I asked, genuinely wanting to know. "We hadn't been in touch for years. I thought she forgot all about me."

"You were all over the news for going after a stalker," Smith said. "It revived her memory."

"Who is your client?"

Foley said, "Wouldn't you like to know?"

"In due time, my dear," Smith said.

Foley walked toward me. His tone was menacing. "In the meantime, why don't you tell us what you did with the evidence?"

"What evidence?"

Foley slapped me hard across the face. "Now is not the time to be cute."

It stung, but I wasn't going to let him know that. "Ten-year-old boys hit harder when I played tackle football as a kid," I said, even though I spit up blood when I uttered the words.

That pissed off Foley. I guess he had a sensitive ego. He slapped me again from the opposite side; my head felt like a ping-pong ball going back and forth.

"What's the big deal with the photos? I already know what you're up to. How can they hurt you now?"

Foley glanced at Smith and smirked. "She doesn't know."

"So let's not waste any more time on her," Smith said.

That got my attention. I was sure I saw everything in the photos. There was a party with lots of people. Was there something in the photos or the DVDs that I missed?

Foley stuck his face up to mine giving me a whiff of the Tequila he consumed just a short time before. "Where are they?"

I stuck my chin out and remained defiant.

He gave me a one-two punch in the gut. "What made you think you could go up against us, anyway? Jillian tried. Look what happened to her. I'm sure it shocked the shit out of her when she felt the bullet."

I snapped! It was like my father was

standing over me, yelling in my ear: "get your ass into gear girl," and it forced me into action. I had to defend myself. My feet were numb from my ankles being taped, but I pulled my knees toward me, trying to block the blows. Then, I let loose. I kicked Foley, hard, centering on his nose as a point of impact. With the force of the kick, it broke his nose. Blood gushed out.

I mocked them with my own wicked laugh. "How's it feel to be kicked by a girl?"

It only pissed them off more. I knew I was in trouble when I noticed the look on Smith's face.

He went ballistic. He rushed towards me, ready to take up where Foley left off. His face was beet-red, and the veins in his arms were bulging. He punched me in the stomach. I doubled over in pain. Then he went for the head.

"You can shake your little ass all you want. Maldonado and Finn aren't here to save you," Smith yelled. "They won't even recognize you by the time I'm done."

I was about to be beaten to a pulp, but all I could think about was getting the last word in. "So you're jealous of my hard ass? What's the matter, Foley checking me out more than you? I didn't know you two were a thing?"

I knew I'd just struck a chord. Using his fists, he went on the attack, with me trying to block every blow with my cuffed wrists.

There was blood, and the pain was immediate. It was agonizing. I believed what he said about nobody recognizing me. Suddenly, there was a crashing noise that rocked the building.

The noise was so loud that Smith turned toward Foley. "What the hell was that?"

"We better check it out," Foley said, still holding his nose. "We can't let anything disrupt the boss."

"We'll be back to finish this," Smith hissed at me. And he hit me one more time before they took off.

With them gone, I checked out his results. Blood was everywhere, making me look like I was straight out of a horror flick. The pain in my head multiplied. The dress would need to be trashed. But I had to put the pain aside and focus on other things. Svetlana bunched under the blanket, her body shaking uncontrollably. When the punching stopped, her petrified eyes slowly peaked out.

Amazingly, none of the others woke up and heard what was going on. I knew they were suffering from the aftermath of whatever drug they forced them to take, but I hoped it wasn't long-lasting.

Not knowing when Smith and Foley would return, I forced myself to spring into action. They battered my body, but I could maneuver my fingers into my breast. I retrieved the jackknife tucked in my bra and immediately set about getting free of the cuffs. Thankfully, it didn't take too long. I could not withstand another round with Smith without access to my own hands.

Once my hands were free, I sliced through the tape on my ankles. Then, I walked over to the door to see where Smith and Foley headed off to. All I could hear was loud music and voices from upstairs. It sounded like chaos. I rushed back toward the girls. Even if it meant getting caught again, and even my death, I wasn't leaving without them.

As fast as I could, I picked the lock to the handcuff securing Svetlana's ankle to the cot. When she was free, I removed the tape and held her for a moment while she cried.

"You're going to be okay, now," I tried to reassure her. "I'm going to get you out of here. But I need your help. We need to wake the others. Can you do that?"

She nodded, and after more urging, she joined me in waking them. Upon seeing me, they were just as terrified as she was, especially when they saw all the blood.

While I quickly went about getting their ankles free, Svetlana told me their names, and gave me their stories of how they came to be captive in the basement. Along with Svetlana, there were Laney, Tara, Jacqueline, Danielle, Mira, Nadia, and Carolyn. The girls were between the ages of fifteen and twenty, except for Laney, who turned twenty-one during her stay here.

They each had a story to tell. Two girls were told their parents sold them to the teacher, and they had to work off their debt. Three others had been living on the streets after being kicked out of their homes or life had been too unbearable and they ran away. Abducted—approached from behind, their mouths covered with a smelly substance—and brought to The Tapestry to be groomed. It was the same substance that knocked me out, no doubt.

They manipulated and groomed Mira and Carolyn on two separate occasions in an internet chat room. Someone pretended to be a teenager with similar interests. They groomed them and convinced them to meet at a local park. When they showed up in the parking lot, a black SUV pulled up to them. Before they knew what was happening, someone covered their mouths from behind, picked them up, and tossed them into the SUV.

Laney's story had me fuming. It was so similar to the grooming techniques of *Jeffrey Epstein* and *Ghislaine Maxwell* that I knew who the guilty parties were.

From what I learned in the short time I had with them, I realized these girls were the perfect selections for these animals. They were probably hand-picked because of their backgrounds. There would be no police report filed on their behalf, and there would be no one out looking for them. Their captors didn't have to cover their tracks.

The minute the girls were free, they were hugging and crying, each holding a glimmer of hope in their eyes. I couldn't fail them. Smith and Foley hadn't returned, and I wasn't sure where they were, but I knew we had to get out of there and fast. I instructed the girls to hold each other's hands and follow me. We left the hellhole that had confined them, cautiously walked along the hall—with me watching for trouble at each door we passed—and finally made it to the stairway.

I saw the hope in their eyes as we walked up. When I came to the pantry door, I turned to the girls and put my finger to my mouth, trying to signal them to keep quiet. I opened the door about an inch to listen and verified it was clear before making a move. We made it this far. Was it possible we could make it to the back door to freedom?

The goons weren't standing at the door, and after verifying the kitchen was clear, I assumed the party moved to the entertainment room. Smith and Foley were nowhere to be found, either. Where the hell did they go? Feeling brazen now, I motioned for the girls to follow me. I led them through the kitchen. When I was just about to open the back door, only steps away from freedom, I heard a loud noise, and my heart dropped. I thought it was Smith and Foley coming back for us. I momentarily froze, and then realized we had to keep moving, no matter what we heard. We had to get out of there.

CHAPTER 44

WHEN I PUSHED the back door open, Nauset Bay P.D. and other agencies had the place surrounded with their weapons drawn. I instinctively jumped in front of the girls to shield them.

"Put your weapons down," Finn ordered, as soon as he saw me bloody and a mess. "And get the paramedics over here now."

I could tell by the distressed look on his face that it pissed him off he wasn't there to protect me. I also heard someone call out my name. When I looked across the parking lot, I noticed Olivia and Madison corralled behind yellow crime scene tape, with two officers keeping anyone from going beyond. "Don't let them get caught up in this," I said to Finn.

He nodded. "They're separated from the folks involved with The Tapestry. They'll be fine."

"I'm okay," I yelled out, more concerned about the victims. At least I think I'm okay. Thank god, the cavalry was here. "Maldonado arrived with the warrant?"

Finn nodded, too devastated to speak.

When I looked around at the rest of the scene, it was complete pandemonium. I noticed Smith and Foley face down on the pavement. Two of their fellow officers confiscated their weapons and badges, while two others handcuffed them and pulled them to their feet. Across the alley, I saw the two goons being searched and handcuffed, and on past them, I noticed Senator Sanders and the public officials being cuffed and placed in the back seat of patrol cars. The other parties in attendance were also being rounded up; Tracy and Jessica were among them. It would take time to weed out the good from the bad, and the innocent from the guilty. But it looked like a good night for the Nauset Bay police officers. There were only three people unaccounted for.

Seeing there was no longer any danger for the victims, I slowly guided them out onto the pavement. It was quite a sight. There wasn't a dry eye in the area when the officers saw them walk out one after the other. The girls looked so innocent, wearing oversized shirts, looking as if they just came from a sleep-over, instead of being held captive inside a basement. I think it dawned on everyone at the scene that the girls could have been their daughters. The predators held them against their will and forced them into doing unthinkable things, all for somebody's greed and profit. The girls remained glued to me, fearful of what was going to happen to them now. They looked at me as their savior.

"We're proud of you, Katie," I heard Olivia yell after seeing the girls come out to safety.

Finn whispered in my ear, "Are these the girls in the photos?" He was emotional as well.

I nodded and repeated all their names. "This is Finn. He is a police officer here to help us."

The girls clung to me, too afraid to trust another police officer. Finn sensed their discomfort, so he called the two female officers from Nauset Bay over to assist. When they still hesitated, I did my best to reassure them. Stands to reason they'd look to me for guidance. I was the one who found them and set them free.

Finn informed me paramedics needed to take them to the hospital to get checked out and advised the female officers to escort them into two separate ambulances. The girls put up resistance. Eventually, I convinced them they were just going to be checked for injuries, and I would be there shortly. Finn reminded me it was necessary to get the girls away from the facility. It wouldn't be long before the media got wind of the bust. Then reporters and all the local television and radio stations would descend on the area for an exclusive, especially when they heard the news about what and who was involved.

Once the girls were safe in the ambulances, and they were on their way to the hospital, I refocused my attention on the scene. I glanced over at Smith and Foley, both of them cuffed and standing next to a patrol car. I looked into their eyes, hoping to see sorrow or guilt. There wasn't any. Smith looked at me with a look of pure hatred, while Foley was wearing a wicked grin. Almost like he knew something I didn't. It would be a waste of words and time, but I wanted them to feel some of the pain of what they'd done.

I walked over and stared at Foley—the corrupt cop who shot my friend. I couldn't see even a glimmer of emotion on his face. Other officers rushed toward me, only to be held back by Finn. When Foley smirked, it infuriated me. I faked a right-hand jab and instead kneed the son-of-a-bitch in the balls. When he doubled over, I said, "You should get used to that position. I understand they like cops in prison."

"Go, Katie!" Madison yelled. When I looked their way, I could see them both smiling.

Finn was watching close, fearing he was going to have to jump and stop me from beating the man, like they did me. He put his arm around me, the lines on his face showing the concern he felt. "You should join the girls at the hospital. Your head looks like you need stitches."

My body hurt like hell, but I still had things to do. "They took my gun. I want it back."

Finn studied me and knew I wouldn't leave without it. He walked over and searched through the weapons confiscated.

They were already bagged and tagged to protect the evidence. When he returned, he handed over the baggie with mine. He kept his eyes locked on me. "Are you okay?"

I nodded.

"I'm sorry Katie."

"For what?"

"For not being there when I should have."

I just looked at him. What could I say? I suspected he was at The Tapestry on his undercover gig, and only escorting the three of us to make sure we got there safely. Even though I couldn't find him at the party when I wanted to go down to the basement, I acted anyway, knowing it could be trouble. I couldn't blame him for that. "We both had jobs to do. My priority was the girls and finding Jillian's killer. I went to the basement. That's not on you."

He studied me and I could tell he was worried this might set our new dating situation back a step. But now was not the time to get into that.

CHAPTER 45

WHEN I WAS sure Maldonado, Finn, and the other officers had control of the crime scene and were busy gathering the evidence, I met up with Olivia and Madison.

"So, how did you like your first trip to a brothel?" I teased, trying to make light of the hell we all just went through.

Both of them hugged me until I complained it hurt. "We're so proud of you, Katie," Olivia said.

"But we're not letting you do that again," Madison added. "I can't believe you tricked us into coming, only to get yourself into trouble."

"You should have taken us with you when you went to the basement," Olivia said. "But now we need to get to the hospital."

"That will have to wait," I said.

"Then we need to get you home and patch you up," she said after seeing the look in my eyes."

I nodded. "You can patch me up, but we have to make it quick. I still have something to do."

They didn't bother to question me. They could see by the look on my face that I was determined.

We walked toward the limo that brought us to the party, stepped inside, and after confirming it was me inside, the officers let it through.

"At least tell me you enjoyed yourselves," I said to both of them.

Olivia laughed. "Madison won $2500 and had one too many white Russians. I nursed a tumbler of chocolate tequila since I was on bodyguard duty. She kept winning at the blackjack table and flirting with the men. Damn, they were eye candy. Too bad they worked in a brothel."

I glanced at Madison. She had a big smile on her face and there was a gleam in her eyes. "I had a great time," she said with all the innocence of someone who had just gone to the prom.

~~~

After Olivia and Madison used their skills to nurse my wounds, they went home to their cottages. I hopped into a shower and ran through everything I now knew. My cell phone buzzed, alerting me I had a voicemail message, but I ignored it. As I stood under the showerhead, allowing the hot water to cleanse the blood from my body, a piece of evidence that had been poking at me for a while now smacked me like a ton of bricks. I stepped out and quickly towel-dried my hair, and put it into a ponytail. I stepped into a pair of jeans and threw on a sweatshirt. Then I retrieved the DVDs from my backpack and put one of them into the machine and hit play.

I sat down on the leather sofa, grabbed the remote, and scrolled through the scene until I had a view of The Teacher. I listened to his voice and watched his mannerisms. "Sonofabitch!"

I hit the exit button, retrieved the DVD, and placed it back inside my backpack. I hurried back into the bedroom, slipped into my Reeboks, and grabbed my gun on the way out the door.

I sped toward my destination, not caring that I was going too fast. Time was critical. I turned off the headlights before turning onto the street to avoid alerting anyone to my presence. The lights were on in Sarah Miles' house, and her black SUV was sitting in the driveway. I parked a few houses away and did a quick check of the surroundings before stepping out of the car. All was quiet, except for the beating of my heart.

With my gun steady, I crept towards the house, watching my back as I went. I snuck up alongside the SUV and peered inside. It was empty. The vehicle was warm to the touch. They must have recently arrived. I checked the front door; she locked it. Staying down low, I hurried past the front window and continued around to the back of the house. The wrought-iron fence blocked me from getting close, but I could see through the French doors.

Sarah Miles was there. She was talking to someone on the phone while throwing things into a suitcase. Somebody else was there as well, only I couldn't see them from my vantage point. Now was not the time for patience, but I had no choice. I pivoted on my feet, moving further along until I could see Howard Moore inside helping her pack. They were making a run for it. As I suspected, the two of them had been involved with the Tapestry for some time. That explained how the imported Italian tile installed in the entryway of his home wound up in the brothel's basement.

Staying low, I headed back out to the front of the house just as the lights went out in the house. They were on their way out. Howard Moore walked out the door carrying two suitcases. I was ready to move, but I wanted to wait for Sarah. If I moved now, she could lock herself inside and a whole other set of problems could ensue.

Howard carried them to the SUV, opened the tailgate, and placed them inside. As he headed back toward the front door, Sarah walked out carrying another bag. Howard reached for it and waited while she locked the door.

I kept my gun steady as I approached. "There was a party tonight. I'm surprised you weren't there. Oh, but you were just not when the cops arrived."

Howard Moore froze in place, completely stunned to see me.

Sarah looked at me and sneered. Her face displayed the same indifference I noticed the first time she walked into the office. "I knew you were going to be trouble the minute I entered your office."

I kept my eyes focused on both of them. "Yeah, I pegged the same about you when you were rude to my dog."

She shrugged with an arrogance I despised. "So, how'd you put it all together?"

"I'm just a P.I. Sarah," I said. "It's not my job to put it together; that's for the police to do. And trust me; they're doing just that. I'll just give them the evidence that helps. But since you asked, there were too many coincidences. And I don't believe in coincidences."

Sarah smirked and looked at me with disdain. "Ridiculous."

I shrugged. "You found out Jillian sent me the photos and tapes, and you had Smith and Foley bug my place, hoping to get to her. Mr. Moore was the only person who could have led you in my direction. I guess he's your attorney."

I glanced in Howard Moore's direction. It infuriated me he could do this to his daughter.

"How did you know I knew Howard Moore?"

It was my turn to laugh. "The same imported Italian tile that the two of you put in the basement of your establishment is also inside his home."

She waved her hand in a dismissive gesture. "Any interior designer could have that tile delivered."

Out of the corner of my eye, I noticed Howard Moore slip his hand inside his leather coat.

"Then you deceived me. You had me tail your cheating husband, knowing he would lead me to The Tapestry. You hid your identity from the business, thinking I'd only connect him to it. When he became an embarrassment and a liability, you conveniently came up with an alibi and ordered Smith and Foley to take him out while you were safely away."

She shrugged and looked at me as if I was describing a faulty personality trait, and not the acts of a stone-cold killer.

"But you made a mistake."

She frowned. "I don't make mistakes."

"And yet, you did. You put the business in the name of a corporation and thought by the time somebody discovered your involvement, you'd be safely out of the country. What you didn't plan on was me searching your home."

Her eyes went wide, and she glared at me at the sudden revelation. Her body shook with anger. "You went inside my home?"

"I was worried about your safety," I said with a laugh, knowing how evil she was now. "You left documents on your desk.

SJM, Inc. That was the LLC you used, wasn't it? Stands for Sarah Jo Miles, does it not? You know it's easy to verify LLCs with the Secretary of State's office, right?"

While I was narrating the pieces to the puzzle, I noticed her body go stiff and her eyes took on a menacing look.

"I'm curious Sarah, whose idea was it to kidnap teenagers and groom them into prostitutes? Was that your idea, Howard Moore, or was it the evil man who calls himself, The Teacher?"

"Stop engaging with her, Sarah," Howard Moore interrupted. "She's using you to fill in the blanks."

"So how'd the two of you get together, Mr. Moore?"

She cackled and looked at Howard with a knowing look. "He was my first paying customer."

"So, you two devised this perfect scheme?"

No response.

"Did Smith and Foley know they were just paid patsies, who would be held accountable while you and Mateo left the country?"

Sarah glared at me. You could tell she was trying to figure out how to get rid of me. "Smith and Foley got what they wanted."

I thought the woman who stalked me was nuts, but Sarah Miles was right up there with her. To the public, they were respectable business associates, carrying on normal lives. Behind closed doors, they were all out for greed and profit, and it didn't matter who got hurt or killed along the way.

"This was all about sick greed," I continued. "I don't care about the illegal gambling or poker parties or the women willing to sell themselves to aid in your endeavors. But I care about the innocent victims you abducted, drugged, and groomed."

"You know nothing," Sarah said with derision.

"I know it was you and Mateo—the good-looking couple—who approached Laney, claiming to need a model. She didn't know your names, but she knows your faces. The others know your faces too. Why do it, Sarah? You had a thriving modeling business. Why ruin it?"

"Thriving business, my ass," Sarah shouted. "Do you have any idea what I had to do to get that business off the ground? Until I got the goods on a few politicians, nobody would give me the time of day."

"Is that why you made all those videos, so you could blackmail people? You're the female Epstein."

While the two of us were battling it out, Howard Moore's hand moved out of his coat pocket. The next thing I knew, he had a gun pointed at me. When I glanced in his direction and saw the malicious look in his eyes, I knew I was in trouble.

Before I could react, he fired two shots. One bullet grazed me in the arm, the second one ripped into my shoulder. The impact threw me back. I immediately went down and rolled out of the line of fire. I clenched my teeth to avoid screaming out in pain. When I was flat on my stomach, I pointed my gun in his direction and fired back. He ducked out of the way. I fired again, this time hitting him in the upper thigh. He went down.

"No!" Sarah yelled in a hysterical voice. She moved toward Howard, grabbed the gun out of his hand, and stormed in my direction. She had the gun pointed, shooting wildly and in a maniacal way.

I kept dodging to avoid being hit and ducked behind a bush for cover. I aimed my gun in her direction and fired. The bullet hit her in the leg, even though I was aiming for higher up. It pushed her back a step, but in her crazed state of mind, she continued toward me in a fit of rage. I fired again. This time, the bullet hit her in the stomach. She went down, screaming.

Howard Moore was back on his feet, looking at Sarah moaning on the ground. He pushed himself to get to her and saw the blood oozing out of her gut. He bunched up the ends of her shirt, placed it into the wound, and put her hand over it. "Hold it there," he ordered. When he looked in my direction, the look on his face scared the life out of me. "You'll pay for this!"

I kept my eyes on him.

He was coming straight at me, ready to attack.

"It was self-defense, Mr. Moore. I had no choice."

He wasn't listening.

I was standing up now, facing off with him, aiming my gun right at him. "Mr. Moore, don't come any closer."

He didn't stop.

"Mr. Moore, I'm warning you—I will shoot!"

He was only steps away from me, and I could see the pure hatred in his eyes. He wanted me dead.

I was just about to pull the trigger when someone fired a shot behind me. Howard Moore went down in front of me and I could tell from the wound that he wasn't getting back up. I turned around to see Finn at the driver's side door of his police-issued vehicle, with his own 9mm Glock raised.

I exhaled with relief. But there was still more to do. I ran toward Sarah, took off my shirt—leaving me in my bra—and replaced her bloodied one to cover her wound.

"Where is Mateo, Sarah? Where were you meeting him?"

Even in her dismal state, she laughed hysterically, sounding like a hyena. "Why would I tell you?"

Finn appeared on the other side of her.

"Tell us and I'll inform the D.A. you cooperated. It might help when it comes time for sentencing. Don't, and they'll throw the book at you. How's life in jail going to be for a woman like you who groomed teenage girls?"

"Maxwell just got twenty years and your crimes are much worse," I added.

She glanced at her watch while pondering over her decision. When she heard the sounds of sirens in the background, she knew her fate was no longer in her hands. "Barnstable Municipal Airport," she finally said, but she wore a wicked smile. "We were supposed to meet there. He has a private plane. You won't make it in time."

~~~

Finn drove at a high rate of speed, traveling down MA-28 and headed toward the airport. It was still fifteen minutes away. I was sitting shotgun and attempting to wrap my shoulder in a ripped shirt from his trunk.

"Can't this thing go any faster?" I whined.

Finn responded, "It's the damn Massachusetts drivers."

He rolled his window down and yelled at the vehicle blocking his way, driving as if he was sightseeing on a Sunday afternoon. "This is the speed lane, moron!"

"We're not gonna make it," I said. "The plane's scheduled to leave in ten minutes."

Finn pulled into the emergency lane and punched the gas while I held on for dear life.

Thirteen minutes later, we turned into the airport drive and headed toward the building. Finn sped past a line of cars waiting to pick up, or drop off passengers, and then pulled to a stop in the emergency lane at the entrance.

We bolted from the car.

Finn flashed his badge to the security guys out front. "Show me the way. We've got a suspect, Mateo Ortiz, taking off in his private aircraft. He's wanted for kidnapping, human and sex trafficking, conspiracy to commit murder, and a whole slew of other charges. He's headed over the Mexican border."

We followed airport security through the maze of travelers. At an intersection, security pointed to an exit at the end of a hall. We took off at full speed. At the exit, Finn pushed it open, and we ran outside, just in time to see a private Cessna airplane taxiing down the runaway. Seconds later, the aircraft lifted off the tarmac and carried Mateo Ortiz into the night.

"Noooo!" I screamed at the top of my lungs. Seconds later, weak from exhaustion and a loss of blood, I collapsed to the ground.

CHAPTER 46

WHEN I REGAINED consciousness, I was lying in a hospital bed; my shoulder wrapped, and an IV protruded from my arm, being poked and prodded by a nurse and doctor. Finn was standing in the background with a worried look on his face. The last thing I remembered was Howard Moore coming at me, and then the sound of a gunshot.

The doctor informed me I needed several stitches over my left eye, from where Smith had tried to change my identity, plus I had a few broken ribs. I had a scrape on my left arm from where the first bullet grazed me, but the second bullet shattered my collarbone. With all the bandages, I probably looked like I came straight from a war zone. They offered me plenty of painkillers, but I declined. Once the doctor made sure I was comfortable, he advised Finn not to stay too long, because I was going to need the rest. Silence filled the room after he and the nurse left. When I glanced in Finn's direction, he was looking uncomfortable.

"Hey," I said, struggling to speak.

"Hey yourself," he said, a smile of relief lighting up his face. "Welcome back."

I tried to sit up. Pain shot through my shoulder and face. He rushed over to help.

"Some night, huh?" he said, reverting to his cop humor.

"I'll say. Everything is hazy. What happened?"

Finn pulled a chair next to the hospital bed and sat down. "They shot you," he said. "Thankfully, one bullet only grazed you, but your collarbone took a hit with the second one. Doc said it will heal, but you might need help for a few weeks." He winked. "That means you'll need some help in the shower."

I smiled at him. "You're just happy that you'll finally get me out of my jeans."

He smiled in return. "There is that... you passed out at the airport."

That reminded me about all that happened and why we were at the airport, to begin with. "What happened with Mateo Ortiz? He got away, didn't he?"

"Don't worry, Katie," Finn said. "We'll catch him. Guys like him can't blend into the woodwork. He thrives on attention."

I scoffed, the anguish seeping through my battered body. "They won't catch him. He's rich and probably in Mexico already. He can hide for a very long time with help from the cartels." She was suddenly despondent.

My injuries were bad, but they could have been much worse. I was more concerned with the victims. Knowing that one perpetrator responsible for abducting and grooming them was still on the loose would impact them. It did me, so I could only imagine what they would feel.

The doctor recommended I not disturb them for a little while. They had finally dozed off after their long ordeal. Thankfully, the doctor said they didn't suffer any significant physical injuries that would do any permanent damage. They found traces of drugs in their systems, which might cause withdrawals and more angst during their recuperation. Specialists were being brought in to work with them. Their mental status was an important factor, and he was worried about their ability to deal with what they had suffered through.

Social workers were also being brought in to deal with what would happen to the girls. Since some were underage, the authorities would have to look into the legal ramifications. There was time to work it all out, though. The doctors planned for the girls to remain in the hospital for as long as necessary. Nauset Bay P.D. needed them as witnesses for the case, so accommodations for their safety were being arranged. According to Finn, they had already been an enormous source of information. It was best if they remained in the area until the trial was over. After that, the powers that be would have to come up with a more permanent solution.

Finn looked at me and I could see him struggling with what he wanted to say. "You've been through a lot in the last few months," he said. "When you collapsed, it felt... I thought I lost you."

Raw emotion surged through him. He leaned toward me and brushed his lips across mine, letting his tongue linger. When he pulled back, he looked into my eyes.

I returned his gaze, brushed my fingers along his face, and offered him a warm smile. "I'm still here."

We stared at each other, both of us feeling things and not being able to show them physically.

His lips grazed my temple, sending a shiver down my body. If they didn't have me bandaged or I wasn't in excruciating pain, I would have pulled him into the hospital bed with me.

Regrettably, Maldonado and Derek walked in, interrupting our moment.

"Did we come at a bad time?" Maldonado teased.

"Yeah, you did," Finn said, "so come back later."

Maldonado smiled at Finn, but nudged him out of the way and leaned over the hospital bed to kiss me. "When you go all-in on a case, you really go all in, don't you?"

I smiled and welcomed his affection.

Derek walked over to the other side of the hospital bed, looking worried at seeing the injuries up close. He hadn't heard just how battered I was.

"How are you feeling?"

"Like somebody used a crowbar."

He looked at me like a caring father would. "Anything you need?"

"I'm only here overnight," I said. "How's Bailey? I've never been away from her before."

He sat down on the edge of the bed. "She looks for you, but she's doing fine. Loretta makes her play ball, and she throws rocks at the beach to keep her occupied."

"Thank you," I said, grateful that they take the time.

"No thanks needed," he said, patting my hand affectionately.

"Katie, you did a helluva job tonight," Maldonado said. "Those young women are free because of you."

"What happened with Sarah Miles?" I knew they had transported her to the hospital, but I didn't want her anywhere near the victims. I was also worried Mateo Ortiz would finagle some legal maneuver to set her free.

Maldonado must have sensed my fear. "Don't worry, Katie. She's in police custody with round-the-clock guards. She won't get near them."

"How bad were her injuries?"

"The bullet on her thigh was a flesh wound, nothing serious. They removed the second bullet from her stomach. She was lucky there, too. The bullet didn't impact any vital organs. It's her disposition that's suffering. She's sorry she ever met Katie

Parker."

"Good!"

"Once the doctor gives the all-clear, medically, they'll transport her to jail."

I thought I would feel better once I knew who killed Jillian, but I felt numb. There was so much more to the case than the death of my friend. She taught me that by putting herself in jeopardy when getting the evidence to me. The victims were safe, and yet, I still felt like I missed something. I kept going back to what Foley said when he and Smith were trying to rearrange my face. Why did they need to get the evidence back? I needed to give the photos and DVDs another look.

"Your friend, Jillian, would be proud of you," Derek said out of the blue, bringing me back to the present. "I know I am."

"Man, you two are going to make everyone weepy," Finn joked, patting Derek on the back.

Maldonado said, "When you get out of here and feel up to it, you'll need to come in so we can go over all the evidence to prep the D.A. for trial. We've got plenty of time. Anything you need, magazines, something better than hospital food?"

"I'm only here overnight," I reminded him.

He grabbed my hand and clasped it in his. "You know, if you need someone to talk to about this case, or whatever else might be on your mind, I'm there for you. I know it was a tough one."

"I appreciate it."

"But, don't think just because you're injured, that gets you out of Sunday dinner."

I laughed. Then I had to grab my ribs because it hurt.

Then we all laughed.

It wasn't too much later when all three of them left, doctor's orders, to let me get some sleep. Finn said he would be back in the morning to give me a ride home. Plus, I wanted to be here at the hospital when the girls woke up. Alone in the room, the weight of all that happened overwhelmed me and I finally cried; cried for Jillian, and for all the victims who suffered the unspeakable. Then, for the first time in several days, I slept like a baby.

EPILOGUE

THE FOLLOWING MORNING, they released me from the hospital, but I made a vow to the girls to visit them every day. The first thing I did was pick up Bailey. When I saw her sweet face running toward me the minute I stepped out of Finn's car, I knew could never leave her again. She's my rock. The one constant in my life I could always count on.

"Hey pretty girl," I cooed, hugging her and petting her. "Did you miss me?"

After several hugs, she stopped her dance and stood still, eyeballing me. "What is it? What do you want?"

Finn laughed. "I know what she wants."

He opened a can of tennis balls and whipped one across Derek's front yard. She ran toward it, retrieved it, and returned, lobbying it at him. Yep, my little traitor will toss the ball with anyone.

We spent a couple of hours at Derek's house, filling him in on all the updates on the case. We had some appetizers and enjoyed the view off of his wraparound deck and played with the dogs. Then we headed back to the RV so I could get Bailey back to our routine. Finn needed some alone time with his son, David, too.

The next few days were complete chaos. The media camped out at the hospital and reporters did everything they could to get interviews with the girls, and anyone else involved in the case, which meant my driveway was blocked. Olivia and Madison helped me to dodge them so I could keep my promise and visit the girls. Madison made some sandwiches and snacks. Then the two of them kept the media occupied while I snuck out in Olivia's SUV.

Finn and Maldonado stopped by several times to meet with the girls as well. They were prime witnesses in their big case. When it was nearing time for the girls to be released from the hospital, there was a scramble of activity to make sure arrangements being made wouldn't harm them.

Social workers discovered some of their home environments weren't healthy, so they couldn't force the underage girls to go back. I had already assumed that, from conversations I had with the girls. That's how they were so susceptible when approached by The Teacher. We put our heads together with reps from the Department of Social Services. Because of all the publicity in the case, they worked relentlessly to find foster situations. Once they found a few families willing to accept them, I followed up with visits to make sure they were good choices. Some girls were even lucky enough to stay together.

Once they settled into their new homes, the media blitz was even worse. The actual trial wouldn't take place for a while, but the media wouldn't let up. To keep the girls out of the limelight, Olivia and Madison agreed to stay on the Cape a few more days and help me. So, we packed up the girls and headed to Casper Island to spend some time in the new home that Jillian left me.

We had to take two SUVs. When we pulled into the cobblestone driveway for the home, my mouth fell open. The house was directly on the water, just like the cottage, only this home was huge. You could literally walk out the back door and see the ocean. The home had three bedrooms, which were all on the second floor with bathrooms off of each. There was also a den that Jillian used as an office and a kitchen that opened into a large family room with a fireplace and another bathroom downstairs. It was all grays and whites, with a wraparound deck out front that extended to the back. There was plenty of space for all of us to enjoy. And more than enough for Bailey to play hide and seek with the girls which she kept doing.

Olivia and I prepped each of the rooms and helped them unpack, while Madison put away the groceries and whipped up some appetizers. Then we all agreed to take a walk on the beach. All eleven of us took our shoes off and stood with our toes in the sand, enjoying the view of white-capped waves. It didn't matter to any of us that it was December. Bailey kept digging up rocks and pushing them with her nose, hinting for the girls to throw them. Moments later, the teenagers and young women were running into the cold waves, chasing Bailey and laughing. I put an arm around Olivia and Madison as the three of us looked on, hoping it was a good sign that they were going to be okay.

When I looked up at the beautiful blue sky, I said farewell to my friend Jillian, and secretly thanked her as well. She was the reason we were all together.

If Only She Knew

When her best friends, Olivia and Madison, are abducted—and used as bait—the chase is on to get them out of the clutches of Katie's tormentor.
https://www.bklnk.com/B0B69TK3MW

CR HIATT writes action-oriented stories with strong female characters as the heroes, and a touch of romance. She also created the series featuring the duo, McSwain & Beck. When she's not writing, she's usually renovating houses, riding her e-bike and spending time outdoors with her Golden Retriever, daughter, and friends, usually somewhere near the water.

Thank you for purchasing and reading Before She Knew.

Readers and word of mouth are crucial to an author's success. If you read the book and enjoyed it, I would be honored if you would consider leaving a one or two-line review on Amazon.

Thank you so much.

For more information on CR HIATT:
Website: http://writercrhiatt.com/
FB Fan Page:
https://www.facebook.com/CRHIATT

Also, feel free to email me to receive updates: authorCRHIATT@gmail.com.

Made in the USA
Middletown, DE
16 August 2023